THE MUTANT SEASON

The
Mutant
Season

ROBERT SILVERBERG
and KAREN HABER

A FOUNDATION BOOK

D O U B L E D A Y

New York London Toronto Sydney Auckland

A Foundation Book
Published by Doubleday, a division of
Bantam Doubleday Dell Publishing Group, Inc.
666 Fifth Avenue, New York, New York 10103

FOUNDATION, DOUBLEDAY, and the portrayal of the letter F
are trademarks of Doubleday, a division of
Bantam Doubleday Dell Publishing Group, Inc.

Library of Congress Cataloging-in-Publication Data

Silverberg, Robert.
The mutant season/Robert Silverberg & Karen Haber.—1st ed.
p.   cm.
"A Foundation book."
I. Haber, Karen.   II. Title.
PS3569.I472M8   1989
813'.52—dc20   89-34894
CIP

ISBN 0-385-24721-4
ISBN 0-385-26647-2 (pbk.)
The Mutant Season copyright © 1989 by Byron Preiss
Visual Publications, Inc.
Introduction copyright © 1989 by Agberg Ltd.
Text copyright © 1989 by Karen Haber.
Front jacket art by Dean Motter.
Jacket design by Alex Jay/Studio J.
Special thanks to Lou Aronica, Pat LoBrutto, David M. Harris,
and Mary Higgins.
All Rights Reserved
Printed in the United States of America
November 1989
First Edition

For my parents—all four of them

INTRODUCTION

Robert Silverberg

THE MUTANT—the stranger in our midst, the secret alien, the hidden Changed One—is one of the great mythic figures of science fiction. If science fiction is, as I believe it to be, a literature of change, a literature of infinite possibilities, then the mutant is a quintessential science-fictional force, bringing the zone of change very close to home indeed, right into the human germ plasm.

The word itself indicates that. *Mutare,* in Latin, means "to change." From that Latin verb the Dutch botanist-geneticist Hugo de Vries coined the terms "mutation" and "mutant" late in the nineteenth century. De Vries, who was experimenting with breeding evening primroses, had observed sudden striking changes in his flowers as he crossed and recrossed different strains. His research led him to the conclusion that all living things are subject to such changes, or mutations, and that mutant forms frequently pass their altered traits on to later generations. Thus the evolutionary process itself can be viewed as a succession of mutations.

De Vries's theories have long since been confirmed by modern genetic research. We know now that the physical appearance of living organisms is determined by bodies known as genes, within the nuclei of cells; the genes themselves are composed of complex molecules arranged in elaborate patterns, and any change in the pattern (or "code") of the genetic material that substitutes one molecule for another will produce a mutation. Mutations arise spontaneously in nature, induced by chemical processes in the nucleus or by temperature conditions or by cosmic rays striking a gene; they can also be produced artificially by subjecting the nucleus to X-rays, ultraviolet light, or other hard radiation.

Mutations are seldom spectacular. Those mutants that are startlingly different from their parents—the ones with three heads, the ones with no digestive tracts—tend not to survive very long, either because the mutation renders them unable to perform the normal functions of life or because they are rejected by those who sired them. The mutants that do succeed in passing their mutations along to their descendants are generally only slightly altered forms: large evolutionary changes result from an accumulation of small mutations rather than from any one startling genetic leap.

The mutant theme has long been a favorite of science-fiction writers. The pioneering experiments of H. J. Muller, who in 1927 demonstrated that radiation could be used to induce mutations in fruit flies, gave rise to a whole school of speculative mutant stories almost immediately. From one of the great early s-f novelists, John Taine (a pseudonym for the mathematician Eric Temple Bell) came *The Greatest Adventure*, in 1929, in which the strange corpses of giant reptiles begin drifting up from the depths of the ocean, and are eventually linked to ancient experiments in mutation carried out by a civilization that had lived in Antarctica. A year later, Taine's *The Iron Star* told of the startling mutagenic impact of a meteor on the wildlife of a region in Africa; and in 1931 Taine's *Seeds of Life* showed a man gaining superhuman powers after being irradiated, and passing them on to the next generation. Edmond Hamilton's "He That Hath Wings" (1938) described the birth of a mutant child to parents who had been exposed to irradiation. And there were many other such stories, most of them taking wild liberties with the scientific knowledge of the day for the sake of dramatic effect.

The explosion of the first atomic bombs in 1945 brought the concept of mutation-causing radiation vividly to the whole world's attention, and, unsurprisingly, it became an obsessive theme of postwar science fiction—so much so that the editor of the leading s-f magazine of the day, who at first had asked his writers to examine the scientific and sociological implications of the atomic era in close detail, finally had to call a moratorium on atomic doom fiction because it was starting to crowd everything else out. It was in that period, though, that some of the finest work on the theme was done —notably Henry Kuttner's "Baldy" series (1945–53), in which telepathic mutants living among normal humans undergo persecution, and Wilmar Shiras's *Children of the Atom* (1948–50), a poignant story of superintelligent mutant children. And ever since, mutants have played prominent roles in the speculations of science-fiction writers. They turn up in Walter Miller's classic *A Canticle for Liebowitz*, in Isaac Asimov's *Foundation* series, in the novels of John Wyndham, in a host of stories by Robert A. Heinlein, and—constantly, always to terrifying effect—in motion pictures. The mutant is science fiction's metaphor for the outsider, the loner, the alienated supercreature. The theme of mutation is one of the most valuable tools science fiction has for examining the nature of human society, the relation of one human being to another, and the ultimate destiny of our species.

A WORD about the writing of this book.

In 1973 I published a very short short story, "The Mutant Season," in which, in just a few pages, I sketched out the notion that mutants have been living among us for many years as an underground group within our society—a kind of secret Gypsy tribe—and are now finally allowing themselves to attain higher visibility. I was content to suggest, rather than to elaborate in any great detail, what effects this might have, both on our society and on the mutants. And there I left it.

Years later my good friend, the indefatigable and ingenious Byron Preiss, suggested to me that there was a lot more to the idea that I might want to explore at greater length—perhaps as a series of novels, even, to be written in collaboration with my wife, Karen Haber, who was just beginning her own career as a science-fiction writer. My first reaction was surprise. "The Mutant Season" was such a tiny story—only about two thousand words long—that the notion of mining it for several novels seemed outlandish. But then I reread it, and realized that Byron was right: I had implied a whole society in those few pages, and then had simply let it slip from my mind.

So here is *The Mutant Season* at novel length—with more to come, as we dig into the fuller implications of a parallel culture of mutants living secretly, and then not so secretly, within modern American society. It has been an interesting experiment in collaboration for us. Karen and I worked the story and its characters out together, basing them (with some considerable modifications) on my original little piece, which by now has been projected into epic length covering several generations. She then went on to write the first draft of the book, after which I edited it line by line, offering suggestions for revisions, both thematic and stylistic; and back she went to the word processor for another round. And so it went over many months of close and mostly harmonious work. Writing a book with your spouse is a little like trying to teach your spouse to drive a car: it calls for patience, good humor, and quick reflexes. I don't recommend it to every couple. But we came through umpteen drafts of *The Mutant Season* still sharing bed and board, and most of the time we're still on speaking terms, too. The other day she handed me the first fifty pages of Volume Two. I have the feeling that these mutants are going to be around the house for a long time to come.

—ROBERT SILVERBERG
Oakland, California
March 1989

THE MUTANT SEASON

1

WINTER IS THE MUTANT SEASON, Michael Ryton thought, slamming the door of the beach shack behind him. The coldest time of the year was the time for their annual gathering. That seemed appropriate, somehow. Especially this year.

The December wind whipped sand against his ruddy cheeks, forcing his fine blond hair back from his forehead to wave like a bright flag in the waning daylight. Behind his filtershades, his eyes watered from the cold.

"Mike, there you are!" His dark-haired sister, Melanie, wrapped almost to her eyebrows in the purple thermal muffler their mother had knitted at last year's meeting, stumbled out of the shack. She was always stumbling over something. "It's four o'clock. You're late for the meeting. They're delaying the sharing until you get there."

"Damn! Let's go."

Michael swallowed his irritation. It wasn't Mel's fault that they had to come to Seaside Heights every winter. Had to stay in these rickety, hard-to-heat bungalows from which generations of paint hung in greenish brown ribbons. Shacks, really. Built sixty and seventy years ago for first- and second-generation Americans escaping the sweltering canyons of

New York City streets in August for the relative luxury of gritty, sun-baked beaches along the nearby New Jersey shore. But the crowds were gone, the beaches deserted. This was December now. Their season.

He stalked toward the meeting house while Mel struggled along the overgrown path, trying to keep up with his long strides. Even without the sand and weeds to hamper her steps, she wasn't the most graceful girl he knew. Not by half. He thought of Kelly McLeod, the way she moved, the way she threw her head back, black hair a shining mane, when she laughed. Now there was grace. He'd never seen her stumble.

Poor Mel. If he hadn't been so pissed off about coming here, maybe he would even feel sorry for her. She was the only null in the clan. That was trouble enough for one lifetime.

They turned the corner, walking into the wind with eyes squinted to avoid airborne sand, passed another row of shacks, and finally saw the blue shingles of the meeting house, the largest bungalow in the compound. He pulled open the aluminum storm door. Mel nearly knocked him over as she skidded to an off-balance halt behind him. Michael gave her a quick, commiserating look over his shoulder —he knew what was coming—took a deep breath, and went in.

THE LIGHT on the desk screen blinked "call waiting" in yellow letters. Andie Greenberg looked up from her screen and ran her hands through her dark red hair. The reception desk was empty. Caryl must be on break. Andie sighed. She'd have to take the call herself, since Jacobsen was expecting Senator Craddick. That Scanners Club speech would have to wait. She saved and cleared the screen, then pushed the button that accessed the call.

The screen stayed dark, which meant the caller was using a

pay phone or had purposely cloaked the call. Andie's stomach tightened.

"Is this Jacobsen's office?" a deep male voice growled.

"You have reached the office of Senator Jacobsen," she confirmed in her coolest lawyer voice. "Please state your business."

"Are you Jacobsen?"

"I'm her administrative assistant, Andrea Greenberg."

"That damned mutant bitch better watch it. We're sick of freaks trying to tell us what to do. When we get through with her, she'll wish she'd never been hatched—"

Andie cut the connection. She took a couple of deep breaths, telling herself to calm down, she should be accustomed to threats by now.

The buzzer from Jacobsen's private line went off. She must have monitored the call, Andie thought. The screen brightened to a view of her inner sanctum, the senator seated behind her rosewood desk. She stared solemnly from the screen, golden-eyed, golden-haired, and mysterious.

"Was that Craddick?"

"No." Andie tried to sound casual.

"Another threat?" Jacobsen asked, contralto voice pitched even lower than usual.

Andie nodded.

"How many this month?"

"Fourteen."

The senator smiled frostily. "I suppose I should feel neglected. When I first took office, that was the average count for the week. They must be getting bored. Don't let them rattle you, Andie."

"I know. I won't." Andie's cheeks reddened. Jacobsen nodded and faded from view. This mutant business scared a lot of people, she thought. Which was why she'd chosen to work for Jacobsen. If mutants and nonmutants didn't learn to cooperate, that fear of the unknown would never go away.

The mail cart arrived, bell chiming. V.J. hopped off the

cart, carrot-colored braids flying, and swung a sack of mail onto Andie's desk. "Hear about Seth?" she asked.

"No. What happened?"

"Letter bomb for the senator went off prematurely. Would have made a real mess up here. Instead, it just made a mess of Seth. The mail room wasn't damaged much. Those steel walls will stand up to a minor warhead."

Andie knew her mouth was hanging open. She shut it and swallowed painfully. "My god! I thought they had metal detectors. What about the X-rays?"

V.J. shrugged. "Somebody got creative."

"Where is Seth?"

"They took him to Sisters of Mercy. Looks like they'll be able to save his hand."

"When did it happen?"

"This morning." She squinted. "Careful of those letters, now." V.J. hustled out the door, jumped back on the cart and was gone.

Andie stared after her, seeing nothing. Even with regenerative technology, Seth probably would never have full use of his hand again. And he is—was—such a good artist, she thought grimly. Two of his acrylic washes, scarlet and blue, hung in her apartment. Poor Seth. A victim of the mutant haters? Or the mutants and their desire for a seat in the public arena?

And what was she doing here? Would she be the next to open a letter bomb? Or catch a bullet meant for her boss? Was she crazy? Maybe she should have taken her mother's advice after law school and become a public defender.

No. She'd made the right decision. Andie reminded herself that she'd applied eagerly for this job. Working with the first mutant senator in congressional history was an honor. She believed fiercely in the cause of integration. And what better place to be than where she was, right hand to the Honorable Eleanor Jacobsen? The senator fascinated her: half saint, half warrior, and totally enigmatic behind those golden eyes.

Andie admired Jacobsen with an intensity that approached adulation. Shaking off her momentary depression, she pushed the intercom button. Jacobsen had to be told about the bomb.

"THAT DEADLINE is absolutely unacceptable, Mr. McLeod. You know we can't build a closed-cycle Brayton generator and have it lift-ready in less than six months. Impossible." James Ryton's voice rang across the conference room.

Despite his irritation, Bill McLeod kept his face impassive. Musn't blow the negotiations now, he thought. I've spent hours putting this deal together. He reminded himself that his consultancy with NASA was a plum assignment; only a few retired Air Force pilots enjoyed the kind of connections he had. But, oh, what he'd give to be home with his feet up, or at the airstrip, working on his antique Cessna ultralight. That orange trim needed sanding. He took a sip of cold coffee and wiped his moustache with a napkin to buy thinking time.

Ryton was a hard bargainer. And that snotty mutant attitude didn't help either. Made it seem like he was doing him a favor just to show up for the meeting. But Ryton's group had the top transmitter engineers in this part of the world. There were a few better in Leningrad and Tokyo, but Ryton was closest. McLeod had to have him on the solar collector project, or rather, the government had to have him. And Ryton knew it, too.

"Well, Mr. Ryton, what do you say to nine months?" He waited. Silence loomed as the two men glared politely at each other.

"Fifteen."

"Twelve?"

"Done."

McLeod did allow himself a sigh of relief. It's those damned government regulations, he thought. Ever since Greenland got 'waved, NASA had been under heavy scrutiny about safety precautions. If not for the French-Russian

Moonstation, the entire solar collector project would probably have been scrapped. McLeod knew that, after Greenland, every NASA administrator had offered a silent prayer of thanks for that Moonbase.

But despite the increased paperwork and procedures, NASA needed the generator flight-ready in nine months. Thank God, Ryton had a reputation for getting work in well ahead of schedule. What with delays and the controversy over Moonstation, the twelve-month framework was realistic.

Business concluded, McLeod shook hands with the mutant, who seemed to recoil from the touch. His palm was warm, almost hot, but dry. Strange, McLeod thought, they look so cool with those golden eyes and honey-colored skin, but God knows what their body temperatures are. Hard not to think of them as freaks. He knew it was considered bad taste to call them that now. But are they really human? And did he really want his kid hanging around one of them?

KELLY McLEOD left the skimmer in the driveway and slung her discpack across her shoulders, the straps slithering against the red plastic of her parka. The yard lights looked warm and inviting against the blue dusk, their amber reflections pooling in the snow that capped the hedges.

She opened the door, dropped her pack in the hall and hung her jacket on a hook. She could see her mother sitting on the couch scrolling through a magazine on the homescreen. Saw the pink wine glass on the table by her side, half empty. The scent of vermouth mingled with warm cooking smells.

Kelly hoped it was only her first martini. Joanna McLeod usually didn't start drinking until after the sun had gone down. It was a habit she'd acquired since they'd returned from Berlin last year. From Germany to New Jersey. What a comedown. Kelly didn't blame her mother for drinking. What else did she have to do, anyway? As far as Kelly was concerned, suburbia was one big green lawn and carwash.

Swimming lessons and computer camp. The American dream. Her dreams led her elsewhere, although she didn't quite know the final destination, yet.

"Hi," she called, preparing to escape up the tan-carpeted steps to her room.

"Oh, Kelly." Her mother glanced away from the viewer, smiled, then looked down at her watch in dismay. "My God, what time is it?"

"Relax. Dad is probably over at the airfield in the hangar, playing with his ultralight."

"You're right. He had a meeting at one, but it couldn't have lasted this long, could it? Since he retired from the Air Force, negotiating these government contracts seems more like a hobby than a job for him." Her mother smiled again, nose wrinkling. Kelly wished she'd been dealt that button nose in the genetic gin game. But it was Cindy who seemed to have inherited all of their mother's sunny blondness.

"Dear, Michael Ryton called. He said he'd try again later. I want to talk to you about that."

Kelly saw trouble coming. "About what?"

"Your father is a little worried about your friendship with him."

"Figures. And you?"

"Well, Michael seems nice, but . . ."

Kelly sighed and imitated a computer voice drone: "Dean's list at Cornell, member of the tennis team, Merton Scholarship recipient, graduated with honors, youngest partner in Ryton, Greene and Davis Engineering . . ."

"Yes, I know all that." Her mother's tone was slightly impatient. "What I don't know is if it's such a good idea for you to be so friendly with someone so much older than you are. You haven't even graduated from high school."

"Oh, come on, Mom. You and Dad practically threw me at Don Korbel when he was home from Yale last Easter. Just because he's the son of Dad's old army buddy. You don't care about Michael's age. You're worried because he's a mutant."

7

Her mother looked embarrassed. "Well, we've seen more of these mutants than you have. They're very close-knit, clannish. And strange. We've seen them floating along the seashore or whatever it is they do that puts them up in the air. They keep to themselves. I'm just afraid of your being hurt."

"Cindy has a mutant friend."

"Yes, but Reta is the same age as your sister . . . and sex."

"So that's it." Kelly wanted to laugh. "I should have guessed. You didn't seem all that worried in Germany when I was dating those soldiers. And they were even older than Michael." She paused, watching her dart hit home. "Don't start worrying now. I can take care of myself. He's a very nice guy, and three times more interesting than those jerks at that dumb backwater school you put me in."

"I'm sure he is. . . ." her mother reached for her glass and took a long sip. "We're just worried. You don't seem very happy."

Exasperation began to erode Kelly's self-control. The last thing she wanted was to get started on this subject with her mother, to bring up questions even she couldn't answer.

"I'd be a lot happier if you'd stop trying to run my friendships," she said. "Why aren't you worried about Cindy, too?" She stared angrily at her mother. "Don't bother answering. I know why. It's because Cindy's always happy. Lucky girl."

"Kelly, I—" Her mother cut herself off as the front door slammed. "There's your father. Why don't you go upstairs for a while before dinner?" It was not a gentle suggestion.

JAMES RYTON sat in the chilly conference room, arms folded, impatiently waiting for the meeting to end. He would be late for the annual clan meeting if McLeod didn't wind things up soon; it was a two-hour drive to the shore. What he was proposing was insane, of course. These normals never thought ahead. No wonder his engineering group was constantly busy with government contracts. The added safety features only made it worse.

"We'll transmit the paperwork to your office tomorrow morning," McLeod said, shutting down the roomscreen.

"Fine. The sooner we can get started, the better." He shook hands with McLeod, nodded and walked toward the rose-carpeted reception area. These face-to-face negotiations were a blasted waste of time, he thought, but government regulations required them. Infuriating when he had a perfectly good conference screen set up in his office especially for these purposes. Stupid. Wasteful.

He hated waste and stupidity. Normals seemed to specialize in it.

He made a mental note to have Michael handle future negotiations. Perhaps he could relinquish this task to his son entirely, since he liked to talk to nonmutants so much.

Ryton thought of the wall he longed to build around his home, his family, his life. It had all started with the violence in the nineties. The murders. Oh, he'd been an idealistic young fool then, hot-blooded and optimistic. But Sarah took all that with her, and more, when she died. His beautiful sister, raped and bludgeoned.

Shivering in the December air, Ryton got into his skimmer. Those fools who sought out unnecessary contact with the normals were asking for trouble, he thought. Mutants had never been accepted. Never would be.

Some interaction with nonmutants was inescapable, of course. They controlled the economy, the government, and the schools. Even worse, their puling, whiny emotions clung to him like cobwebs each time he stepped forth into their world. He cloaked his clairaudience as much as he could, but some leakage always occurred. With a sigh, Ryton turned the skimmer onto the highway access road.

Little people, these normals. With small concerns, contemptible interests. Fearful of strangeness. Otherness. If he awoke tomorrow to find them vanished and gone, he would never miss them. They'd already taken too much from him. His youth. His trust. Sarah. No, he'd never miss any normal. Never.

2

THE MUFFLED POUNDING of the surf stopped in midbeat as the door closed. Michael shrugged off his jacket, grateful for the new space heaters, and saw fifty too familiar faces, one hundred familiar golden eyes, most of his clan, sitting around the large table in the dining area.

His mother gave a slight smile and indicated two gray folding chairs near her. With a sigh, Michael gingerly settled his lanky frame onto the cold metal seat. He could feel it right through his pants. Melanie sat down next to him. He scanned the room; his father was nowhere in sight. Must have been delayed.

"As I was saying," Uncle Halden intoned. "In this year of our wait 672, standard calendar 2017, we've had two births, one death, one disappearance, but that's Skerry, and he's done it before. We've got the usual people looking for him.

"Our outreach efforts have located two singletons in rural Tennessee, and they've joined us. There've been three marriages." A pause. "Two mixed marriages. But we will monitor the offspring." Was it Michael's imagination, or, all around him, had a hundred golden eyes shed tears of woe? Fifty mouths sighed with disappointment?

"The community maintains." Halden said staunchly. He

was Book Keeper this quarter, and the formal words seemed odd coming out of his mouth. Michael preferred to see him at night, by the fire with his banjo, roaring out the old songs, light dancing on his broad cheeks and bald head. The serious mask he'd assumed for this meeting didn't suit his expansive nature.

"And the season was fruitful?" asked Zenora, Halden's wife, as ritual demanded.

"Indeed."

"May it ever be so," came the ritual answer from all attending. Michael nudged Melanie, who appeared to be dozing. She chimed in on the last two words.

"What about the debate on the Fairness Doctrine?" Ren Miller asked. His round face was red with anger, as usual. "When are we going to be allowed to compete in athletic competition?"

"Ren, you know we've approached Senator Jacobsen about it," Halden said. "She's reviewing the possibility of a repeal."

"It's about time."

"Personally, I think you make too much of this," Halden retorted. "Our enhanced abilities do give us unfair advantage over normals. You can't deny it."

Miller glared at the Book Keeper but remained silent.

The clan shifted uneasily.

Michael knew that the doctrine was a sore point with most mutants and had been ever since it was made law in the 1990s.

Halden took a deep breath.

"Let us read from the Book," he said. "The fifth refrain of The Waiting Time." His voice was calm.

He paused to page through the huge old volume. Michael found himself holding his breath in anticipation. The Book Keeper found his place and in a rich voice intoned the familiar passage.

> And when we knew ourselves to be different,
> To be mutant and therefore other,

12

We took ourselves away,
Sequestered that portion of us most other,
And so turned a bland face to the blind eyes
Of the world.
Formed our community in silence, in hiding,
Offered love and sharing to one another,
And waited until a better time,
A cycle in which we might share
Beyond our circle.
We are still waiting.

Halden shut the Book.

"We are still waiting," the little group intoned around him.

"Join hands and share with me now," Halden whispered, lowering his head, closing his eyes. He reached out his hands to either side and grasped others who in turn had reached out, and so it went around the table until every hand held another.

Reluctantly, Michael closed his eyes and felt the familiar tickle of the linkage take hold. He both dreaded and enjoyed this moment, as self-awareness faded, to be replaced by the hum of the groupmind, the mental sound not one of distinct words, but, rather, a reassuring tonality, like several bees buzzing in shifting harmonies. He relaxed, bathing in the warmth of the connection. All was understood, all was accepted and forgiven. Here was love. He floated, suspended in it, stretched in the warmth of the groupmind like a lazy kitten in a golden sunbeam. When, by imperceptible degrees, the subvocal hum shifted, tilting him back toward and into his own lonely head, he swam with that gentle tide as well.

He opened his eyes. His watch told him it was an hour later. As often as he'd experienced it, Michael was always surprised by so great a passage of time in what seemed like only moments. He resealed his green jacket against the cold.

Nearby, people were yawning, rubbing their eyes, smiling gently. His aunt Zenora winked across the table and he grinned, thinking of the wonderful brownies that she had probably hidden away for later. Their aroma hung in the air, a tantalizing chocolate perfume.

The front door opened and Michael's father walked in, his lips pursed.

"James, you've missed the sharing," Halden rumbled at him. "Business, as usual?"

"Afraid so," Ryton said, his expression softening. "You know how I hate to miss a sharing. Especially now that you're Book Keeper, Halden."

"Well, there's always tomorrow's session, Cousin," Halden said. "Come have a drink."

The two men embraced briefly, slapping each other on the back.

What a strange pair, Michael thought. His father was lean and blond while his uncle was swarthy and bearlike. But then, many of his mutant relatives were odd-looking. There was an explanation for that in the Chronicles, he knew. There was an explanation for everything, if you looked hard enough. But the Chronicles were written in archaic, non-scientific language, which did not dispel his uncertainty.

The mutants had first appeared over six hundred years ago. Some kind of meteorological occurrence had apparently preceded them. The Chronicles told of skies raining blood and cows being delivered of two-headed calves. But as far as Michael could tell, that kind of thing was happening all the time in the fifteenth century.

He also knew that mutant scientists and normal theorists believed that a natural tendency toward mutantism was enhanced by exposure to certain kinds of radiation. A comet or meteor shower, maybe, which resulted in all sorts of mutations in the generation immediately following exposure. Many were terminal mutations: peculiar, sterile, doomed. But the successful *Homo sapiens* strains flourished. Mental powers were enhanced. Some mutants developed telepathic skills of varying levels. Others gained telekinetic powers, again, of different strengths. Occasionally, a mutant had more than one power. Precogs. Sense clouders. Telepyros. Occasionally, a mutant with impressiv· strength and skill would emerge. But that was rare. Mutant powers were quirky, often difficult to control.

The eyes were a weird side effect about which there were many theories. Half the time, Michael thought it all sounded like a fairy tale. Until mutant season came around in the year's cycle again.

As a child, he'd listened, riveted, when the tale of his clan unfolded during the ritual telling each year. Now he could almost repeat it in his sleep. How his forebears had struggled to survive, painfully aware of their strange powers and the potential for violent, panicked reactions to them from the "normal" majority. So they'd created enclaves, hidden away from prying eyes and damning questions. For centuries, mutants had lived on the periphery of society as thieves, alchemists, witches, and medicine men. Some were burned at the stake. Some enjoyed lives of unimaginable wealth. Several joined the circus. Mutants made good carnies. And better cat burglars.

Odd, reclusive, aloof, they survived and multiplied, but always under many shadows. Aside from the fear of public discovery and persecution in ages past, mutants had to cope with the knowledge that their life spans were shorter than those of regular *Homo sapiens*. Often, a mutant male lived only into his late fifties. To survive longer was to court madness. Michael had listened with shivers to tales of the storehouses maintained by his clan where their elderly raved, far from normal ears and eyes. The suicide rate among older mutants was twice that of the normal population. In return for their brief lives, they had the use of powers that were, at best, unreliable.

Communities within communities. The mutant strain had been preserved by careful inbreeding. And the price was dear. No wonder people like his father were touchy when it came to public scrutiny. They were proud of their heritage and uncertain of how normals would react, even now. But the thought of spending his life locked in this closet with his family was beginning to feel unendurable. Four years of college had shown Michael a world glittering with possibilities outside the clan.

Michael looked around the room. He saw a big, loving group that probably would never understand how he felt. His Uncle Halden was large-boned, with a generous belly. Against his bearlike solidity, Michael's father looked much shorter, slimmer, golden-skinned and blond. Michael knew he resembled his father, although his mother's Asian ancestry had given his skin a trifle richer hue, his eyes a somewhat more exotic cast. Just another flavor in the mutant pot, he thought. But Michael believed mutants were one hundred percent *Homo sapiens.* Whatever those rogue mutagens were all about, well, leave that to the geneticists in the clan.

He'd heard of mutants with one eye, scaled skin, or seven fingers on each hand, but they were rumored to live on the West Coast, in seclusion. He was grateful that the oddest physical feature he had was the epicanthic fold creasing his eyelids, thanks to Sue Li Ryton, his mother. Melanie appeared a bit more Asian with her darker hair, and Jimmy was the most like their mother of the three. Michael searched around the room for his prankster younger brother but didn't find him. Probably giving somebody a mental hotfoot someplace. And he'd get away with it, too. Somehow, their father managed to overlook Jimmy's transgressions.

The meeting seemed to be over. Michael began to sidle toward the door. These clan meetings were becoming a bore in their predictability, and he wanted some time to himself. There'd be precious little of it once they got home; the trip to Washington loomed, and after that, the NASA contracts.

"Leaving so soon, Michael?" James Ryton's voice, pitched high in disapproval, cut knifelike through the room and stopped him in midstep. "Well, I'm glad you could drop by."

Michael ignored the sarcasm. "I just wanted to get some fresh air."

"In that cold?" His father stared at him. "What's the matter, your family isn't good enough company?"

"I just want to take a walk. To think."

His father snorted. "About some girl, probably. Well, you're wasting your time. You should be thinking about mutant business. Our trip to Washington. It's time you looked upon yourself as a responsible member of this community. You're a partner in the firm. You must consider your future. Our future."

Michael's temper flared. "I think plenty about the business," he snapped. "What about me? What about what I want?"

"Well, what do you want?"

Around the room, conversations stopped as clan members turned toward them. Michael knew what he was about to say would hurt his family and friends, but he couldn't help it.

"I'm tired of worrying about tradition," he said. "This is supposed to be the time in which we come forth, isn't it? We've got Eleanor Jacobsen in Congress now, and—"

His father cut him off. "Some people are not convinced this is the moment for openness with the nonmutant world. I think it's best that we observe the old ways and move cautiously. Normals can be dangerous."

"Yes, I know," Michael said impatiently.

"Then you must understand, I have your best interests at heart," his father said. "We may occasionally socialize with outsiders but we don't marry them."

Michael stared at him in disbelief.

"Who said anything about marriage? And what's wrong with that anyway?"

His father glared back, eyes harsh behind his bifocals. "You know what I've told you about genetic drift. We've got to protect the mutant line. It was hard enough to establish it in the first place."

"I know, I know. Gods, do I know!"

"Then you also know that it's time for you to consider your actions. Your responsibilities. It's time you started paying attention to Jena. She's the right age, and there aren't many others eligible."

A blond-haired girl, slim yet sultry-looking, smiled across the room at Michael. A golden unity pin glinted at her throat. He forced himself to look the other way, stomach knotting. Clan life was a vise in which he was caught, and he feared it would twist the life out of him.

"So that's it," he said bitterly. "Fit in, breed true, conform. Just as I thought."

"You make it sound like a dreadful fate."

"Maybe I think it is." He saw tears in his mother's eyes, but it was too late to take anything back, and he wasn't sure he wanted to. "I didn't spend four years at Cornell just to become part of somebody else's master plan. To be a stud for the clan."

He heard gasps around him. His father's face was turning red, a sure sign of another explosion.

"Michael, if you don't start facing your responsibilities to us, decisions will have to be made for you."

"As if they haven't been already." Defiant, Michael faced him, hands on his hips. "You tell me to act and think like an adult, but when I do, you treat me like a child."

Every golden eye in the room was locked on him. Michael felt as though he was suffocating. If he didn't get out of that room he was going to burst. To die.

With a wrench, he turned and, using his telekinetic skill, opened the door from three feet away. Then he was standing outside the shack, his ragged breath making clouds in the cold air. But where to go? The waves' pounding sent an insistent message. Michael ran for the beach, determined to get as far away from his family as possible.

. . .

JAMES RYTON restrained the urge to wince as the door slammed behind his eldest son. Around him, members of the clan muttered disapprovingly, shaking their heads and moving off to talk in small groups.

"Want some friendly advice?" Halden asked.

"Not really, Hal, but I know you well enough to know I'm going to get it anyhow."

Halden smiled. "You're just going to chase Michael away if you keep that up."

"Maybe you're right." Ryton sighed. "He reminds me of myself at that age. So hotheaded. I'm afraid he'll get hurt."

"You made it through," Halden said. "Intact, so it seems."

Ryton gave him a half smile. "More or less. The mental flares are starting, though, Halden. I can feel them, late at night. The clairaudient distortion wakes me up."

The Book Keeper grasped Ryton's shoulder. "Take heart. We're getting closer and closer to some means of controlling them. Maybe even a cure."

His mouth a bitter line, Ryton pulled away. "I don't want to spend the next twenty years on neural dampers. Rather kill myself." His tone was so low, he might have been talking to himself.

"James, don't talk that way."

"Sorry, old friend," Ryton said. He forced a smile. "Let's discuss something less depressing."

Halden squeezed his arm. "Your son is smart, a credit to the clan. He'll come around. Just be patient."

"Hope you're right. Have you learned anything else about this so-called supermutant?"

"The rumors are heating up," the Book Keeper said. "Reports from Brazil of experiments with radiation. On *human* subjects."

"Brazil this time? Last time, it was Burma. I don't believe any of it. Is there any documentation? Hard proof?"

"Not exactly. But there's been enough noise and thunder

19

to set off discussion in Congress of forming an investigative committee."

"To Brazil?"

"Where else? An informal junket, of course. It won't do to ruffle their feathers just when they're finally paying off so much of their debt to us."

"Thanks to that triobium lode they found in Bahia. And English laser-mining technology." Ryton said. "What about Jacobsen? She'll go, of course."

Halden shrugged. "She'll have to. And we're taking this a bit more seriously than before. I've had reports from the West Coast. Russia, too. Our geneticists think it's possible that whoever these people are, they've isolated and coded the mutant genome."

Ryton laughed harshly. "Oh, don't start that. You know they were talking about genome coding twenty or thirty years ago, in the eighties. It's never been done successfully, especially after that Japanese blunder led to the moratorium on it."

"Perhaps the moratorium never spread to Brazil." Halden emptied his mug in a gulp and poured a fresh cup of coffee. "So what *do* you hear out of Russia?"

"Sketchy reports. They're not as well organized there as we are, of course, but on her last trip over, Zenora saw Yakovsky. He told her that they were worried about Brazil too."

"This should be discussed at the general meeting."

"I thought so. Tomorrow?"

Ryton nodded. "The implications are frightening. After all, the normals don't really know what to make of us now. What will happen if a true enhanced mutant is revealed?"

"Oh, you know, the usual. Mass riots. Pogroms. Lynchings." Halden smiled. "You always look on the dark side, James. An enhanced mutant could be a wonderful thing."

Wounded, Ryton drew himself up. "I know you think this is amusing, Halden. But I haven't forgotten 1992. Or Sarah. This could be very dangerous for us."

"Of course you're worried," Halden said diplomatically. "But that was twenty-five years ago. And after all, aren't we trying to do the same thing in our own way? Create supermutants through inbreeding?"

"No," Ryton snapped. "What we're interested in is survival. Safety in numbers. Staying out of trouble, not making the rest of the human race obsolete. Which is what we'll be accused of if this supermutant thing proves even remotely true. You know the normals are afraid of us to begin with. And if there's any fact behind this rumor of radiation-enhanced mutants, then what happens to us, Halden? What about us?"

ALTHOUGH THERE WERE no sheltering dunes, Michael risked levitating over the waves anyway. It was dusk, and he didn't think he'd be easily seen. He didn't like using his mutant abilities in front of strangers, unlike some of his cousins, who enjoyed showing off to shock the normals. But there was no one on the beach.

A crisp wind carried the hint of snow. A few lonely birds picked at seaweed along the water line. Michael marveled at how they managed to survive, even in the heart of winter. They scattered frantically as his shadow moved over them.

Floating above the water was a wonderful game, he thought. He'd always loved it. When he was little, his mother had occasionally tied a rope to him to keep his levitation powers under control. He remembered her patiently tutoring him when he was four years old. "Take a big step and hop! Come on, Michael. Try again."

His telekinetic abilities had only surfaced in the past three years. He enjoyed experimenting with them. Mentally, he pushed against the surging waters. They pushed back, of course, but he thought that he saw the water give way some.

He was a rarity even in their community; a double mutant. His father was always harping on his precious genes. Preserve. Protect. Marry a mutant girl. Have little mutant kids.

Become Book Keeper someday. Don't show your powers to anybody. Fit in. Fade in. It made him angry just to think about it.

The surf slammed a wave against the shore and the spray came flying toward him. He rose a bit higher to avoid it.

Good little mutants, he thought. They hid like mice, clinging together, sucking up all the breathable air, every personality quirk grating against him like fingernails on a blackboard each time he attended a clan gathering. At least he'd gotten a break from it during college. Seen how the normals lived. And he liked it.

People like Kelly McLeod breathed easily. They were responsible only to themselves, perhaps to their families. But there were no hidden secrets to protect. No claustrophobic traditions to observe, no insular habits to maintain. They were free of the cloying familiarity of clan life. They had no sacred mission, save to be themselves and see what life had to offer.

He admired Kelly's strong personality, her independence. Most mutant women were restrained, careful, some hidden shadow passing behind their eyes. Even Jena. He felt momentarily ashamed for the way he had ignored her. She was a foxy girl, but she had the wrong color eyes. All mutants had eyes that same strange tawny golden brown, oddly reflective in the dark; an easy way to recognize clan members in unfamiliar places.

Kelly's eyes were clear blue. He liked their contrast with her light skin and dark hair, liked her finely modeled, pointed nose, her chiseled cheekbones. The way she'd wear black leather and silver chains one day, the next appear with her hair swept up, tiny earrings, and some old-fashioned blouse with a high neck and lace. When she smiled, she revealed less than perfectly aligned teeth, but that was fine with him. He didn't want her to be a plastic doll. That was part of her attraction.

He thought about kissing her in the McLeod backyard. She

hadn't resisted when he'd put his hands under her bra. If there'd been time, he knew she would have encouraged more, but her father had come out. And he wanted her with a hunger he'd never felt for any mutant girl.

"Call me when you get back from vacation," she'd said to him, dark hair haloed in the lamplight of her back porch. He couldn't wait to see her again. But he'd have to be careful that his father didn't find out.

"A Eurodollar for your thoughts."

Michael jerked around. There was no one there. In the distance, he could hear a shutter slapping in the wind. Had he imagined somebody speaking to him?

"Aren't you afraid that one of the normals will see you and faint?" Somebody was speaking to him, all right, but the voice he heard was in his mind, not in his ears. And that mocking, insinuating tenor could only belong to one person. His cousin Skerry. But Halden had said he was gone. . . .

"Skerry? Where are you?" Michael asked aloud. He had no ability as a sending telepath, and it was forbidden to reach into another's mind to read it even if you had the gift. Skerry could ask him questions, but he would not delve for answers.

"Behind the snack bar."

Michael descended quickly and padded over the sand toward the weathered gray building, boarded up against winter winds. He peered around the far corner. Nothing but beach houses and sand.

"You're getting warmer."

"C'mon, Skerry, stop screwing around!" He knew he could be standing right next to him, but unless Skerry wanted to be seen, Michael could go on searching for him until New Year's.

He heard what sounded like a pack of cards being shuffled behind him. Turning, he saw gray diagonal bars that slowly solidified, like a video image, into his cousin. Same old Skerry. Green U.S. Army parka, jeans and boots, curly brown hair, beard, and those radiant eyes, just like his. But where

Michael ran toward wiry strength and speed, Skerry was big, muscular, with large shoulders and legs that looked as though they could kick a football across a field. Or knock down a tree. His teeth showed white in a teasing grin. Michael liked his cousin, although he didn't exactly trust him. But he didn't exactly distrust him, either. It was difficult to know how to feel about a telepath who pulled disappearing acts.

"You and your old man having words again?"

"Were you at that meeting?"

"Let's just say I keep tabs on what's happening with my nearest and dearest."

"Well, then you know how it is. They want me to marry Jena. Fall in line. Wipe my shoes. Be a good little mutant boy."

"You sound fed up."

"I am."

"So leave."

Michael shook his head, embarrassed. "I can't. Maybe you can, but it would kill my parents if I quit the firm and left town."

Skerry shrugged, pulled out a toothpick, and inserted it into his mouth at a jaunty angle.

"Where've you been?" Michael asked.

"Here and there. Big world out there." He began to saunter down the beach and gestured for Michael to accompany him. They fell into step and walked for several minutes in silence. Skerry paused, looked at him sharply, threw the toothpick into the surf.

"You can't live your entire life for 'em. You'll go crazy. And I don't mean mutant-crazy. You've got more choices than you think, but if you don't take advantage of them now, you never will. Remember that famous mutant life span. Short. Bad ending. Get away and find out who you are."

"Like you?"

"Maybe."

"Easier said than done. Besides, if you've escaped, what are you doing here?"

Skerry shrugged again. "Nostalgia. Besides, what makes you think I'm really here?" He grinned and began to fade around the edges."

"Skerry, wait. Don't go."

"Sorry kid, time's up. Think about what I said. Get away while you still can. I'll be in touch."

It seemed to Michael that the last thing to fade away was Skerry's smile.

MELANIE TOOK A LARGE BITE out of her brownie, savoring the rich, dark taste. This was the part of the meeting everybody looked forward to: catching up on gossip, admiring the newest additions to the clan, and discussing politics. Especially politics. Oh, yes, everyone looked forward to it. Everyone but her.

She watched the younger children levitating in a circle near the fireplace and, for a moment, wished she were a child again so she could join them. But more than age separated her from that happy group by the fire, and from the clan crowding the room. Melanie was a mutant, of course. All it took was a look into her golden eyes to see that. But she was a null. Dysfunctional.

Everybody in the clan treated her politely, of course. Too politely. They acted as though she were mentally retarded. Their pity was as difficult to swallow as the contempt of the nonmutants at school.

Across the room, Marol proudly held on to her infant son, Sefrim, as he levitated peacefully above her lap, asleep.

I don't even have as much ability as a mutant infant, Melanie thought.

She wished she'd stormed out with Michael. Or brought some of her mother's Valedrine with her. She was coming to dread these gatherings as much as her older brother. More. At least he was gifted. She didn't really know what she was.

Don't cry, she told herself fiercely. Don't let them see you cry.

Could she help it that she had the golden eyes but not a shred of mutant power? Oh, how she'd practiced in her room for hours when she thought nobody knew, praying that her abilities were just late in maturing.

She was meant to be telekinetic—she felt it in her bones. But strain as she might, until she'd given herself headaches from concentrating on moving an orange across the room, or even across a table, nothing ever happened. The orange stayed put.

Once she'd gotten her period, Melanie began to give up hope. Almost every mutant girl had developed her power by then. So Melanie tried to understand, if not accept. But when Michael developed a second ability, she realized that she'd been singled out by some cruel and malicious god for special torment. Her older brother had somehow received both his own and her powers!

A hand touched her shoulder gently, affectionately. Melanie looked up to see Aunt Zenora smiling down at her. Uncle Halden's wife was certainly built to suit him, she thought. Big and brassy, just like him. She wore half a dozen golden unity pins along one sleeve: six golden eyes framed by linked arms. Zenora was active in the Mutant Union and was always passing out pins at clan meetings.

Zenora hugged her. "How's school?"

"Okay, I guess."

"You must be, let's see now, a junior?"

"Senior."

"Well, have you been thinking about college?" Zenora asked. "A career?"

Melanie shrugged. "Dad wants me to work with him."

"Sounds like a good idea to me."

"I suppose." The thought of working with her father and brother made Melanie's stomach turn. What she wanted to do was become a video jock. The first mutant video jock. But that was as unlikely as her suddenly levitating and walking across the ceiling.

Zenora was drawn away into a political discussion in which every third sentence seemed to include the name of Senator Eleanor Jacobsen. Melanie shook her head. Politics bored her. She saw her mother sitting on the old red sofa and joined her.

"Zenora's ever the firebrand," Sue Li said, smiling.

"I think she'd rather talk politics than do anything else, even cook," Melanie said. "I'll bet she wears a mutant unity pin to bed."

Jena walked by, eyes cast downward.

Sue Li sighed. "Your brother is causing trouble for us. I'm embarrassed for that girl."

"I'm not," Melanie said. "Jena's got a hundred boyfriends. I'm sorry for Michael."

"What do you mean?" Her mother looked at her sharply. She felt her face grow hot.

"Well, he doesn't like Jena. I mean, he does, but not the way you want him to." Melanie squirmed. "I think it's not fair to try and make him do what he doesn't want to do."

"That's very loyal," Sue Li said, her mouth a prim line.

Privately, Melanie thought that Jena was a smug pain whose only close personal relationship was with her mirror. But she felt perversely pleased to see somebody else subjected to the clan's scrutiny and sympathy, for once. She reached for another brownie and wondered if Zenora was a good cook because she was a mutant, or despite it.

WARM YELLOW LIGHT filled the windows of the Ryton bungalow and spilled out into the dark. The sun had been down for nearly an hour. Michael opened the door carefully, ready to bolt at the first sign of trouble. His mother was sitting at the kitchen table, reading, with her back to him. Melanie and his father were nowhere in sight. She looked up from her notescreen as he entered the room.

"Have you eaten?" She sounded tired.

"No."

"Take off your coat and I'll make a sandwich for you."

The wooden chair legs scraped as his mother stood up and walked into the kitchen. With the light shining on her dark hair, her face nearly framed by the scarlet cowl-necked sweater she wore, his mother reminded Michael of a print he'd once seen, a Japanese print of a geisha in a berry-colored kimono and scarf. He hung up his coat and sat in the chair she'd vacated. He peered at the text onscreen, a horror story from some old collection.

"You like reading this stuff?"

"Yes. It takes me to a totally different world. And then I'm always grateful to come back to my own."

"Wish I felt that way," Michael said. "Where is everybody?"

"Your father stayed behind to talk with Halden and Zenora. Jimmy and Melanie are next door watching Tela's big screen."

She brought a soya loaf sandwich and a cup of cocoa to the table and sat down opposite him, looking pensive.

"Michael, I know you feel resentful of the demands we place on you," she said. "But your father doesn't mean to be harsh with you."

"Then why does he act that way?"

She sighed. "He's worried. You know how important it is to him to build for the future. And he's very proud of you."

"Sure, of having a double mutant for a son. Well, if he's so proud, why doesn't he tell me so himself?"

"That's very difficult for him."

Michael swallowed a mouthful of sandwich.

"I wish he wouldn't make it so difficult for me," he said. "And Mel."

"I know."

"Did you ever feel this way?"

She smiled gently. "Of course. But it was different when I

was growing up. There was much more enthusiasm within the clan. We felt like we were on the cusp of a new age. But that was in the seventies, when anything seemed possible."

"What was it like?"

"Oh, exciting. Confusing. Especially to a child." She paused, old memories bringing color to her cheeks. "It felt like the world was bright with opportunity and color. That all the old ways were changing. And, in a way, they were. But then came the violence. And, in many ways, things stayed the same for us."

Michael leaned back in his chair. "Didn't anybody think the time of waiting might be over?"

Sadly, his mother nodded. "I was too young to remember much of what went on in the meetings. But I do remember that one year, a motion was made to come forth, proclaim ourselves in the public arena. Some of the older members resisted, and in the end, the clan split on the issue. So finally, some of us came forth, back in the nineties. Before that, the meetings were twice as big, twice as many people there as attend now. But we had been divided before that. The sixties and seventies split us, and those looking for openness left. They moved away, some to California. Among them was the boy I thought I would marry."

"What happened to them? To him?"

A shadow passed across her delicate features. "We are starting to come back together again now. Perhaps one day we will all be together, like in the old times. As for that boy, well, he disappeared."

Michael stopped chewing his sandwich and looked at his mother as though he'd never really seen her before. She had an entire private life she'd never shown him. He felt new respect for her.

"Did he die?"

"I suppose so."

"What was he like?"

She reached over gently to brush a strand of his hair out of his eyes. "A bit like your cousin Skerry. Wild. That's what made him so appealing. And would have made him impossible to live with."

Michael was tempted to tell her he'd seen Skerry. The words almost bubbled out, but he decided to hold back. If she told anybody, he'd be grilled about it. Right now, he enjoyed having a few secrets of his own.

3

THE MUSIC from the Hardwired's mechband bounced off the pink tiles in the bathroom in strange, distorted echoes: *waow, waow,* like the cry of a distant, electronic cat. Melanie stared in the cracked glass of the mirror. Her face was flushed from the heat. It was a warm night for the middle of February.

The Valedrine she'd found in her mother's medicine cabinet was buzzing along nicely through her brain, leaving her just the slightest bit numb. She pulled a yellow comb through her hair and studied her reflection. A part-Chinese girl with soft brown hair stared back at her. Just a nice, normal girl out for an evening of fun.

A nice, normal girl with golden eyes.

She stared at her face as though she'd never seen it before, transfixed by the strangeness of those eyes, a double-edged reminder of who she was. A mutant. A null. Who would want her? Mutant or normal, who would ever want her?

Maybe she should wear contact lenses. She closed her eyes with pleasure at the thought; covering that mutant gold with dark brown, or hazel. At least then she'd look like an ordinary Asian girl. Imagine living like a nonmutant, she thought.

How strange. To walk down a street and just fade into the crowd. . . .

The door to the bathroom slammed open and Tiff Seldon walked in, chattering with Cilla Cole. They stopped when they saw Melanie. Tiff shouldered by her toward the stalls. She was a full head taller than Melanie, with a square, athletic figure, her head topped by a bristling yellow crew cut.

"Excuse me," she said with exaggerated courtesy, clipping Melanie with her hip.

Melanie pitched forward, almost cracking her forehead against the mirror glass before she caught herself.

"Hey!" She glared over her shoulder. That shove had been deliberate. She knew it. Cilla leaned against the wall tiles opposite the sink, skinny arms crossed in front of her, a joystick between her lips, double silver rings in each nostril. Her hair was perhaps an inch longer than Tiff's, and bright green. She grinned at Melanie with cheerful malice.

"Hey yourself, mutie. Why don't you do some tricks for us?" Tiff said, her voice booming out from behind the stall.

Melanie threw her comb into her purse, and turned to leave. But Cilla blocked her path.

"Somebody's talking to you, mutie. Don't you pay attention?"

"Get out of my way, Cilla." Melanie's voice was cool but her heart pounded. Tiff and Cilla were tough and reckless, part of a crowd that bashed mutants for fun.

"No manners at all." Cilla shook her head in mock disapproval and, moving in from the right, shoved Melanie backward against the wall. Melanie dodged to her left, but Tiff was suddenly looming over her, grinning nastily. Reaching a meaty hand under her shirt, Tiff pulled out a knife: it flashed silver in the fluorescent lights. Then she grabbed Melanie by the shoulder, waving the small vibroblade in front of her face. Its surface glistened.

"Isn't this nice? My brother doesn't know I took it from his jacket." Tiff's breath smelled of wine or beer, and her eyes gleamed with a peculiar light. "Thought I'd try a little carving. Maybe whittle a mutie." She snickered.

Melanie gulped, staring at the knife. Were they really going to cut her?

The blade danced closer, vibrating, as Tiff faked a pass at Melanie's chin. Melanie shut her eyes. If she screamed, would anybody hear her? Her cousin Germyn was waiting for her at the bar. Wouldn't she come looking for her? Or maybe if Melanie concentrated hard, very hard, she'd discover that she really did have the mutant gift. Then she could fling Tiff away from her with a breath, float to the ceiling and escape. She squeezed her eyes shut, trying desperately to levitate the two nonmutants. But the harder she tried, the weaker she felt. In despair, she gave up. She'd never be able to do anything. And they'd never leave her alone.

Melanie opened her eyes, wondering when the blade would slice her flesh and how much it would hurt. Maybe she'd die, and then Tiff would go to jail for the rest of her life. Maybe that wasn't such a bad idea. The sniper who'd shot three mutants at the World Trade Center ten years ago had gone to jail. But Melanie didn't really want to die.

"Tiff, don't do it," she pleaded. "You'll be sorry."

The bathroom door swung open. Kelly McLeod stood there, mouth open, clutching her purse.

"McLeod, I suggest you use another bathroom," Tiff said menacingly. "This one is occupied," She held the knife steady under Melanie's chin.

Kelly walked in, hands on hips.

"What's going on?"

"Just doing a little mutie carving," Cilla said, giggling. "Want to help?"

"Are you crazy?" Kelly gave her a disgusted look. "What's she done to you?"

Cilla scowled at her. "Why do you care? Are you some kind of mutie lover? Tiff, maybe you should cut her, too."

"Kelly, get out of here before you get hurt," Melanie gasped.

But Kelly ignored her. Instead, she stepped forward, grabbed Cilla's nose rings, and pulled hard. Cilla screeched, flailing at her with both hands.

"Get off her," Kelly shouted. "I said, get off her!"

"Stay out of this, McLeod." Tiff said, turning from Melanie to point the vibroblade at Kelly.

"Go 'wave yourself."

Tiff lunged for her, but Kelly released her hold on the other girl and dodged. Instead, Tiff nicked Cilla's arm with the knife. Cilla clutched the wound and started to wail as blood seeped around her fingers.

"Shut up, Cilla!" Tiff yelled. "There's some plaskin in my purse. God, I barely touched you."

Cilla closed her mouth in midsob and began rummaging in Tiff's purse for a bandage.

Kelly laughed. "Do you always do whatever she tells you to do?"

"Mutie lover!" Cilla yelled. She spun around and caught her with a back-handed slap that rocked her head to the right, spraying blood on the wall in red streaks. Tiff cursed, shoved Melanie away from her and turned around, knife hand poised to strike Kelly.

Melanie saw her chance. She leaped at Tiff, grabbed the hand holding the knife and drew it toward her mouth, sinking her teeth into the flesh above the wrist bone.

Tiff howled with pain. Melanie clamped her jaws and hung on as the larger girl tried to shake her loose. She could taste the salt of Tiff's blood. The knife clattered to the tiles at their feet. Melanie kicked it into the corner by the door. She saw Kelly struggling with Cilla. The room was crowded now, noisy and suddenly filled with people. Loud voices echoed around her.

"Ow! Let go of me, you damned mutant!" Tiff yelled.

Go to hell, Melanie thought.

34

"Ladies! Break it up!"

Jeff, the Hardwired's bouncer, waded in among them, dark head bobbing as he ducked punches. He pried Cilla and Kelly apart, getting kicked twice in the scuffle. His bald, burly partner, Ron, grabbed Melanie and Tiff.

"Let go of her, girlie." He shook Melanie, not gently.

Reluctantly, Melanie opened her mouth to release Tiff's wrist, now bloody.

With a look of disgust, Jeff shoved them toward the door. "The girls are always the worst," he said to Ron, who gave a connoisseur's nod.

"Yeah, vicious," he said gruffly.

"Well, I don't care what this is about or who started it." Jeff's voice was harsh. "You know the rules: no fighting in the Hardwired. Your memberships are revoked for two weeks. Out."

The club was silent; even the mechband had been turned off. Rows of faces watched as Tiff and Cilla hurried out the door, cursing. At the bar exit, Tiff paused.

"Mutie, I'll be looking for you," she yelled.

Melanie made an obscene gesture at her. Tiff returned it and walked out, clutching her wounded wrist.

Jeff held the door open. "Out, ladies. That means you two, too."

Melanie scanned the crowd for Germyn, then gave up the effort. She knew that her cousin had probably gone home at the first sign of trouble, taking her skimmer with her. Just as well, she thought. Germyn was never the greatest company. Grabbing her orange parka from the wall hook, Melanie walked out into the parking lot. Kelly followed, quietly. Melanie watched her out of the corner of her eye. Why had she helped her? Aside from a few classes together, they barely knew each other.

The silence grew between them. Finally, Melanie couldn't stand it any longer.

"Thanks," she blurted out. "You didn't have to do that, you know."

Kelly shrugged. "I couldn't just stand there and let them cut you, could I? Besides, I can't stand either one of those gorks. But you ought to be more careful—they're easy to antagonize."

"Don't I know it," Melanie said bitterly. "But they caused the problem. I was just minding my own business."

"I guess." Kelly kicked at a loose piece of gravel.

Melanie stopped walking as she made a sudden connection.

Suddenly she said, "You're dating my brother, aren't you?"

"Yeah."

She looked closely at her rescuer. Kelly was pretty in a nonmutant way. All that dark hair and those big, blue eyes. But what did Michael see in her, really, besides that? Jena was much sexier, she thought, and she was terrific at telekinetic sports and gymnastics. But maybe Michael didn't care.

Kelly seemed nice, much nicer than Jena. Normal guys at school were always sniffing around her; half the football team, at least. Not that she paid any attention to them. Well, she might have a thing for mutants. It happened sometimes. Melanie remembered the freckle-faced boy who had followed her around for half a year when she was a sophomore. Mutant-groupies, she called them. Well, maybe her brother was a normal-groupie. But he was crazy to risk clan censure just to date a normal, even one as nice as Kelly McLeod.

"Need a ride home?" Kelly asked.

"Yeah. It looks like my cousin forgot about me," Melanie said. "Hope you don't mind."

"No problem. Come on." Kelly led her to a silver-gray skimmer.

"Nice," Melanie said enviously. "Yours?"

"My mother's. Hop in." Kelly unlocked the door.

She pressed the starter, but the only response was a dull growl. She tried again. The engine refused to turn over.

"Damn." Kelly popped the hood open and got out of the skimmer. A moment later, she was back, clutching a handful of orange wires. Her face was grim.

"What happened?" Melanie said.

"The starter's been cut," Kelly said. "I'll bet that bitch Tiff did it. Didn't think she had the time." She walked to the back of the skimmer and began rummaging in the trunk.

Melanie followed her. "Now what?" she asked, feeling helpless. She'd never understood much about skimmer mechanics anyway.

"I think I can jury-rig it with some wire from my dad's tool kit," Kelly said, pulling something out of the trunk and striding toward the front of the skimmer. "He always keeps an extra in this skimmer. Here, hold this." She handed Melanie a flashlight. "Keep the light over here."

Leaning over the engine, she began to fiddle with what looked to Melanie like twin rows of metal plugs, looping braided green wire over and under them, occasionally tightening a wire coil with a small screwdriver.

"Hold that light higher, will ya?"

Hastily, Melanie complied.

With a grunt, Kelly stood up, wiping her hands on a rag. "There. Let's hope it works."

She leaned over the driver's seat and pressed the starter button. For a moment, nothing happened. Then, with a grinding complaint, the skimmer came to life. The girls smiled at one another in relief. Kelly threw the tools back into the trunk.

"Where did you learn to do that?" Melanie asked, amazed.

"My dad's a mechanical freak," Kelly said. "I think it comes from being a pilot. I just hung around until he started to teach me how to fix things." Kelly turned the skimmer out of the parking lot. "Michael thinks it's funny that I know how to use tools."

"How long have you two been going out?"

"About two months. Ever since you got back from that meeting-vacation or whatever it was."

"You must really like him," Melanie said carefully.

"Yeah. I do." Kelly said. She stopped the skimmer at an intersection, waiting for the light to change, and looked at Melanie. "You sound like you don't approve."

Melanie hesitated. It was no secret that mutants kept to themselves, but she didn't want to give away information to an outsider. Still, if Kelly wanted to get involved with Michael, she might as well know the truth.

"It's okay with me. He seems happy. But my father would have a fit if he found out."

"Why?"

"Mutants aren't supposed to date outside the clan."

Kelly stared at her. "You're joking."

"No. Nonmutant friends are tolerated. Barely. But that's it. You have to marry inside the clan. They're trying to maintain and protect clan numbers in case things get ugly again, the way they were in the nineties."

"Circling the wagons?"

"Sort of."

The traffic signal switched from red to green.

"And if you don't marry within the clan?"

"You risk censure. Or worse."

"Censure?" Kelly laughed. "What does that mean? Do they slap your hands? Send you to bed without supper?"

"It's nothing to laugh about," Melanie insisted. "It's tough. Censured clan members are outcasts."

"Hard to imagine." Kelly flipped a strand of hair out of her eyes. "It sounds like some antique cult."

"Maybe to you," Melanie said coldly. "But this is the way we live. And if you want to see my brother, you'd better understand the risks he's taking for you."

Kelly was silent for a moment, concentrating on the road. Skimmer lights streaked past them, red, yellow, white.

"Thanks for the warning," she said softly. "I didn't mean to be rude or upset you."

"Forget it." Melanie said. "How do your folks feel about you dating my brother?"

Kelly shrugged. "They're not crazy about the idea, but they're trying to live with it. I know my mother likes Michael. My father, well, he's polite anyway."

"At least you can bring Michael home to meet them. I doubt you'll get to meet my parents. And I don't think you'd enjoy meeting my father."

"Well, my folks enjoyed seeing Michael levitate. I had to really beg him to do it. What's your talent?"

"What do you mean?"

"What mutant ability do you have?"

"Nothing. I'm a null." Melanie sank back in her seat, trying to keep the bitterness out of her voice.

"Really? I didn't know there were mutant nulls."

"Yeah. Happens occasionally. I'm the only one in my family not to have a milligram of ability. Hard to believe, isn't it? My parents try to be nice about it, but I know they're disappointed. Sometimes I think that I'm not really a mutant at all. Maybe I was just switched for a mutant baby at birth, at the hospital."

"Then where'd you get those eyes?"

Melanie sighed. "Even my theories are dysfunctional."

Kelly chuckled sympathetically and pulled up in front of Melanie's house. She shut off the motor and turned toward her.

"Look, I appreciate your telling me this stuff, Melanie. I really like your brother. And, despite everything you've told me, I hope we can be friends."

"Y-yes. Sure, if you want."

Kelly nodded.

"Thanks for the ride." Melanie got out of the skimmer and closed the door. She watched Kelly back out of the driveway, yellow headlamps burning a path through the gathering fog.

How odd, she thought, to have found a new friend because of a fight. And she's nonmutant.

BILL MCLEOD stared in horror at the bruise on his eldest daughter's face. What was that reddish stain on her clothes? Beside him on the couch, his wife looked up from her reading with alarm.

"What happened?" he demanded.

"I walked into a fight at the Hardwired."

"A fight?"

"Yeah, in the bathroom. Two girls were riffing with Melanie Ryton. They had a vibroblade."

"A knife?" McLeod's stomach tightened. Was that blood on his daughter's shirt? "Were you cut?"

"No. And the knife was a small one."

"I'm relieved that you're such an expert on knives," he said acidly. "And who is this Melanie Ryton? Any relation to Michael?"

"His sister."

McLeod shook his head. Yet another Ryton. Would he never get away from that damned family?

"You're sure you're all right?" Joanna asked.

"Fine, Mom. Just messy."

"Did you have to get involved?" McLeod demanded.

Kelly gave him a disgusted look. "What was I supposed to do," she asked, "stand there and watch?"

The tone in her voice infuriated him. "Kelly, you could have gotten hurt. And I'm beginning to think you might have deserved it."

"What do you mean?"

"I mean that you're looking for trouble," he said. "Hanging around with mutants. See what it brings? Don't you have any other friends?"

"Bill!" Joanna sounded shocked.

Kelly leaned against the wall, hands in her pockets.

"Dad, Melanie is harmless. She doesn't even have any mutant powers. Just weird eyes. But everybody gives her guano for being a mutant. I don't like it."

"Of course not," Joanna said. "We've always told you to stick up for your ideals, haven't we, Bill?"

He nodded impatiently. "Yeah, of course we have. But that's not the point," he said. "Don't you know enough to keep your nose out of trouble? Mutant business is not yours. Why can't you find some nice friends with normal eyes?"

Kelly's eyes narrowed in anger. "Fine. First thing tomorrow, tell Cindi that she can't see Reta. Let's have a moratorium on mutants. We'll become known as the McLeods, famous mutant haters." Her voice was shrill. "I don't care what you think about the mutants. I like them."

"Bill, this is giving me a headache. Can't you let up for a while?" Joanna said irritably.

McLeod began to feel like the entire situation was his fault. "I will not let up," he said, his tone defensive. "Kelly, I don't want to forbid you to see any of these mutants, but I'd be a lot happier if you'd spend more time with others besides them. And if you'd stop this romance with Michael Ryton. You've always had your pick of boys. Why must you date a mutant?"

"God, half the time I feel like a mutant in this family," Kelly said. "Why shouldn't I like them? I don't want to stop seeing Michael. He's more interesting than any other boy I've ever met. And if he's a mutant, well, so what?"

"Kelly, calm down," Joanna said. "Your father is just upset about the knife fight," Joanna said. "And can you blame him? You come in with a bruised face, clothes covered in blood—"

"It's just a few spots."

"—and tell us you were in a fight in some bar."

"Yeah, I know." Kelly shifted from one foot to another, looking uncomfortable. "I'm sorry. But would you rather I lie about it?"

"No, of course not. And I'm proud that you stuck up for Melanie. Your father is too."

McLeod felt his temper flaring again. "Jo, don't talk about me as if I'm not even here."

"Dad, she's just trying to let you calm down."

McLeod wondered when his daughter had started using that condescending tone with him. He didn't like it.

"You can see our point, can't you, that it can be dangerous to be too friendly with mutants?" Joanna asked.

Kelly shrugged. "I understand what you're trying to say, Mom. But if it had been me in Melanie's position, wouldn't you have wanted my friends to try and help me?"

"Of course."

"Then what's the difference? So what if Melanie's a mutant? She's my friend. And she can't even do anything mutantlike."

"I've never heard of such a thing," McLeod said sharply.

"Well, it's true."

"That must be rough on her," Joanna said, frowning.

For a moment, McLeod's mood softened. Poor little Melanie, caught between worlds. Then he thought of her father, the coldly aloof James Ryton, and his irritation returned.

"Look, I'm sure Melanie has a hard time at school. But so do a lot of other people. And some of them aren't even mutants. She's got other friends. Mutant friends. So save your sympathy, Kelly."

"I wish I'd been a mutant for about fifteen minutes back there in that bathroom. I'd have floated Tiff Seldon right into the john and washed her hair for her." Kelly giggled.

McLeod knew she was trying to amuse him, and he smiled reluctantly. But an image formed in his mind of Kelly's face, familiar in every regard save for golden eyes, and he repressed an urge to shiver. His anger had burned out, leaving only flickering embers and depression.

"Let's just forget about this, okay? Why don't you get some clean clothes on." He turned away from his family and switched on the roomscreen, dialing up the zero-g basketball finals. He wanted to think about something other than mutants.

THE HOUSE WAS DARK, lit sparsely by track lights in the usual blues and greens soothing to mutant eyes. A guttural chant wafted toward Melanie from the tubular copper speakers in the living room. The prayer for endurance from the third book of the Chronicles; it was one of her father's favorite invocations. The rest of the house was silent, brooding. The entire world outside seemed remote. Banished.

"I assume there's an explanation?" James Ryton's voice was icy as he took in the sight of his disheveled daughter. Melanie cringed inwardly, wanting to hide. She'd known better than to expect comfort from her father. If only she could have gone home with Kelly.

"Well? What have you got to say, young lady?"

Melanie looked toward her mother, sitting curled like a cat on the sofa. She smiled encouragingly. With a deep breath, Melanie plunged in.

"A couple of girls jumped me in the bathroom. One had a knife. She'd been drinking. She wanted to cut me."

"Damned normals. They won't be satisfied until they've killed us all!"

"James!" Sue Li gave him a sharp look. Then she turned to Melanie. "Keep going, dear. What happened next?"

"Kelly McLeod came in and helped me fight them off."

"McLeod's girl helped you? A nonmutant?" Her father sounded surprised.

"Y-yes."

"How do you know this girl?" her mother asked quietly.

"She's in two of my classes."

Melanie watched her father pace angrily across the blue carpet. His face was haunted. A vein throbbed in his forehead, always a bad sign.

"And what were you doing that made these girls attack you?"

"Nothing. Combing my hair."

"Alone?"

"Yes."

"I don't understand why you'd want to go to a nonmutant place to begin with," he said. "Where was Germyn? I thought you were going out with her tonight."

"She took off as soon as the trouble started. As usual."

Melanie watched her mother's mouth twitch in what might have been a smile, quickly concealed. Her father, however, did not look amused.

"Wandering off on your own, you become a target," he said.

"So this is my fault?" Melanie said angrily. "I asked to have a knife pulled on me?"

"Don't use that tone with me, girl."

Her mother cut in. "James, you're too upset to discuss this now. Let's talk about it later."

"Don't try to placate me, Sue Li. You know how I feel about socializing with normals. The dangers."

"Yes, of course. But I think you're overreacting. After all, this isn't the nineties, James. And I don't see any harm in Melanie spending some time with nonmutants occasionally." Sue Li paused. "All the kids go to the Hardwired. She didn't ask for any trouble. If somebody occasionally takes a drink from the wrong bottle and gets aggressive, well, that's not our daughter's fault. It seems to me this all could have been much worse."

Melanie thought that her mother looked like a tiny female Buddha wrapped in her ginger-colored sweater. Serene. She wondered if she was trying to influence everybody's mood. It wouldn't be the first time she'd ended a family argument through subtle telepathy.

"Sue Li, I won't allow you to distract me," Ryton said. "Our children's continued involvement with normals is dangerous. I don't like it."

"I don't see how I can avoid it," Melanie said. "There's not enough of us to start a private mutant school. And I can't live my whole life avoiding normals."

"Well, you can be smarter about where you choose to go, what you choose to do." Her father's voice was hard. "And I forbid you to see that McLeod girl again."

Melanie's lower lip trembled. "But Dad, she helped me. And she wants to be my friend."

"You have friends within the clan."

"Oh, sure. You know that nobody in the clan really wants to be friends with me. Yeah, they're all very nice, but they treat me like I'm brain-damaged instead of just a null. And so do you."

For once, her father was speechless. He stared at her as though he'd never seen her before. Melanie knew she should stop, retreat to her room and safety, but she couldn't help herself. The words she'd dammed up for years burst out.

"I can't seem to make anybody happy," she cried. "At school, I get picked on for being a mutant. At home, and at clan meetings, you look at me like I have three heads. Oh, I know you think I don't see you, but you're wrong. And I know what you're thinking, too: 'Poor girl, a null, who'll want her? Who will we find to marry her in the clan? It's such an embarrassment having a dysfunctional daughter. Why did this have to happen to us?'"

"Oh, Melanie, you're wrong," her mother's voice was anguished, all serenity shattered.

Melanie turned on her. "Really? My own father is so busy blaming me for everything that he doesn't seem to realize that somebody threatened to stab me! Of course, that would have made everything easier for you all, wouldn't it?" She paused, feeling a sense of satisfaction at the sight of the color draining out of her mother's face, the rigid, shocked posture of her father.

"Melanie, you don't know what you're talking about. How can you say these things?" Her mother's voice broke on the last word. Melanie felt a prickle of guilt: she didn't really want to hurt her, but wasn't this the truth? Wouldn't they all be better off if she wasn't around?

Her father shook his head in dismissal. "You're talking foolishness. Childish nonsense. Everyone likes you and treats you well. You're imagining demons. Nightmares."

The three of them stared at one another in frozen silence. Finally, her mother stood up.

"It's late. We're all tired. Let's just go to bed. Tomorrow it will all look better."

Melanie felt sorry for them. They couldn't stand the truth. But she could handle it. She had to.

"Good night, Mother. Father."

She left them standing behind her and went to her bedroom. Once she'd closed the door behind her, she turned off the infrared switch before it automatically responded to her body heat and illuminated the room. She wanted the darkness.

Sitting on the bed, hugging her knees to her chest, Melanie reviewed the evening one more time. The fight in the bar. The conversation with her parents. She couldn't keep living this way. She wouldn't.

Bill McLeod rolled over and stared at the wall clock. It gleamed the time at him in soft amber numerals: four in the morning. Beside him, Joanna breathed deeply and evenly. He longed to join her but the sound of Kelly's voice echoed in his head each time he closed his eyes, keeping sleep away.

Half the time I feel like a mutant in this family.

Well, it was just said in anger, he told himself. Kelly was fighting back against her old man and his bullheaded comments. She probably didn't mean it.

But what if she did? She seemed so far away these days. A stranger. What had he done—or not done—to alienate her? Oh, hell, all kids felt alienated occasionally. It came with the territory. He remembered spending an entire night walking on the beach when he was fourteen. And his father had tanned his hide when he got home. But he'd grown out of the need for lonely beach walks, especially in the Air Force. And now, anchored to a desk job, he didn't have time for much alienation. Too many contracts.

Joanna did a heroic job with the kids. He tried his best to share, to be there for them, to withhold his judgment whenever he thought they needed to learn for themselves. . . .

His damned judgment. He clenched his fists in frustration. McLeod knew he ought to be decent about the mutants. But they gave him the creeps. Even in the service, he'd steered clear of them. His daughter had nearly gotten beaten up because of them. Or worse. And now she wanted to date that boy. . . .

Half the time I feel like a mutant in this family.

"Bill, if you don't stop rolling around, I'll never be able to sleep." Joanna sounded cross and groggy. "What are you stewing over? Kelly?"

"Yeah."

"You've got to be patient. You know it's her age."

"Thank God you can only be seventeen once."

"Amen." She snuggled up against him in the dark. "What in particular is bothering you?"

"That comment she made about feeling like a mutant. Do you think she really meant it?"

Joanna chuckled. "Sure. At the time. She was just trying to shock you. And it looks like she succeeded."

"Well, she seems unhappy. It bothers me."

"I don't think she's more unhappy than I was at her age. Or you were."

"It's not like we deprive her of anything."

"Bill, you've got to stop worrying about this. You're a terrific father. Just ease up on this mutant thing for a while. I think it gives her something to rebel against. I'm sure she'll lose her fascination with them eventually. Be patient."

"That's your area, not mine."

"Well, I've got an idea that should completely distract you

from your impatience. . . ." She began kissing his back, rolled over to nuzzle his chest, then slowly moved lower.

"Why do I get the impression I'm being treated like a sex object?"

Despite the glow of the clock, he couldn't see her smile in the dark. But he heard it in her voice. "Stop complaining. Just lie back and enjoy it."

4

GLEAMING SILVER in its track, the elevator door slid closed with a pneumatic whisper.

"What floor, please?" came the electronic drone of the cab's voice.

"Fifteen," Andie said, curtly. She disliked talking to machinery. The elevator rose smoothly, silently. Stretching in the luxury of the empty cab, Andie stared at her distorted reflection in the door's burnished surface. Wondered idly what it would be like to go through life with a neck of Modigliani-esque proportions topped by a Picassoid face with two eyes on one side of the nose. That was how she'd first imagined mutants when she'd heard about them as a child. Before they were in the schools, the streets, the seat of government.

The cab stopped and the door whooshed open to admit Karim Fuentes, Senator Craddick's senior aide, and Carter Pierce, chief lobbyist for Korean superconductors, Brazilian gene splicing and French plasalloys.

"Andie—looking good." Fuentes gave her one of his dazzling smiles. "You know Carter?"

"We've met." Despite herself, she liked Karim's dark good looks and easy charm. But Pierce's political connections and French silk cuffs left her cold. She'd never cared for blonds anyway. For his part, Pierce avoided Jacobsen's office with almost phobic consistency. "How are you?"

"Perhaps we should be asking that of you," Pierce said, smugly, staring into his reflection and straightening his tie.

For a moment, Andie wanted to get off the elevator. But the slow climb up eight flights by foot was unappealing. She decided to stay. She could always kill Pierce, she told herself.

"Pardon me?" she said.

Pierce smiled slyly at her. "Well, we heard about the letter bomb. And that's not the first one, is it? Doesn't this kind of thing ever make you just a little bit nervous? I mean, you are working for a target when you work for Eleanor Jacobsen."

Andie shrugged. "I consider it a privilege to work for somebody like Senator Jacobsen. Public office can be dangerous, Carter. Anybody can become a target. Even you." She looked at his metallic-striped yellow tie and considered choking him with it.

"B-r-r-r." He paused. "I'm not inventing these facts, Ms. Greenberg. It's obvious that working for certain people is especially perilous."

"So?"

"I'm just curious as to how you can stand it."

"Carter . . ." Fuentes looked nervous.

"Well, it certainly beats hell out of working night and day to underbid the remnants of our country's industry on behalf of foreign interests." Andie smiled sweetly, dripping venom. "Excuse me, this is my floor." The door opened and she strode out, fuming.

"Andie, wait."

She spun around, ready for an argument. But Fuentes had followed her, alone.

"Well?"

"I'm sorry about Carter. You know he's got this thing. . . ." Fuentes looked nervously around the crowded hall, moved closer.

"What thing?"

"About . . . you know." He almost whispered.

"About mutants?" Andie asked between clenched teeth.

"Yeah. He thinks they should all be sent to Marsbase when it opens, or something like that." He shrugged.

"Funny, that's usually how I feel about Carter."

Fuentes snickered. She felt better.

"And how do you feel about them, Karim?"

His smile vanished. He looked down for a moment, then met her eyes with a sober, searching gaze. "I think they have a right to representation just like anybody else. And the right to be left alone. I don't know any mutants very well, but Jacobsen seems sharp, dedicated and efficient. She gets her job done despite all the media attention. What else can you ask for in a senator? I don't see you cleaning up after her all the time the way I do for Craddick."

"That's for sure."

"Look, some people may have a problem with Jacobsen, but it's not my concern. Mutants seem all right to me. And I say, if they've finally gotten themselves a senator, good for them. Besides, my grandmother would spin in her grave if she thought I was putting down another minority group. She was the first one in our family to finish college. She believed in equality and she made sure everybody in her family did too."

"I'm glad you feel that way, Karim. There aren't many people I know who do," Andie said. She was liking him better by the moment. "I admire the hell out of Eleanor Jacobsen. And I'll do anything I can to help her bring mutants and nonmutants together." She turned to leave, stopped as he took hold of her arm.

"Andie, would you like to have lunch?"

The charm was stripped away. He looked exposed. Earnest. Even more appealing. Andie smiled.

"That sounds like fun." She glanced down at her gold watch. "But it'll have to be late, say one-thirty. In addition to the usual business, I've got to get Jacobsen, and myself, ready for that Brazil trip."

"Yeah, I thought so. Craddick may go too."

"Well, I won't mind escaping wet, cold Washington in March for the sunny beaches of Rio."

"That makes two of us. Listen, a late lunch sounds fine. Let's talk about Brazil then, okay?" He smiled eagerly.

"Great. See you at one-thirty in the lobby?"

He waved and was gone.

Andie held her holocard up to the door. It slid open, wishing her a good day in a grating voice that she hated.

There was a letter for Jacobsen from Senator Horner, "the reverend senator," as Andie called him. She buzzed for admittance to Jacobsen's inner office. No response. Well, it was early yet. Jacobsen usually appeared around nine.

Cracking the seal on the folder, Andie read the contents and shook her head. Another crazy proposal about unifying the mutants with The Fold, Horner's fundamentalist constituency.

"If only every mutant man, woman, and child would join our flock, our prayers would be answered," the senator wrote.

What a hypocrite, Andie thought. But every special interest group had its representative in Washington. Last week, it had been the United Muslim Liberation Front through Emir Kawanda. They'd already tried, and failed, to beat the mutants, running their own candidate against Jacobsen. Now they wanted to join them. And who could blame all these minority groups? The mutants seemed to reach goals easily that it had taken others generations of marching, demonstrating, and petitioning to achieve.

Maybe demagogues like Horner and his ilk wanted to grab a ride on mutant coattails. But their underlying philosophies of greed, racism, and religious imperialism seemed incompatible with mutant concerns. Not that Horner would care, Andie thought. Beneath all that sanctimony, the "reverend senator's" heart pounded to a shrewd political rhythm: votes, votes, votes.

"Good morning, Andrea." Jacobsen strode through the office, a screencase in either hand. She smiled, then disappeared into her private office. Andie followed, poking her nose through the open door.

"Senator, we've got another appeal from Horner. The usual stuff."

"Then give it the standard response."

"Right. Thanks but no thanks."

"Exactly." Jacobsen was already at her deskscreen. She looked up briefly. "Has Stephen Jeffers confirmed our meeting at nine-thirty?"

"Yes." Andie paused. "I must say, he's certainly turned into an ally."

"What did you expect?"

"Well, since he ran so hard against you in the primaries, I thought he'd keep his distance."

Jacobsen smiled. "Andie, a polished old pol like you should know that political feuds can be the most fleeting of all. And when it comes to getting business accomplished, especially mutant business, Stephen is too much of a professional to allow our onetime rivalry to get in his way. Good thing, too. If he hadn't gotten behind me after the primaries, I doubt I'd have been elected. It would have been too easy to split the mutant vote."

"Even with the huge mutant population in Oregon?"

"Absolutely. His assistance was invaluable."

He's not hard to look at either, Andie thought. All that hair. That square chin and killer smile. Those golden eyes.

Jacobsen gave her a sly look. Andie turned away, suddenly uncomfortable. She knew Jacobsen was a limited telepath, but weren't they supposed to respect privacy?

"Are you ready to discuss the Brazil trip?" Jacobsen asked.

"I'll be right in." Andie pulled the file, grabbed her note-screen and swung back into Jacobsen's office.

"You remember the supermutant rumors?"

"Of course."

"Naturally, I have a great deal of interest in this. It seems my interest is shared by others, so much so that a congressional investigation has been suggested. Unofficially, of course."

Andie nodded. "And you're the logical choice to head up this 'unofficial' junket?"

"So it would seem." Jacobsen smiled wryly. "Everybody's favorite mutant."

"Have they asked you yet?"

"No. But they will. A shame. Frankly, the last thing I want to do right now is take a silly trip to Brazil. I don't even speak Portuguese."

"Get an implant."

"Not until they ask me." Jacobsen reached for her white porcelain coffee cup. "Which I assume they will do this afternoon. So I think you'd better schedule a hypnotic implant for both of us, Andrea. The usual cultural background and language package. We'll be briefed by the State Department just before we leave. And plan on being away for at least two weeks."

"Done. I'll program enough cat food to last Livia until April, just in case you want to open a satellite office down there."

Jacobsen smiled at the jest. She seemed unusually light-hearted this morning. "Don't tempt me, Andrea. I need you to act as a good influence around here. Oh, and don't forget to notify the appropriate media agencies."

"Of course." She paused. "Senator, a question off the record?"

"What is it?"

"You don't give much credence to this supermutant rumor, do you?"

Jacobsen's eyebrows arched upward in surprise, but the

unguarded moment lasted mere seconds before the smooth mask was back in place.

"I think it's healthy to maintain a skeptical attitude until hard proof is available," she said. Her voice was calm. Careful. "What we are dealing with here are rumors. And I hate wasting time on rumors."

"What will you do if they're not just rumors?"

"I'll worry about that if and when the time comes."

JAMES RYTON shot his cuffs and turned to his son.

"Nervous?"

"A bit. Excited." Michael looked serious in his gray suit, a younger version of his father, save for the bright-pink braided tie he'd insisted on wearing. James didn't begrudge him the vanity, but preferred his own sedate, old-fashioned burgundy neckwear. The tube car swayed and they held on to the handrails. Stations shot past the windows, squares of white light and pale faces framed for seconds, gone.

"You've met her before, haven't you, Dad?"

Ryton nodded. "Yes, and it's always a pleasure to see her. Eleanor Jacobsen has been in office now for an entire term, and it's something every mutant can be proud of."

The tube deposited them at the Capitol station. They flowed up the moving stairs and took the silver elevators to Jacobsen's office. The receptionist greeted them.

"Mr. James Ryton and Michael Ryton? Please come in and sit down. The senator is in a meeting, but I'm sure she'll be with you shortly."

Ryton nodded impatiently. He was anxious to get on with business. After fifteen minutes had passed, he approached the receptionist again.

"Do you think it will be much longer?"

She smiled sympathetically. "I'll remind her that you're here."

"Thank you."

· · ·

AT THE SOUND OF THE BUZZER, Andie looked up from her note-screen. The senator and Stephen Jeffers were oblivious, locked in debate.

"You mean to tell me you'd allow further restrictions to be placed on mutant athletes?" Jeffers asked angrily. "Good god, Eleanor. Pretty soon we'll have to wear weights and blindfolds before we set foot in the public arena."

"Stephen, calm down," Jacobsen said in smooth tones. "You're exaggerating. Of course I won't support these restrictions. But your demand for the repeal of the Fairness Doctrine is premature. You know we don't yet have the support in the Senate to call for such a vote."

"Then let's get that support."

"I wish it were that easy."

Jacobsen's screen buzzed again.

Andie intercepted the call.

"What's up, Caryl?"

"A James Ryton and Michael Ryton to see the senator. "They've been waiting for half an hour."

"Thanks."

She turned to Jacobsen. "Senator, I believe your eleven o'clock meeting is here."

"Already?"

Jacobsen checked her screen. "Andie, I need another ten minutes or so with Stephen. Can you pacify them until I can get clear?"

"Of course."

Jeffers winked at her. "Eleanor should clone you, Andie. Then you can be in two places at once."

"Or three." Jacobsen corrected him. "Thanks, Andie."

She closed the door behind her and walked into the outer office, Jeffers's smile still glowing in her mind. The Rytons were waiting by Caryl's desk.

"Gentlemen, please excuse the delay. I'm Andrea Greenberg, Senator Jacobsen's assistant. She'll be with you in a moment." She shook both men's hands, fighting the urge to chuckle. Talk about clones. The younger Ryton looked as though he'd been cast in exactly the same mold as his father. No, on second glance, there was something unusual about his eyes, a bit of a slant. Interesting. Mutants were always interesting, she thought. And attractive. An electric tingle moved up her spine.

Andie shepherded the Rytons toward two chairs by her desk.

"You've met the senator before?"

"Yes, on a previous visit," James Ryton said. "We want to talk to her about the Marsbase appropriations bill. The regulations that are being built in will strangle the space engineering business, and we've only just regained our competitive stance with Russia and Japan."

"Are you aware that the bill will be put to a vote tomorrow?"

"That's why we're here today."

Andie's private line buzzed once; Jacobsen's code.

"Excuse me." She turned away and picked up the earpiece.

"Andie, I'll have to reschedule with the Rytons. How about tomorrow?"

"I'll tell them."

She turned to the two men apologetically.

"The senator's meeting appears to be going into overtime. I'm afraid I'll have to ask you to come back tomorrow—"

"But that might be too late," Michael Ryton blurted out. A quick look from his father silenced him.

Andie started to tell them she was sorry, but she stopped in midsentence. They looked so crestfallen. She checked her desk chart. By the time Jacobsen could meet with them tomorrow, the vote would already have been called.

"Wait," she told them. "Let me see what I can do."

She buzzed Jacobsen.

"Senator, I'm sorry, but I really think you ought to make time for the Rytons today. They want to see you about the

Marsbase appropriations bill, and tomorrow, you won't have time for them before the bill comes to the floor."

"Is it that urgent?"

"I think so."

A pause while Jacobsen conferred with Jeffers off the line. Then, "Would they mind if Jeffers sits in?"

Andie turned to the Rytons.

"Stephen Jeffers is with the senator now. Would you mind if he's part of your meeting?"

"Not at all."

"They'll be right in."

"Thanks, Andie."

"Okay, folks, you're in." She almost winked at the younger Ryton, he looked so relieved. Even his father seemed to have thawed a bit. "This way."

As they walked into Jacobsen's office, James Ryton paused at the door.

"Miss Greenberg. Thank you." James Ryton smiled. Andie had the feeling he didn't do it often.

"JAMES? It's good to see you again." Jacobsen shook his hand briefly. "And this is your son?" She took Michael's hand. He was impressed with the firmness of her grip and her authoritative air. Dressed in a sober gray business suit, she commanded the office space with ease, gesturing for them to sit down on the padded red leather chairs in front of her desk. Michael saw·that she was not wearing a mutant unity pin. Probably not her style, he thought. She seemed conservative and low-key, far more so than he'd expected. And her office had an old-world feel enhanced by the mellow wooden paneling, the elegant blue upholstery on the sofa, and the wine-colored Oriental rug on the floor. No twenty-first-century poured acrylic furniture for Senator Jacobsen.

A handsome man with a square jaw and golden eyes was already seated by the desk. A unity pin sparkled on the lapel of his navy-blue business suit. Michael's father nodded to him.

"You've met Stephen Jeffers?" Jacobsen asked.

"At the Western conclave three years ago," Ryton said.

"Good to see you again, James." Jeffers shook his hand, then turned to Michael. "I see you've joined the firm since then. A good move. It's one of the best space engineering firms in the business, from what I hear."

"James, I understand you're handling the solar collector contract," Jacobsen said.

"Yes."

"It's about time that the American space program got competitive again."

"Well, we'd like to keep it that way. But these damned regulations are crippling us."

Jeffers nodded. "The legacy of the Greenland accident."

"Safety regulations have become a noose around our neck. I already employ a dozen people just to cope with these new specifications. It's impossible to stay competitive given these conditions. I can't just farm out the work to Korea the way Russia and Japan do."

"James, safety regulations are a fact of life in the space industry," Jacobsen said.

"Safety, yes. And all of our work is state-of-the-art in that regard. But most of these recent regulations are just window-dressing, something your colleagues can point to whenever the moronic public raises some outcry about space safety."

"Now hold on, James—"

"Senator, you have no idea how knotted regulations have become. That's why we're here. With the rising cost of parts and labor, and competition from abroad, if any additional safety restrictions get tacked on to this legislation, I won't be able to stay in business."

Jacobsen shook her head. "You know this is a sensitive issue. I can't just walk in and announce my opposition to federal safety regulations on Marsbase. I'd be laughed off the

Senate floor. Rightly or wrongly, it's a political necessity that we satisfy critics of the space program or there won't be any space program. We'll have a replay of the eighties. And that will be even worse for your business."

"I'd be happy to testify as to the impact of existing safety measures," Ryton said. "We've had to increase prices tenfold just to stay in the same position as before Greenland. I'm sure that if you surveyed my American competitors, you'd find the same to be true. Perhaps the taxpayer would be interested to know how much it's costing them to pay for the psychological comfort of these redundant systems."

"So you feel that these safety regulations are unnecessary?"

"Some of them, yes."

Michael felt a surge of respect for his father as he held his ground.

"And what do you think?" Jacobsen asked him.

"I agree with my father. It's obvious that the regulations were a necessary sop to critics after the Greenland accident, but frankly, they're a waste of time and the taxpayers' money. What's more, they don't really make the system any safer than it already is. Which is *very* safe. We've brought documentation of just how safe it is even before we add the additional features." He pulled a memorypak out of his pocket and handed it to her.

Jacobsen sighed. "You're as persuasive as your father. Very well, gentlemen. I can't promise miracles. But let me see what I can do."

James Ryton stood up. "We'd appreciate hearing about the vote, Senator."

"My assistant, Andie, will contact you."

Michael shook the senator's hand again and walked out of the office feeling relaxed, almost gleeful. Jacobsen's good-looking red-haired assistant gave him the thumbs-up sign as he walked past her desk, and even his father nodded at her.

So that was the famous Eleanor Jacobsen, he thought. Well, she certainly lived up to her reputation: sharp, intelligent, and politically wily. The right mutant in the right place. He couldn't wait to tell Kelly about her.

5

THE NIGHT SHUTTLE rode silently above the clouds. Above the atmosphere, in fact. An all-night flight had been reduced to half an hour's span, thanks to the intercontinental shuttle. Barely enough time to unseal your screencase, Andie thought. She peered out the window at the dark field of space, studded with stars. Below her, the marbled blue ball of Earth slept under its blanket of clouds. The moon winked on the horizon, round and silvery, a friendly night-light. She wondered briefly what it must be like to live on the surface of that arid satellite, on an airless, reflecting plain, under domes, terraforming slowly, painfully, knowing that your children will inherit and enjoy the work you do now. She'd never been to Moonstation. Yet. As for Marsbase, well, she hoped to see it as soon as it was finished. She could never live off-Earth, but she'd love to visit.

Andie leafed through a brochure attached to her shuttle ticket. It invited her to invest in Moonlodge, a resort "now under construction in the beautiful mountain ranges near the Bay of Tranquillity. Open to members only, of course." She resisted the urge to snicker. In photos and video, the moon-scape had always struck her as strange and dramatic. Eerie. Never beautiful.

Across the aisle, Karim was holding the same brochure. Andie caught his eye and winked. He smiled, then cocked his head toward the row in front of him where his boss, the august Senator Leon Craddick, had managed to fall asleep. Craddick's great shaggy head of white hair nodded forward gently as he snored. Eleanor Jacobsen glanced across at her colleague, frowned, and went back to the dossier she was scanning. What endurance and concentration, Andie thought admiringly. And it certainly paid off in the Senate.

She saw Senator Joseph Horner sitting several rows back, muttering over his laptop, scalp glistening between thin strands of hair. Probably praying for more well-heeled converts, she thought. What was he doing on this junket? He wasn't even supposed to believe in evolution, much less evolved mutants. Not that that stopped him from soliciting mutants as converts to The Fold. Andie was willing to bet he'd twisted more than one arm for a shuttle ticket. Regardless of his personal beliefs, Horner couldn't allow the search for the next step in human evolution to begin without God's personal representative to Congress on the team. The temptation to push him out an airlock was great, but she banished the fantasy and resolved to stay as far away from him as possible.

Closing her eyes, Andie imagined sitting in a Brazilian bistro ordering a Cuba Libre. What a shame that Stephen Jeffers hadn't come along. She'd have enjoyed sharing a café table with him. Well, perhaps Karim would provide some company. Her implanted memory of Rio showed her sprawling beaches, glorious flora in full bloom, a sparkling city filled with white buildings reaching to the sky, moving to a sensual beat that never seemed to stop. The shuttle slowly nosed down in descent. Andie silently practiced her Portuguese and waited to see the white lights of the landing strip outside Rio.

THE HOME-SCREEN flashed amber at Sue Li Ryton from across the room. She put down her grocery bags on the cool blue tiles of the entry hall and keyed up the messages. The first appeared; she could almost have predicted its content. The words, when they appeared, confirmed her suspicions.

"Mom, I borrowed the keys and the skimmer. See you around eleven. Michael."

Sue Li sighed and took off her pink coat. She knew Michael was taking Kelly McLeod out again. Should she tell James? The less he knew, the better. He was so much against this kind of thing. Harmless, as far as she was concerned. But it looked as though Michael intended to spend all his free time with this girl. Sue Li couldn't cover for him indefinitely. Especially with the summer clan meeting coming up. They were due back in Seaside Heights in June.

The screen scrolled up the second message: a request for James to contact Andrea Greenberg, code 3015552244. Andrea Greenberg? Sue Li felt suspicion gnaw at her. It wasn't like James to receive messages at home from women. Who could this be? A business acquaintance?

She trusted her husband, more or less. In a marriage of this duration, trust was almost beside the point. Theirs was a union cemented by time and family.

Once, she'd expected more. With Vinar. How she'd thrilled to his touch, lived for the moments when they could be together. Of course, she'd been very young. One couldn't expect the same passion in maturity. And yet, after Vinar disappeared, Sue Li had hoped she and James could achieve a true unity of mind and body. Well, with telepathy, they could at least connect mentally, although she often found the experience unsettling. Especially now, with James's mental flares beginning. As for their bodies, well, she'd stopped expecting a sexual feast long ago. But that didn't keep her from feeling possessive of her husband.

Hanging the coat in the hall closet, Sue Li wiped her sweaty forehead with the back of her hand and rolled up the sleeves of her suit. The temp display on the wall clock registered 15C. Warm for April. She touched the intercom toggle.

"Melanie?"

No answer. Probably out sulking somewhere. She'd been even quieter and more withdrawn than usual since that incident at the bar two months ago. Sue Li smothered a pang of guilt. What could she say to that girl? Was it her fault that Melanie was a null, and had such a hard time because of it? She'd done everything she could for her daughter. Sue Li kicked off her shoes and wiggled her toes, closing her eyes in relief.

"Jimmy?"

"Yeah, Ma."

"What are you doing?"

"Nothing."

As usual, Sue Li thought. He was probably levitating all the furniture in the master bedroom, waiting to surprise her later. "Well, since you're doing nothing, would you carry my packages into the kitchen and put them away, please?"

"Sure, Mom."

The packages floated upward and around the corner. By the time Sue Li reached the kitchen, boxes were disappearing into cabinets, vegetables into the refrigerator. So far, so good, she thought. She turned to put a glass in the sink. A bright orange package whizzed past her face, almost colliding with her nose, circled around her head, and back again, like a small satellite. She grabbed for it, but it danced out of reach. Sighing, she closed her eyes and summoned all her irritation into the mental equivalent of a slap. She threw the image at her youngest son at half power. The box fell to the ground with a clatter. The intercom clicked on.

"Ma! You didn't have to do that!"

"I've had a day full of cantankerous art dealers and ultrasensitive conservators. I'm not in the mood for your jokes." She picked up the fallen container. A box of condoms. Open.

"Jimmy, where did you get this?" She tried to sound calm.

"I found it in Michael's drawer."

"Well, put it back. We must respect people's physical privacy, not just their mental rights."

"Are you gonna tell Dad?"

Did she detect a note of glee in her youngest son's voice? She'd put a stop to that right now. Steel in her voice, Sue Li snapped at her son.

"You'd better mind your own business, young man, or I can intensify that spanking. Or maybe you'd prefer to be compelled to repeat the seventeen chants for patience and caution for a few hours? You're not too old for it." She left the threat suspended in air for a moment. "I want that package back where you found it. Now!"

"All right." He said, all the life in his voice extinguished. Sue Li was relieved when she heard the intercom click off. Jimmy was becoming a little too unpredictable. They'd really spoiled him. He got bolder each year, more disruptive. He'd hidden Halden's clothing for an entire morning at the last meeting. She began to fear group censure as childish pranks gave way to malicious mischief. Of course, James was as blind to the flaws in his youngest son—and namesake—as he was to the gifts of his eldest son. Sue Li shook her head.

As the box of condoms levitated up and out of the kitchen, she sank down into the green floatchair by the basement door and felt the cushion conforming pleasantly to her shape. She felt a peculiar urge to laugh and cry. Michael was hardly a child any longer, but did she need such definitive proof? She tried to repeat the chants for calmness. On a busy day, she often invoked them. But they failed to provide the insulating tranquillity she'd felt so many times before.

There were joysticks in the bar. Occasionally, she used one when James worked late. And there was Valedrine in the medicine cabinet. For a moment, she was tempted. Then the front door slammed.

"James?"

"No, Mom, it's me." Melanie said quietly. She walked into the kitchen wearing a blue tunic and green leggings, opened the refrigerator and stood there, staring into it. Sue Li reached around her to retrieve a package of instant squid. Finally, Melanie selected a bunch of kiwi wafers and closed the refrigerator, idly munching. Sue Li nodded approvingly. Keeping the mutant metabolism balanced required many small meals.

"How'd your day go?"

"Okay."

"Dinner won't be ready for a while."

Melanie shrugged. She walked toward the living room, but turned suddenly, as though she'd remembered something.

"Mom?"

Sue Li opened the package of fish, waiting for the reconstituting chemicals inside to react with the air. She didn't bother to look up.

"Yes?"

"Cousin Evra is having an all-night party on Friday of graduation week. She wants to work on a skit for the clan meeting. Can I go?"

"Who else is invited?"

"Tela, Marit, Meri. Just girls."

"I thought you didn't get along with Tela." Sue Li frowned, concentrating on cutting the fish into delicate slices. She envied Zenora's finely tuned telekinetic skills. She could slice sushi from fifty yards away.

"Oh, she's all right."

Sue Li turned on the convection oven. If Michael were home, she'd have asked him to cook the fish quickly, telekinetically, but Jimmy always burned food. So careless, she thought. Michael had much more control over his gifts. She turned to her daughter.

"It seems fine, if you'd like to go. Your father will be pleased to see you're getting involved in clan affairs."

"I'll bet."

"Don't get wise, Mel." Sue Li dipped the fish into flavored

maikon crumbs and set it into the oven's airflow, where it floated, undulating gently.

"We can drive you over if you want to wait for me to get home."

"N-no, that's okay. Michael said he'd drive me." Was it Sue Li's imagination or did Mel seem uncomfortable? But Michael was a fine driver. Sue Li was grateful for his help in chauffeuring the younger children. And when Melanie graduated from high school in a few weeks, she'd be allowed to apply for a license, too.

"Whatever you wish. Now if you'd finish those crackers, I could use some help here."

THE CLOCK read twelve-thirty, bright-yellow numbers radiating from the far side of the dark room, next to the screened window. Michael rolled over on his back. In bed beside him, Kelly stirred. He reached out and lightly ran his hand over her hip, savoring the satiny feel of her flesh.

"Mmmm." She snuggled closer. "Stay all night?" He kissed her cheek. "Can't. I'll be late as it is. I think my father keeps one eye open until he hears the front door close."

"Why do you live at home? Don't you want your own place?"

"Sure. But it's clan tradition. We don't move out until we're married."

"And everybody adheres to it?"

"Almost everybody."

"Wow. Mutant tradition sounds amazing. The biggest tradition in my family is to go see my aunt for Easter. And my parents didn't even make a fuss when I didn't want to go."

"How'd you'd get out of it?"

"I told them I had a report due. Our family isn't close the way yours is. They know I'd be bored chipless." She rolled over and gently traced her finger down his chest.

"Your family seems pretty tight."

He shivered at her touch, a pleasantly teasing sensation he

wanted both to stop and continue. "Claustrophobic is a good word for it. I'd be happy to skip the yearly clan meetings, for all the good they do me."

"What's it like?"

"What do you mean?"

"To be a mutant. To go to clan meetings?"

He sighed. "A pain. I get an earful from my father, mostly 'Thou shalt not mix with normals.' And I have to listen to the year's report: how many births, how many deaths. Then there's the reading of the Chronicles. And, of course, my cousins."

"By the dozens?" Kelly giggled.

"Nearly."

"It sounds interesting." She leaned back and stretched. She looked like a lovely silhouette to him, outlined in the yellow glow of the chronometer.

"Maybe it is. If you're nonmutant."

"Well, then I'm qualified. Tell me again about the sharing."

"We all join hands around the table and link telepathically. Even those who aren't gifted in that way can manage it in the group circle. You feel a floating sensation. Close, kind of. Friendly."

"Love?"

"I suppose." He was uncomfortable using that word, or even accepting it, in reference to the clan. Did he love them? Did they love him? Did their feelings matter in a situation where they had no choice but to cling together?

"That doesn't sound so awful to me. In fact, it sounds nice." She paused. "Doesn't it make you feel special?"

Special? He shook his head. "More like peculiar."

Kelly grabbed his shoulder and pulled him around to face her. "Look, Michael, all my life I've felt like a stranger. An outsider. I don't think I've spent more than a year in any one school. The Air Force keeps you moving, constantly. And the idea of having a group of people around who you know well, who love you and connect with you, sounds pretty good to me."

"That's because you don't do it."

"Maybe." He thought she sounded hurt. He regretted his words, but it was so hard to explain his feelings about being a mutant. And he'd met people before who looked upon the mutants with a sort of dazed amazement, as though they were . . . well, special. It made him uncomfortable. He didn't want Kelly to treat him that way. He reached over and put his arms around her possessively, pulling her close.

"I can't talk to anyone about this the way I can talk to you," he whispered fiercely. "No one, in the clan or out, but you."

"Really?" He cupped the side of her face in his palm, stroking her downy cheek. "Perhaps the clan meetings sound good to you, but in a way, they're like living in a small town where everybody knows you but nobody understands you. No privacy. It doesn't make me feel less lonely." He rested his forehead against hers. "But I don't feel lonely when I'm with you. When I was in Washington, I thought about you all the time. Thought about doing this. Wondered if you wanted it too."

"God, that's all I've been thinking about," she said. "I couldn't wait for you to come home."

He nuzzled her right breast, taking the nipple between his lips and teasing it with his tongue until it was erect. Kelly moaned gently and moved her hand lower, between his legs. In a moment, he was hard, throbbing against her palm. He took a deep breath and let it out in a lingering sigh.

"Do you want to do it again?" she whispered. He could barely hear her.

"What do you think?"

6

ANDIE WALKED BRISKLY through the deserted
lobby of the Cesar Park Hotel and waved her ID badge before the front door's sensor to unlock it. The doors rolled
open and she walked out onto the street. She had time for a
quick look at the beach before the meeting at ten.

The city that greeted her was surprisingly silent. Andie
knew that the Nunca Mais purges of '97 had cleared the
favelas, those raggle-taggle villages clustered on the hillsides.
The new regime had been quick and brutal, despite public
outcry. Where were the favelitas now? Andie imagined them
working sugarcane plantations in the country's steaming
green interior. If they were still alive.

Andie had expected to see straggling partiers heading home
from all-night discos, lovers still walking dreamily, arm in
arm, along the beach. But perhaps this was not the case during the week. She had absorbed the legends of Rio. Now it
was time to learn the truth.

Carefully, she crossed the bustling Avenida Atlantica,
heeding her implant's warning about unpredictable Rio drivers. She stepped onto the mosaic pavement at the beach's
edge, kicked off her shoes and buried her feet in the white
sand of Ipanema. Blue-green waves rolled toward her, break-

ing upon the wet sand. A few dedicated sunbathers sat in chairs, staring out to sea. But the beach was mostly deserted. She walked along the sand, wishing she'd brought a hat. Even at this early hour, the sun was fierce. She began to feel thirsty, although she'd just finished a generous glass of mango juice in the hotel. But her mouth was dry, tongue cottony. She visualized a glass of water, condensation beading it, and thought longingly of a cool ice cream bar. Down the beach to her left, a fruit ice vendor approached, a tanned boy of about fourteen, wearing filtershades and white jeans. She decided to splurge on an ice bar. As the boy counted out the change, he raised his shades up to the top of his head. When he looked at her, Andie was startled to see a pair of golden eyes, bright as coins, gazing steadily into her own. She nearly dropped her change. The vendor smiled. "Obrigado," he said, and sauntered down the beach, out of sight.

Had she imagined it? Andie put the pop in her mouth. It tasted stickily sweet. She really didn't want it after all. She looked for a trash receptacle and disposed of the cloying thing. Did that boy really have golden eyes?

Confused, she left the beach, put her shoes on, and walked across the street, nimbly dodging manic taxi drivers. She passed several cafés, blinds drawn, chairs upended on tables. Where was this legendary hedonistic culture? Even the shops were closed. At the corner of Avenida Rio Branco, she saw one small café open, with a waiter idly polishing glasses behind the bar. As she passed, she caught his eye. He smiled gently and she nodded. Had his eyes gleamed with gold? Perhaps it was just a reflection, she told herself as she entered the Cesar Park. Whatever it was would have to wait. It was time for the briefing.

Eleanor Jacobsen got down to business immediately, as usual.

"As you know, we are here, unofficially, to investigate the rumors of next-step mutants. Personally, I don't believe any of them. However, I will discount nothing until the end of this trip. We will begin with a visit to the gene-splicing laboratories of Dr. Ribeiros this morning. Of course, officially, we represent American-Japanese medical research interests looking for more laboratory space. After lunch, Mr. Craddick, the Reverend Mr. Horner and I will meet with Dr. Ribeiros to interview him about his laboratory's capacity for contract work. Meanwhile, I encourage the rest of you to utilize the lab's library and research as time permits. Remember, we can't risk offending the Brazilians. Be careful. We will meet again at four to compare our notes. Questions?"

MELANIE TRIED TO BALANCE the armload of discs she was carrying, but she shifted too much to the left, and the first ten volumes of *The History of Civilization* clattered to the floor of the school library, followed by her purse, coat, and discpack. She looked down at the pile at her feet and sighed loudly.

"Can't you be more careful?" the librarian said, glaring from the monitor in the corner, by the door.

Mel's face grew hot. She tried to brush her bangs out of her eyes. The librarian hated her. She might be two rooms away, but she was watching her every move and she hated her.

"Yeah, Ryton. For a mutant, you're pretty clumsy. Why don't you just float yourself and your stuff out of here? To Marsbase." Gary Bregnan, fullback for the Piedmont Eagles, said in a piercing whisper. Two of his football buddies sitting nearby snickered. Led by Bregnan, they began chanting, sotto voce, "Mutie, mutie, mutie." Mel's eyes began to sting with tears of frustration. Everybody hated her. Well, she hated them, too. She'd send them all to Marsbase, if she could.

She gathered up the discs with her belongings and found an empty PC booth. The April rain drummed against the clerestory windows, a cold, depressing tattoo. She could hear Bregnan still laughing behind her. So he hated mutants, did he? Well, soon he'd have to find some other target. Meanwhile, the least she could do was return his contempt. Oh, her mother was always talking about trying to understand normals. But her mother didn't have to face Gary Bregnan and his friends each day.

Mel spent forty-five minutes taking notes for her humanities presentation, "Comparing the Impact of Sea Travel on Ancient Spain and Space Travel on Contemporary America." She rubbed her eyes, tired of staring at the white letters on the screen.

Thank God for Kelly McLeod, she thought. If she hadn't agreed to work with her on this report, it would have become a nightmare. Kelly had suggested using maps and even constructing a gameboard. Without her, Melanie would have given a flat, two-minute talk. In her opinion, the Spanish empire had come about because of Spain's naval superiority, and then been destroyed by the results of its voyages. She didn't want to draw any similar conclusions about things now. Melanie yawned, made a backup disc and turned off the PC. At least the rain had stopped.

On her way out, she stopped by the front desk. Bregnan's laughter still echoed in her ears. Scanning the catalog, she stopped at "Perverse Human Sexual Practices Throughout History" and "Venereal Diseases," then checked out both files under Bregnan's name. It was easy to fake his ID with the dumb, old-fashioned computer. On the way home, she dropped the discs off in a Salvation Army chute not far from school. Serve Bregnan right if he has to pay to replace them, she thought. She might not have mutant power, but she wasn't entirely helpless.

"Mel, wait a minute!"

Melanie froze in horror. She'd been discovered. She couldn't even get revenge without being caught. In despair, she turned to confront her accuser.

Jena Thornton hurried up the street. "Hi! I've been looking for you."

"You have?" Melanie said, voice quavering. Had Jena seen her deposit the discs?

"Yeah. I wanted to talk to you. Want to get something to

drink?" Jena smiled, her long blond hair dancing gently around her face in the wind. She didn't seem very suspicious.

Melanie's heart stopped pounding. She was safe. But what did Jena want? At clan meetings, she'd rarely done more than nod at her. And at school, Melanie might as well have been invisible for all the attention Jena paid to her. While the football players teased and tormented Melanie, they whistled whenever Jena swayed past them.

"What do you want to talk about?"

"Oh, you know. School. Clan stuff. C'mon, let's get a chobashake." She took Melanie's arm and drew her toward a choba and sushi shop.

Once inside, Jena ordered two shakes and maguro rolls from the mechwaiter.

"How're your classes?" she asked.

Melanie swallowed a mouthful of tuna and rice. "Okay. I'll be glad to graduate next month. All my credits are in."

"Are you going to State in the fall?"

"I don't know. My folks want me to. I might just work for my father."

Jena smiled. "He's got a good business going. And Michael works with him?" She seemed to linger on the name, savoring it.

"Yeah. They just got back from a trip to Washington, to see Eleanor Jacobsen."

Jena shivered. "She's so fine. The thought of her makes me float." She levitated a few inches off her seat, then sat down on the blue banquette, giggling. "I'd love to meet her. Maybe Michael will tell me about her at the next clan meeting."

"Ask him about it." Melanie was beginning to feel uneasy. What was Jena getting at?

"Oh, I'm having a party on the seventeenth. I wondered if you and your brother would like to come."

"Sure. I mean, I'd love to, but you'll have to ask Michael."

"All right, I will. And you can bring a date if you want. He can too. I guess he'll bring Kelly McLeod. It'll be interesting to have a nonmutant at the party."

"What makes you say that?"

Jena's eyes were wide, innocent. "Well, I saw Michael and Kelly at the movies last week. They are going out, aren't they?"

"I don't know."

"Well, they'd better be careful," Jena said. Her smile had faded. "If the clan finds out, Michael could regret it."

Melanie bristled. "Is that a threat?"

"Of course not," Jena said smoothly. "Just an observation. Well, I guess it'll be a good experience for your brother to taste forbidden fruit." Her laugh was hard-edged.

"Look, Jena, it's getting late—"

"You know Stevam Shrader?"

"He's Tela's cousin, isn't he?"

"Yeah. I've been seeing him. Nice muscles." Jena giggled. She glanced down at her wristchron. "Oh, God, I've got to go. Promised to get the skimmer home, and I'm meeting Stevam in an hour. Stay and finish. See you on the seventeenth." A blur of blond hair and blue jumpsuit, and she was gone.

Melanie gathered up her discpack. Jena made her jittery. What was she getting at about Michael and Kelly? Sometimes mutants were as difficult to figure out as nonmutants, she thought. But she wouldn't have to worry about that much longer.

JENA PRESSED THE ACCELERATOR of the vermilion skimmer to the floor. The highway was a concrete ribbon beneath the skimmer, the passing landscape a yellow-green blur of budding trees.

She told herself she hadn't lied to Melanie Ryton. Of course she'd invite both Mel and Michael to the party, even if they both knew whom she was really after. And she *was* dating Stevam, although he bored her silly.

If only she could forget what she'd seen last night. Michael with his arm around Kelly McLeod. The two of them laughing together as they walked out of the theater. Happy together, ignoring the stares they received as a "mixed" couple.

At the word "couple," a knot grew in Jena's stomach. Those two had seemed very much coupled last night, glowing with a special intimacy that made her worst nightmares pale by comparison.

From the age of twelve, Jena had adored Michael Ryton. At each clan meeting, she'd watched him play floatball or leaper with their cousins, loving the way he moved, the way he smiled shyly at her. She'd hoped that, with time, he'd come to feel the same way about her. After all, she was close enough to him in age. A suitable choice. And his choosing time was upon him. Why not her?

She'd realized early on that her looks were a potent tool, effective even on nonmutants, not that she cared about those silly, boring normals. At clan meetings, she saw the way the men looked at her. Even men her father's age allowed their gaze to linger as she walked by. She'd considered it a pleasing game. But the only man with whom she really wanted to play seemed to have his mind on other things. Nonmutants.

Jena gripped the steering wheel tighter. She'd missed her exit. Damn.

She'd taken Michael's rebuff at the clan meeting last winter as a sign that he just wasn't ready to settle down. Fine, she'd told herself. He'll come around. Give him time and space. His rejection had hurt her, but she'd shown no one, not even her mother, just how deeply the scars extended. Sooner or later, she vowed, he'd be hers.

How could Michael be interested in dating a nonmutant? Kelly was all right, but she was a normal. An outsider! To go against clan custom, Michael must feel more than a gentle infatuation for her. Possibly even enough to risk clan censure by marrying her.

No. No. No.

Jena told herself that it couldn't happen. Wouldn't. She'd waited long enough. Now she knew that she had to do something, and soon. She took the next exit off the freeway, turned the skimmer around and headed home, a plan forming in her head.

"JAMES, you can't just wrap Michael up with Jena and expect things to take. They're not sushi," Sue Li said. She watched her husband pace the room, moving restlessly in and out of the pools of blue and green light, a sure sign the mental flares were bothering him. "Besides, betrothals are old-fashioned."

"I don't give a damn about fashion. It worked with us, didn't it? If you give these young fools too much choice, they make dangerous decisions."

"Oh, those were different times. You can't generalize." She wished the topic hadn't come up, but James had asked about the missing skimmer, and, reluctantly, she'd told him about Michael's date with Kelly. Now he was raging. With a sigh, she turned away from *Art History Monthly*, leaving the screen on, and sank back against the cushions of the couch.

"Trying to force Michael to your will won't work," she said. "I'm afraid you'll chase him away." And I'll never forgive you if that happens, she thought, wondering if he could read her clearly. His clairaudience was a quirky, uncertain gift.

Ryton stopped pacing, a look of dismay on his face. She felt a small tingle of triumph. Hers had always been the superior telepathic power.

"I'd never force my son away from home," he said softly.

"I don't think you know how hard you push him," she said, pulling the plum-colored kimono more snugly around her.

"He has no idea of the kind of force that could be brought to bear upon him," Ryton said harshly.

Sue Li stared at him in horror. "You aren't thinking about petitioning the groupmind? Against our son?"

"It's been done before. Infrequently, of course. Only for the good of the clan. There's been talk of calling for a censure against Skerry. Bring him in line. I'm tempted to vote for it. Michael likes him. This might be a good lesson."

"A group censure could destroy Skerry's telepathic gifts!"

Ryton shrugged. "What good is it to us? He's abandoned the community. If nothing else, we could still use his contribution to the gene pool."

"And of course, you'd compel that as well. Is that all you think about?"

"Of course not. But you know this is important, Sue Li. Always has been. We're so few. And now that we've revealed ourselves, our young ones only think about mixing with the normals." Ryton rubbed his temples wearily. "Crazy idea. Dangerous. Nothing good will come of it. The normals are no more ready for it than we are."

"You make it sound like they're prehistoric apes."

"In certain ways, compared to us, they are."

"You know I hate it when you start saying things like that." Sue Li turned toward the computer screen. For the second time that evening, she longed for telekinesis, just enough to shove her husband into the wall and knock these hostile, paranoid ideas out of him.

"Encouraging him in this infatuation with the McLeod girl will only make it worse," he said. "And I don't want my son to be so exposed to irrational normals, where he can be hurt. Or worse."

"He's managed to survive so far," Sue Li said drily. "Even college didn't kill him. And he was surrounded by thousands of normals there." She snapped off the screen's power switch. "We can't keep him locked away forever, James. He's already chafing to move out, live on his own. And he should. If we try to separate him from Kelly, this could all backfire on us. Be patient. They're both very young. Maybe it will just run its course."

"Well, I hope you're right." He settled into a chair and

began to fill his pipe with tobacco, a sign that the discussion was over.

Sue Li gave a mental sigh of relief and keyed up the power again on her scanner. Turning back to her magazine, she congratulated herself on avoiding the issue of her son's sex life. She would have to talk to Michael about that later.

7

ANDIE SWITCHED OFF the old-fashioned microfiche machine.

"Damn!"

Her hunch had not paid off. There was a small mutant population in Rio, maybe two thousand people, barely a noteworthy percentage of the ten million Brazilians packed into the city. Not enough to fill every café with the golden-eyed waiters and clientele. The size of the mutant population here didn't support the bizarre theories she'd been formulating. Perhaps she'd imagined that beach vendor's golden eyes.

Most of a day wasted chasing down a wild hunch. What was she going to tell Jacobsen? This investigation was turning into a fiasco, one with which the General Accounting Office would have a field day. Not to mention how many votes this might cost Jacobsen come election time. She had to turn something up.

Around her, the Rosario do Madrona medical school library hummed. Monitors at regular intervals in the white circular wall stared out at her somberly. Well, there was nothing here to support her suspicions. Maybe it was time to be more direct.

She turned to Catalina Jobim, the reference librarian.

"Can you recommend additional resources concerning unusual eye pigmentation? Golden eye pigmentation?"

The green-clad librarian looked confused.

"But Miss Greenberg, what are these golden eyes you speak of?" she asked.

"Oh, just people I've seen on the street," Andie said. "I thought their eyes were, uh, so beautiful. I was curious. After all, your mutant population is rather small." She paused, watching Jobim carefully. "Surely there's some documentation of this?"

"No," the woman replied in crisp tones. "Nothing. What you've seen are probably contact lenses. I'm sure of it," She smiled. "You would be amazed by the crazy fashions we see here. Last year, everybody had red hair. Everybody. Now, golden eyes. And tomorrow, something different."

Andie wanted to believe her, but the odd way she looked at her only increased her suspicions. She thanked the librarian and excused herself. It was almost noon.

At lunch, Jacobsen seemed more remote than usual.

"Any leads?" she asked, toying with a dish of orange melon.

"None," Andie said. "I'm beginning to pray for a clue, a hint, even concrete proof of supermutants. Just so we'll have something to go home with."

"I know what you mean."

Andie wondered if her boss had hit a snag in her investigations. Somehow, she couldn't believe it. If anybody could slice through smoke screens, it was Eleanor Jacobsen. But the senator looked tense and preoccupied. Over dessert, Andie questioned her.

"It's nothing, Andie," Jacobsen said. "And spare me that Jewish mother look. The tropics are just not my ideal climate. That's all."

Reluctantly, Andie let the subject drop. With a free hour after lunch, she considered taking a walk on the beach, then decided against it; the midday sun was too hot. But she felt restless cooped up in the air-conditioned hotel. She had to get out, even if it was just for a walk around the block.

Turning at the corner of Avenida Rio Branco, she hurried away from the sleek, low-slung skimmers with their shaded windshields, the quiet streets—too quiet at noon—and walked for several blocks through the fashionable district, admiring corner vid displays for colorful boutiques in Rio do Sul Mall. The street was almost deserted, save for a pink-uniformed maid scolding two tiny children. A side street looked inviting, and Andie stopped at a café, lured by bright tablecloths and the shade of a jacaranda tree in full purple bloom.

Most of the tables were empty. A skinny man in a bathing suit sat at one, smoking, staring at his watch, scanning something. Near the compubar, another man, bearded and wearing dark glasses, nursed a beer.

Andie selected a table by the tree. The waiter, a hazel-eyed mulatto with blond, curly hair, took her order in lilting Portuguese.

"Cup or caffeine hypo?"

"Cup, please."

Andie watched him insert her order into the bar. She leaned back in the curved plastic chair and surveyed the street. Even the distant tempo of traffic was muted here. She was tempted to wander down the block and out of sight, to forget about congressional investigations and strange eyes.

A deeper shadow fell over her.

"Excuse me," a tenor voice said in perfect American English. "Is this seat taken?"

Andie looked up to see the bearded man from the table by the bar standing at her side. Before she could protest, he had seated himself.

"I'm not looking for company," she said stiffly. The man smiled and removed his glasses. His eyes were bright gold.

"Are you certain you wouldn't like my company, Ms. Greenberg?" He sat back in his chair, studying her. The waiter brought a tiny cup of steaming black liquid. Mechanically, she spooned sugar into it until she'd almost filled the cup to the brim. When the waiter withdrew, Andie quickly turned back to her companion.

"H-how did you know my name?"

"Why wouldn't I know the name of cousin Eleanor's administrative assistant?" He shrugged, took a sip of beer. "My name's Skerry. And I'll save us both a lot of time and trouble, Ms. Greenberg. I know why you're here. I might have some information you can use."

"Such as?"

"You're worried about this supermutant thing, even more than my lofty relative. Well, you should be. She's wrong. Try to get her to see that, before it's too late."

"You mean there *are* supermutants here? It's not just a rumor?" In spite of herself, suddenly Andie wanted to believe him.

He shrugged. "Hard to say. Right now, all we know is that they've come up with some kind of mutagen that not only isolates but enhances the potential for specific mutations. At least, that's what their results indicate. Don't ask me how they do it. And I have no idea how far they've gone."

"Who's involved with this?"

"Most of the medical research community here. Ribeiros is your point man, all right. But don't waste your time. You'll never get through him. He's too well protected, as, I believe, the sainted Eleanor is discovering."

"Why should I listen to you? How do you know this?"

He smiled. "I've got connections—and ways of finding things out. And I'm not hampered by official rules and regulations."

"What are you doing here anyway?" Andie demanded.

"Do you think the Congress of the United States is the only organization interested in this supermutant rumor?"

"But how did you hear about supermutants? What's your source?"

"I've got ears. Better than most of those in Congress, in fact." He leaned back in his chair. "Your coffee's getting cold."

Andie took a sip and grimaced at the sugary taste. She put the cup down. "So I'm supposed to believe that some stranger who pops up out of nowhere, speaking perfect American English, is conducting his own private investigation of the same issue we're looking into, only he's got all the answers? Is it too much to ask whom you represent?"

"Let's just say it's a very special interest group."

"Special as in mutant-special?"

He gave her a mock salute. "Very good. You're even smarter than I thought."

"Are you down here alone?"

"No, there are a couple of us looking around."

"Why not talk to Jacobsen?"

He shook his head. "A waste of time. She's a by-the-book lady. And I'm not exactly welcome in certain well-established mutant circles."

"I see. Well, what if I go to her for you?"

"She would believe that even less."

"Then why approach me?"

"You've got official access, and you're on the right team. You can steer them towards the appropriate directions. To facilitate the involvement of, shall we say, appropriate agencies."

"The CIA? I'll need some hard proof for that."

"Try this." Skerry took a memorypak from his pocket and dropped it in her palm. She looked at it skeptically.

"What is this?"

"A record of genetic experiments on human embryo splitting from a clinic near Jacarepaguá."

"What? But that's illegal. And how'd you get it?"

He smiled. "I stole it."

Andie pushed her chair back from the table and shook her head. "I can't accept this. I'd be an accomplice to the crime.

Not to mention how much trouble this could cause if somebody learns we have stolen information. . . ."

His laughter cut her off. "You might not be as smart as I thought. Don't admit it's stolen. That clinic will never say a word. Believe me."

"I'd rather play by the rules."

He stopped smiling at her. "This isn't the United States, Ms. Lawyer. There are no rules here, save for who you know and what you know. And, even more important, who knows what you know. So be very careful. Take this information, but don't show it to Jacobsen until you're back in Washington. She's being watched here."

"By whom?"

"A hundred eyes. The police. A few foreign interests. And other mutants, of course."

Andie imagined a crowd of strangers staring through lenses and keyholes at her boss. At her. An army of spies, if she could believe this stranger.

"How do you know?" she demanded. "And why do you care, anyway?"

"To borrow a phrase, if not me, who? And if not now, when? Look, toots, this is serious business. For you as well as me, not to mention the cast of characters watching your boss. And while everybody's wasting time going through official channels, these experiments continue."

"On human subjects?"

"It seems that way."

"Are you sure?"

"Yep. So look sharp. And be careful." He wavered before her as if a gust of torrid wind had passed between them. Andie rubbed her eyes. Was she suffering from eye strain, or was he fading from view as she watched? The trunk of the jacaranda tree was visible right through his T-shirt. She tried to keep her jaw from dropping.

"Wait! What if I need to find you?"

The chair opposite her was empty. A cool breeze blew past her cheek.

"I'll find you." It was a whisper in her ear, in her mind. She looked down, half expecting to see the memorypak vanish as well. But the blue plastic oval nestled in the palm of her hand like an egg. She tucked it into her belt pocket and looked at her watch. If she ran, she could just make that meeting at the Cesar Park.

BILL McLEOD reached for the airbrush. The nose of the Cessna ultralight needed a touch-up, and he had just mixed a fresh batch of silver paint especially for the job.

Behind him, he could hear Kelly chatting with that mutant girl, Melanie Ryton, as they chipped paint off the Cessna's tail. Kelly insisted on hanging around that family, despite his misgivings. Well, maybe it was just a phase. Melanie was a nice kid. And, as Joanna kept telling him, so was Melanie's brother, Michael.

The hell with nice, McLeod thought. He'd promised Joanna that he'd keep his mouth shut on the subject, but he didn't like his daughter dating that mutant boy. And McLeod had a fair idea of how far his daughter and Michael Ryton had ventured into matters sexual. He didn't like that, either. But she was eighteen. As long as she behaved with discretion, he could at least try to respect her privacy.

McLeod laid down a bright patch of liquid silver in a gleaming, controlled arc. The crysacrylic pigment dried instantly, upon contact. He eyed the new paint critically. Some detail work here wouldn't hurt, he thought.

"Kelly! Are you interruptable?"

"Sure, Dad."

"Would you bring me the small kit in the trunk of the skimmer?"

"Okay."

He watched her jog toward the skimmer with Melanie close behind. The May sunshine glinted off her hair and her yellow pantsuit. For a moment, he imagined her jogging across a runway toward a plane, her slender figure covered by a different sort of garb, a gray flight suit. What a fine pilot she'd make. He'd tried to talk her into applying for the Air Force Academy. If only she'd set her mind to something besides mutants.

"YOUR DAD'S TERRIFIC," Melanie said, trying to keep up with Kelly's long-legged stride toward the car park. The April wind blew her fine hair in her eyes and she envied Kelly's neat black braids.

"What do you mean?"

"He's funny. Nice. And handsome." Melanie giggled. "I know I make him uncomfortable, but he's good about trying not to show it."

"He doesn't understand mutants."

"Didn't he work with any in the Air Force?"

"Only occasionally. They seem to avoid the draft pretty easily."

Melanie smiled. She knew how deftly her older male cousins had influenced draft boards with a little telepathic push.

"Don't take it personally," Kelly said. "But you're a mystery to my father. To most people. And that makes them feel uncomfortable."

"How do you think it makes me feel?" Melanie said. "Do you think I like it? People either try too hard to be nice and overshoot, making things worse, or they're rude." Melanie leaned against the blue skimmer while Kelly rummaged in the trunk.

"Yeah. I don't know why mutants even bother to try and get along with nonmutants. Most of the time we act like such waveheads around you." She pulled a green pack out by its handle and sealed the car.

Melanie shrugged. "We can't hide forever. Besides, we don't have a choice. There's more of you than of us."

"Haven't the numbers of mutants increased each year?"

"Sure. But we'd have to spend all our time making mutant babies if we wanted to catch up."

"Sounds like fun." Kelly swung the pack in a circle, then stopped, midtwirl. Her face was serious. "What about half-mutant babies?"

"There aren't many."

"Do they have mutant abilities?"

"Some. But the clan discourages intermarriage."

"So you've said." Kelly stopped walking and gazed off into the distance.

"What's wrong?"

"Nothing."

"Really?"

"Yeah. I'm just thinking about the future." She turned toward Melanie.

"You're thinking about my brother, aren't you?"

Kelly nodded. "I'm in love with him," she said, her voice almost a whisper.

"You are?" Melanie grabbed her by the shoulder. "Have you told him?"

"No." Kelly's voice cracked.

Bewildered, Melanie hugged her. "Don't cry," she said. "I'll bet he loves you, too. Why don't you ask him?"

"I'd feel silly. He has to tell me without my asking, or it doesn't mean anything."

"I guess." Melanie released her. She felt torn between wanting to help and not wanting to get involved. She had her own plans. And she'd taken enough of a chance lying to her parents about this afternoon. Her brother's love life was his own concern. But Kelly was her friend. How could Melanie tell her that what she longed for most was impossible?

"Come on. You don't want your father to see you crying, do you?" She handed Kelly a tissue.

"Thanks. Let's talk about something else." Kelly wiped her face. "What are you going to do after graduation?"

"I think I've lined up a summer job in Washington." Melanie's eyes began to shine at the thought of it. "After that, I don't know. I don't want to go to college right away."

"Doesn't your father want you to work for him?"

"That's what he keeps saying. But I'd rather work someplace else. Arrange something on my own and show them I can take care of myself." In her mind, she played back the ad she'd seen on the vid: "Are you eighteen or older? Jobs for the summer in Washington. E-mail code 7172A. . . ." She thought of the fat envelope sitting in her closet. She'd filled out and sent off the applications last week. Yesterday, the notice had arrived. A job as a hostess at the Washington Convention Center! Maybe she'd even meet some vidjocks there.

"I wish I knew what I wanted to do," Kelly said. She sounded envious. Melanie gave her a sympathetic look while she tried to remember the last time anybody had envied her for anything. It was a nice feeling.

8

A BIT BREATHLESS, Andie seated herself at the long teak conference table. The tablemech had already served the first round of coffee in the obligatory tiny white cups. The entire city seemed fueled by Brazilian caffeine. For those who wanted more concentrated dosages, syringes were arranged in sterile paks on a silver tray on a serving table by the door. Craddick had two empty hypos by his setting. Andie wasn't surprised. She'd seen his head nodding drowsily through more than one conference on this trip.

Jacobsen sat at the center of the table, notescreen open before her, a cup of what looked like tea cooling beside it. She nodded at Andie as she entered, but continued speaking.

As Andie had suspected, there was little to report. Horner and his aide sat, smugly silent throughout. Craddick made an occasional comment, but it was essentially Jacobsen's show. And the mutant senator looked tired.

"Doctor Ribeiros appears to be cooperating fully," Jacobsen said. Was that an ironic note in her voice? "In the week left, I suggest we divide our efforts. Beginning next week, I propose that Senator Horner make use of his religious connections to meet with the archbishop here. Senator Craddick, perhaps, could visit the clinics in Jacarepaguá. I'll continue the interview with Dr. Ribeiros."

Jacarepaguá? Wasn't that the clinic where Skerry had found the information on genetic experiments? The hell with spies. Andie had to talk to Jacobsen, alone. She waited impatiently until the meeting ended, and watched the room clear. Karim waved at her. She'd see him later, at Ribeiros's clinic. But as she turned to Jacobsen, somebody loomed over her.

"Young lady, excuse me. A word with you and the charming senator?" Reverend Horner sank into the chair between her and Jacobsen, who smiled frostily.

Andie took a deep breath and fought the urge to grab the arms of Horner's chair. Just one good push, and he'd roll back and back, crash, through the plate-glass window, mouth rounded in an O of surprise. And slowly he'd sink, backward and down, twenty stories, to the street pulsing with traffic. She imagined the thin scream floating on the humid air. Closing her notescreen with a snap, she gave the senator a big smile.

"What can we do for you, Mr. Horner?" Jacobsen asked. Her tone would freeze saltwater, Andie thought.

"Well now, pretty lady, I've been thinking that, rather than divide our efforts, it is imperative that we combine. We must come together to maximize the results of this trip." He was using the same voice he invoked for his vidnews sermons. His words coated the air like an oil slick. Treacherous. If she touched him, Andie wondered, would he feel as oily as he sounded?

Jacobsen crossed her arms and leaned back in her chair. "How so?"

"Let's admit that the interests of your constituents and mine are one and the same. Present a united front, so to speak."

"Similar to the United Moslem Front?"

Jacobsen's sarcasm was unmistakable. Andie tried not to giggle.

"Well, yes . . . I mean, no." Horner seemed flustered. "What I'm trying to say is, won't you reconsider my suggestion? It would certainly make me inclined to pass along any information I might come across—"

"Senator Horner, as you know, you are legally required to share with the committee any information you may uncover during this investigation. Otherwise, you have no business being here. And if I suspect you're withholding anything in order to buy favors or force compliance, I'll reach right into your mind and pull out the information myself!" Jacobsen's voice was almost a whisper. "I've told you before that I have no interest in aligning myself with any special interest group."

"Aside from the one you already represent." Horner's voice no longer sounded oily. He was braying like a donkey.

"I represent the state of Oregon," Jacobsen said quietly.

"You represent the mutants! And mindrape is against the law!"

Andie held her breath, wondering what Jacobsen would do. To her amazement, her boss started laughing.

"Oh, come on, Joseph. You can do better than that. Mindrape?"

Horner's face was red with anger. "I wouldn't laugh too hard, Senator. You do your constituency a disservice by denying it the aid and comfort of The Fold."

Jacobsen smiled wryly, but the laughter was gone from her eyes. "Joseph, it doesn't take a telepath to know what you're after. I'm sure that The Fold would dearly love to have a group of talented mutants. Would, in fact, welcome them with open arms. And purses. And any mutant who wishes to join you is free to do so." Her tone hardened. "But I will not sponsor a blanket endorsement of any group, yours or others. I don't have the authority. Or the interest."

"You may regret that."

"Is that a threat?"

"An observation."

Jacobsen placed her palms against the table and stood up. "Save your observations for the investigation, Senator. Now if you'll excuse us." She moved away from the table. Andie followed gratefully.

In the corridor, Andie took a deep breath and let it out noisily. "He's certainly annoying."

Jacobsen nodded. "I tried to keep him off this trip, but he's got clout. And I can only push so hard before there's a leak. The media vampires would love to get ahold of this kind of thing."

"Do you think he'll cause more trouble?"

"No. But I'll be relieved when we're back in Washington. Have you had any luck at the library?"

"Nada. The official line is: What golden eyes? Oh, those? They're contact lenses."

Jacobsen smiled wanly. "Well, keep trying."

"I'm going back there this afternoon."

"Perhaps the clinics at Jacarepaguá will give us some better leads than we've found so far."

Andie considered telling the senator about the meeting with Skerry. But what if Jacobsen didn't believe her? Even with the memorypak? Skerry had warned her not to reveal it until they were back home. A mechmaid rolled down the hall past them, blue lights blinking, sensors beeping. Andie felt a chill. Skerry had said that Jacobsen was being watched, perhaps by machines as well as people. She'd have to wait to reveal what she'd learned until they were back home. Safe.

"What was it you wanted to discuss, Andie?"

"Oh, I . . . I just wanted to find out how you felt about Ribeiros."

Jacobsen's eyebrows arched in confusion. "I thought I covered that. He's very cool. Appears to be cooperating, but I wonder about appearances."

"So you're suspicious?"

"Yes. And with nothing to go on."

"Well, I'm sure we'll turn up something soon." Andie hoped she sounded more confident than she felt.

"If there's anything to turn up at all." Jacobsen gave her a quick squeeze on the shoulder. "Come on, I'll give you a lift to the clinic."

Two hours later, the amber letters and figures on population movement rippled across the screen in blurry columns. Andie rubbed her eyes and decided to see if Karim had learned anything new. Maybe he'd discovered a pod of supermutants sitting in a jacaranda tree. Or driving every taxi in Rio. Anything.

She found him in the garden talking to some patients wearing head bandages. Some of them were wrist-linked to radar headsets, for their own eyes were bandaged against light. The door swung open with a mechanical whine as Andie approached it. Karim looked up and smiled. He excused himself and walked to meet her.

"I didn't know you could gain access to the patients here." Andie looked around the room, admiring the flowering bromeliads, lush, potted plants, and artificial brook.

"Well, I didn't exactly ask permission," Karim said, smiling. "I just took a walk to see what I could find."

Andie chuckled. "You mean you snooped around and waited until the place was deserted, then snuck in here."

"I thought that was what I said. What's up? Did you find something?"

The middle of her back prickled as though somebody was staring at her. She took him by the arm and peered over her shoulder, but the corridor was empty.

"Let's get out of here for a while," she said. "Want to take a walk along the beach?"

"Sounds good. We can borrow Craddick's skimmer and driver. The senators are in another endless meeting with Ribeiros. They won't be finished talking with him for hours. Shall we?" He motioned toward the exit.

"I wonder what they're talking about," Andie said as she

strode across the asphalt parking lot. She could almost see the heat shimmering in waves, caught by the ferocious midafternoon sunlight. If she squinted her eyes, she wondered if she'd see Skerry between the shimmers.

"Well, whatever it is, I don't think they'll get any answers out of Ribeiros. That guy is smoother than a samba." Karim waited for her to climb into the back of the sleek, scarlet skimmer and got in after her.

"To the hotel," he told the driver. They sped away, nimbly dodging other skimmers, weaving through traffic at high velocity. Andie restrained the urge to shut her eyes. The chauffeur glanced back at them through the rearview mirror; he was wearing mirrored sunglasses. She wondered what color his eyes were.

Fifteen minutes later, they were both walking along the water line at Copacabana, comfortable in the minuscule bathing garb favored by the cariocas. Around them, bathers frolicked in the water, splashing, laughing, and shrieking as each wave hit.

"So what have you learned?" Andie asked.

He shrugged. "Not much. It's certainly not a genetics lab. That clinic specializes in plastic surgery. Ribeiros made his fortune that way; a tuck here, a tuck there, and now every rich woman in Rio wants him to fix her nose, breasts, or behind."

"What about eyes?"

"Ribeiros seems to do a lot of eye surgery, doesn't he? And now that I think about it, that doesn't make sense for a plastic surgeon."

"Of course, he could bring a specialist in. Those patients we saw might have just had their crow's feet removed. From what I've heard, new skin is terribly light sensitive, and regenerative drugs only make it worse."

"Well, that probably accounts for the bandages."

"Unless the reason they're in there is to change the color of their eyes." There, she'd said it.

"What?"

Andie pressed on. "I mean, if they wanted to change their eye color to, say, gold, maybe they could have Ribeiros or one of his associates do it."

"Gold, as in mutant gold?"

"That's right." Karim shook his head. "Assuming they could, why would they want to do that?"

"To pretend they're mutants. To fit in with the coming master race."

"Master race? The mutants?" He stared at her for a long moment. "Andie, I think you've been spending too much time out in the Brazilian sun. You've got visions of supermutants dancing in your head just because you think you saw a beach vendor with golden eyes."

"You can laugh, but I saw him, and I know what I felt. And since we've been here, I've noticed people all over whose eyes seem to catch the light in odd ways."

"I know. You've hardly talked about anything else."

"Well, it all seems very suspicious to me. This city gives me the creeps. It's certainly not what I'd expected. Don't you think it's strange that Rio is so quiet? Didn't you expect to find it an all-night, all-day party?"

"Now that you mention it, aside from the traffic, it is much quieter here than I thought it would be. A couple of discos are open, but it's no more lively than Georgetown on a Saturday night."

"Almost as though something is controlling things."

"Maybe." Karim kicked at a piece of dark-red seaweed. "Just because the nightlife's dead and you think you've seen some oddly colored eyes doesn't convince me that a bunch of invisible, so-called supermutants have staged a coup here. You can't even convince me that they exist. Half the time I have to work at believing in regular, garden-variety mutants. Like your boss."

Andie shook her head. "Don't you wonder why Dr.

Ribeiros never takes off his dark glasses? Even indoors? We've never seen the color of his eyes."

"So now you think Ribeiros is a mutant?" Andie could hear the pent-up laughter in Karim's voice. "If he is, couldn't Jacobsen tell?"

"I don't know." She felt a pang of doubt. Maybe she was wasting her time looking for plots and conspiracies. Hadn't Jacobsen told her she doubted the existence of the supermutant? Who would know better than she? What if Skerry was wrong, just a renegade mutant looking to make trouble? But what if he was right?

"Okay, Karim, you've made your point. But once and for all, I'd really like to find out if the supermutant exists."

"You and the Congress of the United States." Karim stopped walking, put his hand on her shoulder and drew her toward him. "What you need is a little r-'n'-r."

"What are you suggesting?"

"Let's take forty-eight hours in Teresópolis. Go see the summer palace. It's cooler up there. Get our minds off mutants and senators. We'll be back in Washington by Thursday." His gaze was frankly seductive. Andie admired his lean, tanned body. His small red bikini. Her pulse quickened.

"That sounds nice. But can we get away?"

"Why not? Your boss is no hard-ass, and mine certainly believes in vacations."

"For himself, maybe. But what about loyal aides?" She disengaged her hand from his.

"He's been positively benevolent ever since we got here. In fact, everybody looks like they've spent the afternoon at a tea party after an hour or two with Ribeiros."

"Except for my boss." The image of Jacobsen, pale and tired, flashed before her. As if she was under some sort of strain and not even aware of it. Andie pondered the image. Something was wrong. If only she knew what it was. Supermutants? Paranoia? The longer she was in Rio, the more confused she felt. A weekend in the hills might clear her head.

"I can be ready to go by six. I'll leave a message on Jacobsen's screen. She's been so preoccupied, she'll hardly notice I'm gone."

MICHAEL WATCHED KELLY get into the skimmer. She was wearing a sleeveless purple tunic cut low in front and back. Her dark hair fell to her shoulders in graceful waves. Lavender crystals glittered at her ears. She leaned over as she clambered in and kissed him gently. As she pulled back, he saw that she was wearing very little beneath the tunic.

"Very nice," he said, smiling.

She gave him a sly look. "Well, it is graduation week."

"Yeah, although you'd hardly know it since they stopped having graduation ceremonies in ninety-eight."

"There were too many bomb threats back then."

"Not anymore. But I guess it saves them money. Cheap, this younger generation."

Kelly jabbed him in the ribs. "Well, 'old man,' where are we going tonight?"

"Isn't your friend Diane throwing a party?"

"Yeah, but that's later, after the clubs close."

"Then why don't we go to the Hardwired, then check out Club Centauri?"

Kelly looked puzzled. "I thought your cousin had invited us to a party."

"My cousin?"

"Jena Thornton. Remember?"

Silently, Michael cursed. Why had he told Kelly about that invitation?

"It's just mutants. You won't enjoy it."

"How do you know?"

"Believe me, I just know."

"Michael, that's not fair. How will I ever meet your family?"

"This wouldn't be a good time." He set his lips in a thin, determined line.

"Why not?"

"Dammit, Kelly, won't you listen to me! This is an all-mutant party."

"Are you ashamed of being seen with me?"

"No!"

"Then let's go to Jena's."

Michael sighed. "As you wish. Don't say I didn't warn you." Furious, he backed the skimmer out of the driveway. The last thing he wanted to do was take Kelly to a mutant party. But he couldn't turn back now without a real fight. He did a quick mental chant to regain his composure and turned the skimmer in the direction of his cousin's house.

Traffic was light. In twenty minutes, he was parking the skimmer along the curb near the house.

Jena answered the door. She was wearing a shimmering, skintight blouse almost the color of her hair, with leggings and boots to match. A quick look of surprise flitted across her face and was gone. She smiled brightly.

"Michael! And Kelly, is it? Glad you could come. Everybody's back in the den. Come in."

The room was filled with mutants and the sound of mutant pleasure chants. In the corner, two couples sat locked in mental rapport, arms linked. Expressions flickered across their faces; humor, surprise, ecstasy. Nearby, two boys in black jumpsuits floated near the ceiling, passing a glowing glass ball back and forth without touching it. A girl with red hair twisted into loops and coils leaped up and joined them. Near the couches where mutant couples flirted and teased, trays of food floated above each armrest.

Michael reached for Kelly's hand. The chants faded. Every golden eye in the room was trained upon the new arrivals, silently assessing. Condemning.

He moved forward, wordlessly daring anybody in the room to make a rude gesture, an unkind comment. He nodded coolly at his clan members. His cousins returned his salute and returned to their play.

Michael felt a warm hand on his arm. Jena had walked up beside him. Around her neck she wore a golden choker: a necklace of unity pins linked by a chain. He inhaled the scent she wore; something pleasantly musky. What a beautiful girl, he thought. A guilty prickle of desire warmed his loins. What was he doing here?

"Michael, let me show Kelly the house. I'll bet she's never been in an actual mutant's house before," Jena said, putting an arm around Kelly. "Would you like to see the sanctuary where my father chants?"

Kelly nodded, but Michael thought she looked confused and a bit doubtful.

"I'll come along," he said.

"Oh, you'll just be bored," Jena said, waving a hand in dismissal. "Besides, you've seen the house before."

Michael didn't like her insinuating tone, but he couldn't protest further without making a scene. Helplessly, he watched Jena lead Kelly away.

"Dating a normal, Ryton?" Stevam Shrader asked.

Michael eyed Shrader with dislike, irritated by his condescending tone. Shrader always stumbled over the group chants at clan meetings. He was a dull, muscle-bound clod. What could Jena see in him?

"Yes," he said coldly. "I'm dating Kelly McLeod."

Vala Abben joined them, silver crystals glittering in her dark hair. "Aren't you worried about censure?" she asked. With her sharp chin and inquisitive manner, she reminded Michael of a carnivorous rodent sniffing around for fresh meat. "And isn't she kind of, well, boring? Limited?"

"She's refreshing," he said, snagging a choybar as it floated past. "She's bright. Funny. And attractive."

Shrader nodded. "Yeah, she's not bad. Might be interesting to screw. But she's not mutant."

"Thank God for that," Michael said, and turned away angrily. If they'd been anywhere else, he'd have put Shrader through the wall for that comment. But this wasn't his house, or his party. He went to find Kelly and Jena.

"AND THESE ARE THE CHANT STICKS which we use on special days," Jena said. She floated one toward Kelly.

The teak wand was richly colored, its surface rubbed to the consistency of silk from long handling. Kelly stroked it gently.

"Interesting," she said, and placed on the table by the window. Jena was being nice to her, but it made her feel uncomfortable. Maybe Michael was right. She didn't belong here.

"Come out and see our deck," Jena said. The iridescent glass door slid back smoothly, although she hadn't touched it.

Kelly gazed out into the dark, green lushness of the backyard.

"I've always thought my cousin Michael was killer sexy," Jena said, her voice a throaty whisper, inviting confidences.

"Oh. Really?" Kelly's tone was heavy with irony; Jena's interest in Michael was more than a little obvious.

Jena moved toward her. "Yes. Don't you think so? Have you ever slept with a mutant before? How is he?"

You'd love to know, wouldn't you, Kelly thought. Well, get 'waved. I've had enough of this strange party, especially your curiosity. Kelly started to tell her that she had a hell of a nerve when Jena touched the side of her face. It could have been a caressing movement, but there was a firmness to it that almost had the feel of an assault. Kelly wanted to protest, but she was rooted to the spot, head pounding. Was she fainting? Yes, and Jena was holding her to keep her from falling. Good Jena. Kind Jena. She was really her friend. Of course she'd tell her about Michael. . . .

"What's going on here?"

Michael stood in the doorway, his face hard with anger. Kelly felt herself being pulled from Jena's grasp by invisible forces. In a moment, Michael's arms closed protectively around her. She shook her head to clear it.

"Nothing, Michael. Kelly started to feel dizzy and I was telling her to lean on me," Jena said. "That was a nice little telekinetic display of possessiveness, though."

"Save it, Jena." Michael looked at Kelly. She seemed disoriented. "We're leaving." He half led her out of the room. Jena followed them to the door.

"Sorry you can't stay. We were just getting set to play some party games; mind strip and search. I'm sure Kelly would have enjoyed them." She stared at Michael for a moment. "See you later."

Michael turned away, walking swiftly, Kelly in tow. Behind him, he could almost feel the cold winds of mutant season howling.

JENA WATCHED the skimmer's taillights disappear around the corner. She felt disappointed and elated. She'd barely had time to get a glimpse into Kelly's head, but what she'd learned had been instructive. Kelly and Michael had been intimate. Very intimate. And Michael's parents didn't know it. Yet.

"Did you tell Michael to leave?" Vala asked, floating almost at eye level.

"No, silly," Jena said. She turned from the window, a false smile covering her frustration. "Why should I do that?"

"Well, he brought that normal with him. Why'd he bother?"

"He likes her." Jena's voice sounded shrill, even to her own ears. Control yourself, she thought. You've got time to deal with this. "What kind of hostess tells a guest to leave just because his date is inappropriate?"

Vala smiled sharply. "Just as well he did leave, if he's going to date a normal."

Jena didn't have to look around the room to know that every head was nodding in agreement.

9

I'M SORRY, Miss Ryton. We simply don't have anything for you." The pale face on the screen stared at her without expression. The nameplate on his desk read PAUL EDWARDS, EMPLOYMENT COUNSELOR.

Melanie stared at him in disbelief.

"But I filled out an application," she said. "You sent me a letter telling me I had the job. See?" She held the printout in front of the monitor.

Pale Mr. Edwards scanned the letter.

"I'm afraid that must have been a mistake."

"What kind of mistake?"

"Obviously, we overcommitted. You're the third applicant I've had to turn away today."

I'll bet, Melanie thought. And did they all have golden eyes too? She crumpled the letter in her fist. Aloud, she asked, "What should I do now? I've spent all my money just getting here."

The pale face remained impassive. "I'm sorry. I suggest you call your family and ask them to send you a ticket home. Now if you'll excuse me." The screen faded to black. Melanie bit her lip and gathered up her pack. The pink linen suit she'd worn itched. She wondered if the job would have still existed if she'd worn contact lenses to cover her mutant eyes. Blatant discrimination was against the law, of course. But a job suddenly evaporating owing to clerical error? That wasn't discrimination, was it?

She walked out of the interview cubicle and passed through the vast office, empty save for one receptionist, the only human being in the convention employment office that Melanie had seen face to face. She left the air-conditioned sanctuary, stepping through sliding glass doors into the full heat of noonday Washington in late May. The leaves on the maples lining the sidewalk hung motionless. The air smelled cloying with the scent of roses past their prime. A few people moved slowly past the building, like sleepwalkers, weighed down by the heat. Melanie stripped off her jacket.

What was she going to do? Go home? No. That was admitting defeat. She'd come here and now she'd stay here. She'd show everybody she could take care of herself. Melanie fought back the impulse to sob in defeat and frustration. She saw a kiosk on the corner, and with a few of her precious remaining credit chips she purchased a printout of the want ads. Surely there was something she could do in Washington.

MICHAEL WATCHED KELLY WALK, naked, across her bedroom to get a joystick. Although he usually admired the sight of her trim body in motion, tonight he felt irritated.

"Why do you have to go away for two months?" he asked, testily.

"My father rented a cabin at Lake Louise for July and August," Kelly said, offering him a joystick as she put one in her mouth. He shook his head in refusal.

"I didn't know you were such an outdoors type."

She smiled. "I'm not, although I wouldn't mind some cooler weather."

"Don't go."

"I have to. Honestly, Michael, it'll only be for a month. You make it sound as though it's forever."

"Your father's just trying to break us up." Michael stood up and started pacing the room.

"You're paranoid. I'm the one who should be worried, after meeting your 'charming' cousin."

"Jena?" For a moment, Michael remembered the scent of musky perfume, the warmth of her hand on his arm. Angrily, he banished the memory. "Don't be ridiculous. Besides, I told you we shouldn't have gone to that party. I still think she was attempting a mindrape."

"Don't be so melodramatic." Kelly leaned back against the pillows. "I just got dizzy, that's all. Besides, you said she was telekinetic."

"That's what I thought."

"Well, whatever she is, I don't like it. She's too friendly. Too interested in you."

"That's the clan's doing," Michael said. "Don't worry. The feeling is definitely not mutual."

Kelly smiled. "Good. And I've satisfied my curiosity about mutant parties for quite a while. Maybe a lifetime."

"But you're still going to Lake Louise?"

"Yes." She put down the joystick and reached for him. "Now give me something that will make me want to come home."

BENJAMIN CARIDDI locked the door of his office. The laser key also unlocked the desk, and with a simple command from him, the deskscreen rose out of the keypad like an electronic flower blooming. He checked the deskchron: eleven P.M. Keyed in a code with a cloaking prefix. The screen rang three times before his call was answered.

"Ben?" A resonant male baritone asked. The screen stayed dark on the other end as well, but Benjamin had seen that face so often he could sketch its features.

"Who else?"

"Any luck?"

"Two fifteen-year-olds and a thirteen-year-old."

"All fertile?"

"Of course."

"Good, you know the procedure then."

"Sure. I'm running low on narcodane."

"You'll have a new case in the morning. . . ." A pause. Benjamin knew the next question even before it was asked.

"Any mutants in this group?"

"No."

"Well, keep looking."

"Always."

JAMES RYTON tried to stop pacing, but his legs seemed compelled, beyond his control. From kitchen to front door, to living room, from wallscreen to window, he made the circuit of the room, pacing back and forth over the blue carpet. His wife watched from the couch, eyes unreadable, face pale. He lit his pipe, watched it go out, relit it, but did not smoke it. Should he call the police? Halden?

"James, you're making me dizzy," Sue Li said.

He turned toward her, feeling a hundred outraged voices singing in his head. "No note, no message. I don't know what to do." Never before in his life could he recall feeling this indecisive. This helpless.

"Let's just wait until Michael comes home. Maybe he'll have some information we don't."

"And if he doesn't?" Ryton's head throbbed. His mental flares were recurring, and their clairaudient cacophony was giving him a headache. These damned flares usually hit whenever he was agitated, like a migraine with echoes. His father had suffered from them, and his father before him.

A small voice whispered to Ryton that this was the first step on that slow journey to madness that so many of his brethren had made. Would he end his days gibbering in a locked room, tormented by the distorted echoes of his own clairaudience? He shoved the thought away with a prayer for a quick death, and turned back to his wife.

"Then we'll decide what to do."

"You're awfully calm." He felt irritation, suddenly, at her impassive glance, her cool demeanor. Sue Li and her Buddha face.

"I only seem that way. Of course I'm concerned. But it doesn't make sense for both of us to be wearing a hole in the floor pads." She paused. "Let me put on the chants. They'll help to clear your head."

"No! Nothing." He knew that not even the clan chants could soothe him nor silence the antiphonal Greek chorus that chittered and yowled at him. Tranquilizers might help, but then his judgment would be impaired. He felt as though he was walking across the floor of a noisy convection oven in which the power had just been turned up. He loosened his collar.

The front door opened with a hiss and Michael walked in.

"Mom. Dad." He paused. "What's up?"

"Michael, did your sister say anything to you about taking a summer job in Washington?" Ryton asked hoarsely.

"Mel? No. I thought she was visiting cousin Evra."

"So did we," Sue Li said.

"She's not?"

Ryton shook his head. "We called a few hours ago. Evra is visiting her sister in Colorado. They haven't seen Melanie since school closed for the holidays." He felt the roaring sensation building in his head. Gingerly, he sat down in his chair. "We finally found the message on the homescreen. No address. Just a note that she'll be in touch with us once she's settled."

"Have you checked her room?"

"Of course. She only took a few pieces of clothing. Everything else is here."

"How about her money—her credit chips?"

Ryton felt annoyed. He hadn't thought of looking for them. He turned to his wife. "Did you look for them?"

"No."

"Where does she keep them?"

"In the third drawer of her desk."

He took the stairs two at a time. But he knew, even before he reached the room, that the drawer would be empty. He came back shaking his head.

"Gone."

"Could Jimmy have hidden them?" Sue Li asked.

Ryton tried to restrain his anger. Jimmy was asleep, and blameless, he was certain. He couldn't imagine waking him for this. Not yet.

"Of course not."

"So she's finally done it." Michael smiled in a peculiar way that Ryton didn't care for. He leaned back against the wall and crossed his arms in front of him. "Good for Mel."

"What do you mean?"

"I mean, Dad, that you should have seen this coming. She's wanted to prove her independence for a long time."

"Why didn't you tell us?"

"I thought you knew. Besides, I never suspected she'd really do it."

Ryton reached for the message screen. "We have to call the police. Halden as well."

"She has to be gone twenty-four hours before you can report her as a missing person."

"She's been gone all weekend."

"Would Kelly have any idea where she's gone?" Sue Li asked quietly.

"I don't know. She didn't say anything about it tonight." He stared at his father defiantly.

"So that's where you were." Ryton felt chagrined. His son said nothing. "Well, first thing in the morning, better call that girl and tell her, in case Mel tries to contact her."

"I will, for all the good it will do. They're going away for a month."

Ryton stared at Michael, looking in vain for a shadow of the child he had been. His children were growing up, becoming strangers with cold faces. Running away. The world was going crazy. He reached for the screen keyboard and punched in Halden's code. The screen remained blank, dark green. After a minute, the audio switched on.

"Halden, James here."

"A problem?" Halden's voice sounded thick, furry.

"Afraid so. My daughter has disappeared."

The screen rippled with motes, which solidified into Halden's face, rumpled from sleep. He turned away from the screen for a moment as if answering a query from somebody out of range. Zenora, most likely. When he turned back, he looked grim.

"A runaway?"

"So it appears. She lied to us about some party, then left a message about getting a job in Washington."

"How long has she been gone?"

"Two days."

Halden whistled tunelessly. "Why'd you wait to call?"

"We thought she was visiting Evra."

"I've warned you before that Melanie was unhappy."

Ryton felt his self-control waning. "We all knew she was unhappy, Halden. But what was there to be done about it? I didn't call you for a lecture on child care."

Halden nodded. "You're right, James. No use bringing that up now. Could this job be legitimate?"

"Unknown."

"I'll spread the word. You realize how difficult it will be to find her, especially since she's a null?"

"Yes, yes," Ryton said, feeling impatient. "I'm fully aware of the limitations on telepathic netting. Even we have our limits."

"Not to mention Melanie's dysfunction acting almost like an echo screen."

"Then look for a blank space which repulses our efforts. That certainly would describe her." Ryton could hear the hiss of Sue Li's breath, the emanation of horror at his statement.

Halden grimaced. "James, I realize you're under tremendous stress, but if that's how you talk about your daughter, I'm not surprised she left with so little notice."

"I'm sorry, Halden. This is very unsettling. She's just a child."

"Do you know anyone in Washington?"

"No. Wait, yes, in Jacobsen's office."

"I suggest you get in touch first thing in the morning. I'll let you know as soon as I hear something." The screen went dark.

Ryton turned to his family. Sue Li had her lips pursed in a way that he knew meant trouble later. Michael was frowning, his face red.

"Way to go, Dad."

"What do you mean?"

His son shook his head. "Uncle Halden is right. You are un-fucking-believable."

"Don't use that kind of language with me." The voices in Ryton's head resumed their arguments. He massaged his forehead wearily.

"I'll bet you're not half as concerned with Mel's safety as you are about how this will look at the summer clan meeting."

"Michael!" Sue Li sounded shocked.

Ryton's head pounded. This was just one more noisy voice added to his torment. "Don't be ridiculous."

"Michael," Sue Li said. "Your father is terribly upset. And you know he gets mental flares when he's agitated."

"Yeah, I know. Well, I also know that my sister is out there someplace, maybe in trouble, and all you can do is whine to Uncle Halden."

"Michael, that's enough!" Sue Li said.

Ryton turned away from both of them and walked toward the bathroom. He had to get something to stop the noise, the pain.

. . .

THE LIGHTS in the movie theater dimmed as the promo started again. The now familiar images of Moonstation filled the screen. Mel had watched it three times already. She could almost recite the narration by heart. Moonstation looked like an interesting place to visit. The little domes, the smiling people in the bright-blue suits. Even the machinery they drove looked strange and exotic. Maybe they didn't care about mutants on the moon. Maybe she'd go there someday.

She pulled her jacket up sleepily around her. The theater was almost empty. She could probably stay here all night. The Hyde Rider film marathon would last until noon the next day. She would decide what to do tomorrow. Maybe she'd fake her father's credit number and take the monorail to Denver. Maybe she'd find a job. At least there was nobody telling her what to do and how to do it. She fell into a light sleep, dreaming of floating under a dome, pink ribbons tied to her ankles as though she were a balloon.

10

THE PRINTOUTS from the solar collector reports fanned across James Ryton's desk in a yellow arc, but he stared at them with eyes blinded by guilt and fear. Why had Melanie gone? They'd done everything they could for her, hadn't they? She was an unworldly girl, innocent and at risk. He didn't want to think about the kind of perils waiting for her. Melanie belonged at home, where people cared about her and would take care of her.

Fear had made him speak harshly about his daughter to Halden, fear and those damned mental flares. Sue Li had prepared a calming herbal mixture for him this morning, and the flares had subsided to faint echoes, thank the deities. By the time he called the police, Ryton felt his self-control was back in place, like armor.

They'd been polite, of course. The police were always polite. A bit cavalier, but courteous.

"We'll put a tracer on your daughter," Sergeant Mallory had told him. "This happens all the time after graduation. In a week or two, she'll be back."

After he signed off, the cops had probably all shared a good laugh about how even mutants had to cope with rebellious children. Normals, Ryton thought. What good were they?

He stopped drumming his fingers on the gray plaswood desktop. While he had little use for most nonmutants, one *had* been sympathetic and cooperative when he needed her help. And she was in just the right place, too. Ryton turned to his deskscreen and requested the dial code for Andrea Greenberg. She answered on the fourth ring, looking moderately surprised.

"Mr. Ryton? Did you get my message about the Marsbase allocations bill?"

He nodded rapidly. "Yes, and thank you for your help on that. We were gratified by the vote."

"I thought you might be. So what can I do for you today?"

"Ms. Greenberg, I have a problem."

"More NASA regulations?"

"No. This is . . . personal." He paused, his voice trailing off self-consciously. How could he involve a nonmutant he scarcely knew in his problems?

"Yes?" Was that impatience in her voice? He was wasting her time. But what did he have to lose? Desperation gave Ryton strength.

"It's my daughter. She's run off. At least, I believe she has. She left a message about taking some job in Washington."

"How old is she?"

"Eighteen."

Andrea Greenberg frowned. "Mr. Ryton, legally, she's an adult. And I should think an adult mutant would be able to take care of herself."

"You don't know my daughter," Ryton said. "Melanie has led a sheltered life. And she's a null."

"A null?"

"Dysfunctional. She doesn't have any mutant abilities."

Andrea Greenberg stared at him, green eyes wide with surprise. "I've never heard of dysfunctional mutants before."

"It's rare," Ryton admitted. "And we don't publicize it."

"I'm beginning to see why you're concerned."

Ryton leaned closer to the screen. "Ms. Greenberg, I think my daughter has set out to prove something to us. Or to herself. I'm afraid that what she'll prove is how much trouble she can get into on her own. My wife and I are terribly worried."

"I'm sure you are. But could Melanie's story be true? Perhaps she really has found a job. In which case, you don't really have anything to worry about."

"But she didn't leave us any address. We don't even know how to contact her. I don't know what to do. She could be raped. Murdered. I've seen it happen before." Ryton felt as though he were squirming, naked and exposed, before Andrea Greenberg. Just as he began to despair of gaining her help, her expression softened.

"I understand," she said. "Look, why don't I contact some people I know on the local police force and see what I can find out? I can't promise anything, of course."

"Ms. Greenberg, I'm very grateful." Ryton's voice shook.

She looked embarrassed. "Well, I'll do what I can."

"This is the second time you've helped me. I hope that someday I can be of service to you. Thank you."

"I'll contact you if I learn anything. And you're welcome." Her image faded.

Ryton picked up the scattered yellow papers before him. He could not condemn all normals, he told himself. Not as long as he knew Andrea Greenberg.

THE STAR CHAMBER was dark at noon, redolent of stale beer and old cigarette smoke. Melanie peered through the gloom and tried not to look nervous as the bar's owner stared at her with beady-eyed interest. His prominent front teeth reminded her of the hamsters she'd seen once in science class.

Antique neon lights, blinking pink and green along the walls, and cryolights on the mechband in the corner were the only source of illumination. Each time Melanie moved, something crunched under her feet. She leaned against a bar stool, trying not to upset the brimming ashtray attached to it.

"Turn around, girlie." His voice was hoarse. He inhaled on a cigarette butt that he held casually between thumb and forefinger, then flicked it into the sink behind the bar.

She made a quick spin, feeling horribly self-conscious in her tight jeans.

"Slower."

Melanie did it again.

"Your legs are all right. Ass is good, too. Okay, lemme see your tits."

"What?"

The man gestured impatiently. "C'mon. The job is for an exotic dancer. Exotic dancers gotta have good tits. Now do you want this job or not?"

Melanie wanted to run out the door. But she told herself she needed the job. She had to stay and prove herself. With fumbling fingers, she pulled up her blouse.

"The bra, too."

She unhooked it, grateful for the dark room. He stared at her for what felt like an eternity.

Finally, he nodded. "Nice. Small, but nice. Funny, somehow I didn't think mutant tits would look just like the rest. Okay, kid, you got the job. Get here about six-thirty so one of the other girls can show you the routines. There'll be a costume for you in locker number four downstairs. You're responsible for keeping it clean. You get three hundred fifty credits a week, plus tips."

Melanie almost flew out the door. She had a job! She'd show everybody she could take care of herself. She hurried back to the tiny room she'd rented off Avenue J; she wanted enough time to get ready for tonight, and the hall bathroom was usually busy after five.

When she returned to the Star Chamber, the bar was already filled with people drinking and smoking. She could feel the vibrations from the mechband all the way downstairs.

Her locker was in a tiny space that looked as though it had started life as a root cellar. The room was crowded with women in various stages of undress. Melanie found her locker, opened it, and stared at her costume in shock. It was a red lace g-strip and garters attached to black stockings that flashed with purple cryolight arrows.

"What are you looking at? Haven't you ever seen a g-string before?" the red-haired girl next to her asked. Her breasts were large and pendulous. She was applying green cryolight stars to them as she spoke.

"Where's the rest of my costume?"

Raucous laughter was the only response Melanie heard for a minute.

"That's your costume, sweetie," the redhead said, not unkindly. "You must be the new girl. Dick said I should show you around. So get dressed. And don't forget those purple arrows. No, not on your ears. On your boobs. Here, let me help you."

She cupped Melanie's left breast in one hand, took a purple arrow, licked it, gently affixed it to the nipple. Then she did the same to the right. Each time, her hands lingered a bit longer than necessary. Melanie felt her nipples hardening at the unfamiliar touch.

"You're a sweet little thing, aren't you?" the redhead said huskily. She rubbed the back of her knuckles across Melanie's breasts.

"Don't. Please."

"Call me Gwen." She put her arm around Melanie and drew her closer. Casually, Gwen reached a hand under Melanie's g-strip and explored there, stroking gently, a look of friendly curiosity on her broad features. She seemed oblivious to the racket around them. Girls slammed locker doors, pulled on their skimpy costumes, and hurried upstairs.

Melanie tried to squirm away from that insistent hand. She leaned back against the lockers, but Gwen held her close, breathing heavily. Melanie felt dizzy, as if she was going to smother between Gwen's enormous, perfumed breasts. She began to breathe in shallow gasps.

"I can see we're going to be good friends," Gwen said, licking her lips. "There's a whole lot I can teach you." Her busy fingers worked in tighter and tighter circles.

"Please," Melanie said, her voice weak. That wicked stroking. Make her stop it, she thought. Oh, God, it was beginning to feel good. As if her legs had a mind of their own, they opened to let that friendly hand get at more of her. Gwen took her nipple in her mouth, arrow and all. Melanie moaned. She wanted her to stop. No, to continue. Yes, to continue licking and stroking, and. . . .

"Gwen! Dammit, what have I told you about hitting on the new girls!" The bar's owner stood in the doorway, hands on hips.

Gwen released Melanie's breast and withdrew her hand.

"Sorry, Dick." The redhead looked repentant. Then her eyes met Melanie's and she winked.

"Get upstairs. The new girl can serve drinks and Terry will show her the ropes."

"Okay."

With mingled relief and dismay, Melanie watched Gwen's broad backside vanish up the stairs. She shook her head to clear it and told herself that she'd only imagined enjoying Gwen's assault. Shivering, she vowed to stay away from her.

"You," Dick said, pointing his cigarette toward her. "Upstairs too! And don't make time on my time!"

Melanie blushed and hurried up to the main floor behind him.

Under the tutelage of Terry, a tall mulatto girl in pink g-strip and stockings, Melanie served drinks and sterile hypo packs for the first show.

By the time the second show started, the clientele of Star Chamber was sprawled around the cavernous room in various stages of intoxication. There were chuters and joy heads; a breenfreak with orange stripes tattooed on his bald head and down the middle of his nose; a couple of androgs in blue skinsuits; middle-aged businessmen with screencases and thinning hair; and tourists in travel sacs. Melanie had never seen such an assortment.

The first time a customer grabbed her ass, she jumped so hard she nearly lost her drink sling. Terry pinched her in irritation.

"Wavehead. That's how you get the big tips. Let 'em have their feel. Just make sure they pay for it."

Melanie quickly learned to smile and endure the rough hands that groped up her legs as she made change. She got a bigger tip that way. Everybody seemed to want to touch her. All right, she decided grimly. As long as they pay for it.

She watched Gwen dance a sweaty bump and grind accompanied by pounding drumbeats and horns from the mechband. The big redhead came off the stage grinning, her g-strip bulging with credit chips. Terry did a desultory belly dance, arms slowly writhing while the mechband whined a vaguely Mideastern tune. Each song included an extended musical vamp to allow patrons to stick credit chips in g-strips. Once the music started, the customers, drunk and feverish, crowded around the stage, whistling and yelling.

"You're on," Terry told her, hurrying down the stairs on the side of the raised dance floor.

"But I don't know what to do."

"Then fake it. Just get up there and shake your boobs at 'em. That's all they care about. And make sure you get close enough so they can put the tips in."

Melanie mounted the stairs in a daze. The mechband asked the audience to welcome "Venus, the erotic mutant dancer," then laid down an undulating rhythmn. She stood frozen in the smoky orange spotlight, terrified. The customers booed and began rapping glasses and hypos on their tables in an irritable tattoo. The mechband started the melody again. Still, Melanie couldn't move. She looked toward the bar. Dick was glaring at her. Terry hissed from the side of the stage.

"Get with it, stupid!"

Melanie shook her head and began edging toward the stairs. She couldn't do it. She wanted to cover herself. To run and get away from the hunger she saw in the men's eyes. It was the same hunger she'd seen in Gwen downstairs.

"Hey, what is this?"

"Dance, you stupid cow!"

"Boo! Get her off!"

She cringed back from the jeers of the crowd. The sting of a hypo startled her. Terry had jabbed a drink into her leg. She staggered, feeling things shift in her head. Her stage fright ebbed and disappeared as the warmth of the chemical uncurled in her bloodstream. These jerks wanted a show, did they? She'd give them a show, all right.

She took a deep breath and began to move her hips in mimicry of the other girls. The men gathered at ringside stopped complaining and sat down. Melanie closed her eyes and pretended she was alone, dancing for herself. As she began to shimmy, the crowd yelled its approval.

"All right, mutie!"

"Come on, honey. Show us that goodie!"

Feeling the rhythmn of the music now, she became bolder and, opening her eyes, turned the shimmy into a strut that took her past the row of men in front. They waved credit chips at her, but she backed away teasingly.

A chuter with gray hair and dark circles under his eyes waved a three-hundred-credit chip at her.

"I've always wanted to feel mutant titty," he shouted.

Melanie shook her head and danced away.

He held up two more three-hundred-credit chips.

"C'mere, darlin'."

She waited until he held out twelve hundred credits. Then she shimmied up to him and leaned over. His hands were rough, and she flinched as he pawed her, but after a minute, he let go and slipped the chips under her belt.

After that, it was easy. Each time she saw a credit chip waving in somebody's fist, she slowed her movements, teasing until the amount was increased. Then she danced close enough for the customer to cop a feel and deposit the tip.

Step right up and touch the mutant dancer, she thought woozily.

A pale young man with short, dark hair and old-fashioned eyeglasses hung over the stage's edge, repeatedly surging forward to insert more chips in her g-strip. Each time, his grip on her leg was harsh and bruising. The fifth time she shook him off as the music ended. With relief, she hurried off the stage.

"Not bad. Five-minute break, then get busy at the tables," Terry told her. "Dick wants us to push breen hypos; he's overstocked."

Melanie nodded gratefully and cut through the crowd toward the bar.

"Breen, please," she told the barmech.

"Hypo?" came the mechanical query.

"Yes." She pulled the credit chips out of her costume and gasped at their total. Over five thousand credits. She'd never had so much money before. Jamming the credits back under her belt, she grabbed the hypo, holding it up against the bar lights. The plump, disposable syringe glinted with amber liquid. Melanie closed her eyes and jabbed her upper arm. In seconds, the narcotic went to work, drawing a gentle curtain between her and the world.

"Miss Venus?"

"Yes?" She turned carefully, intent upon maintaining her balance. It was the pale young man with glasses, the one who'd grabbed her leg so many times.

"My name is Arnold," he said. "Arnold Tamlin. I've always wanted to meet a mutant."

Melanie forced a smile. "Well, now you have."

He stared at her hungrily. "I enjoyed your dance very, very much."

His speech was slurred. She wondered how much liquor he'd had. And what else, besides.

"Very, very, very much."

"Thank you."

He repeated himself again, then leaned toward her. She moved back, butting into the breenfreak, who scowled at her.

"Sorry."

Arnold Tamlin continued to lean toward her. Then he seemed to fold in half, and began to slide, face down, to the floor. He didn't try to get up. Dick appeared, nudged Tamlin with his foot, and when he got no response, leaned over the bar.

"Bouncer!"

A sturdy gray mech with padded claws rolled out of a slot at the end of the counter, latched on to the unconscious man, and dragged him toward the door. The last of Arnold Tamlin that Melanie saw was the gray soles of his shoes.

Two hours later, Dick told her she was off-duty. Gratefully, she put down the drink sling and joined some of the girls downstairs. Exhaustion so dulled her senses that she barely noticed the others around her until someone came up behind her and cupped her breasts.

"Want me to help you get out of that costume?" Gwen asked. Her breath was warm on Melanie's neck.

"No! Leave me alone." Angrily, she pulled free. She'd had enough strange hands grabbing at her body for one night. Tearing off her costume, she dressed quickly and hurried upstairs, out of the bar.

Twenty minutes and two tube stops later, she was sitting in the faded blue bathroom at Avenue J, watching water run into the rusty tub. Her watch read two A.M.

She eased herself into the steaming bath, glad for the silence of the late hour. There were bruises on her thigh and near one nipple. Five thousand credits balanced against six bruises. So this is independence, she thought wearily. A tear slipped down her nose and fell into the water without a sound.

11

CARYL, GET ME JOE BAILEY at Metro D.C.," Andie said. If anybody could locate Melanie Ryton, it was Bailey. Besides, he owed her a favor. Several favors.

"He's on line five," Caryl said.

The deskscreen flickered, brightened. Bailey's homely, long-jowled face smiled at Andie around a donut.

"Hey, Red. What have you got for me?"

"A missing girl. Mutant. Age seventeen or thereabouts. Chinese-Caucasian. Her name's Melanie Ryton."

"Right." Bailey fiddled with his keyboard, chewing. "Where'd she come from?"

"New Jersey."

Bailey stopped chewing.

"Jersey? That's not my beat. At least, not lately."

"She told her parents she got a job here."

"So?"

"They don't believe her. I figured you could check on it faster than I could."

"Give me a minute." He wiped his hands and turned away from the screen. Then he was back, shaking his head.

"Negatory. No Melanie Ryton nowhere. I've checked employ, juvey, even the screw parlors. Nada."

"Damn."

"I thought your mutants kept all their kids at home in boxes."

"Not funny. And not true."

"Hope she's careful out there. You heard about the sheikh who wants to buy a mutant girl for his harem?"

"No. But I believe it. Keep an eye out for this one, okay?"

"Andie, do you know how many kids, parents, grandparents, and missing pets I get asked about every day?"

"For me, Joe?" She leaned forward and gave him a flirtatious look, eyelids at half-mast.

Bailey sighed. "All right."

A yellow message band from Caryl cut across the bottom of the screen: HORNER NEWSBYTE STARTING, CHANNEL 12. URGENT!

Andie glanced at the note. "Joe, I've got to go. Don't forget about Melanie Ryton. And you've got powdered sugar on your chin."

"Right. Ciaocito, Red."

His image vanished, replaced by that of Senator Joseph Horner, smiling his best Sunday-morning-come-to-prayer-meeting smile at the camera. Then he turned back to his host, Randall Camphill.

"As I was saying, Randy, we've got to be vigilant against this supermutant threat," Horner said.

Uh-oh, Andie thought. What is that son of a bitch up to? She hit the record button. Jacobsen was in a meeting, but she'd want to see this.

Camphill turned so that his best profile faced the camera. "Senator," he said, "can you explain to our audience what you mean by supermutant?"

"An unnatural product of eugenics, of ungodly genetic tampering. The supermutant is a danger to the rest of us," Horner said, voice cracking. "While we have come to accept our mutant brothers and sisters who are the result of natural, if unfortunate, processes—or so they tell us—we cannot accept, and must prevent, the defilement of human beings in the service of science. Who is to say that the supermutant, a product of the laboratory, is even human?" Horner's eyes gleamed with righteous concern.

"And you say you've seen these so-called supermutants during your fact-finding trip to Brazil?"

"Well, now, Randy, I haven't exactly seen them. But there've been signs. Clues. And we must be careful. We must be vigilant. Even now, they might be among us. At first, one or two, a mere drop of water in the population pool. But remember that a mighty ocean began with only a single drop. Be wary, lest we are all drowned in this coming flood."

"Thank you, Senator Horner. We're out of time. . . ."

Andie turned away from the screen.

"Oh, hell," she muttered. "One cat, unbagged. That bastard."

Should she buzz Jacobsen out of her meeting? She'd have to respond. Quickly.

The call waiting light began to blink on Andie's screen, multiplying until every line into the office was ringing.

"We're in for it now," Caryl said, running toward her desk-screen. "What do I tell them?"

"No comment," Andie said. "The senator's in a meeting and they'll have to call back. If they insist, take their name and number. Record all calls, but it's strictly no comment if they ask questions."

"Got it."

In her imagination, Andie could hear Horner's words repeated a hundred times across the country, around the world, booming from every vid kiosk on every street corner, spawning hysteria. People were already edgy enough about mutants. The riots of twenty years ago were a terrible, lingering memory. Fear of some monstrous supermutant could cause panic, perhaps worse. Was that what Horner was after?

And was he right? Could the world really handle enhanced mutants? She remembered the memorypak Skerry had handed her in Rio. She'd planned to show it to Jacobsen as soon as they returned from Brazil. But that had been weeks ago. The demands on her time had been overwhelming. And whenever she thought of Skerry's request, it had sounded more and more like paranoid fantasies. She'd promised herself to show the memorypak to Jacobsen this afternoon. Would there be time now?

The call waiting lights continued to blink despite Caryl's frantic efforts. She was fielding calls as fast as she could, shaking her head furiously.

"No. I'm sorry. We have no statement to make at this time. No. Absolutely not."

Andie took a deep breath and punched in the priority override code to summon her boss.

"WHERE DID YOU GET THIS?" Jacobsen demanded. The screen was empty. They'd scrolled through the contents of the memorypak twice.

Andie sighed. "I've already told you. . . ."

"That some mysterious stranger in Rio approached you, seemed to know me, and gave you this?" Jacobsen leaned back in her chair, eyes wide in disbelief. "Don't you realize that by accepting it you could have compromised the entire bunch of us?"

"Yes, but—"

"Well, I suppose it's too late now. But you should have come to me immediately."

Andie had never seen her look so exasperated.

"Perhaps I should have let you push Horner out the window in Rio. Damn the man."

"I thought you didn't read minds without asking permission," Andie said, her cheeks reddening.

"I don't. But you were practically broadcasting. Even non-mutants can do that, occasionally." Jacobsen's expression softened into a smile. "Why didn't you tell me about this, Andie?"

"I thought we were being watched."

"You were probably right. Nevertheless, I wish I'd known sooner. And now I have the proof I've been searching for, if this is trustworthy, that genetic experiments on human embryos are taking place in Brazil. And, somehow, I must find a way to undo the damage that fool Horner has done without outright lying."

"I think you'd better hold that news conference tomorrow morning, "Andie said. "Before this gets worse. I've already had two answermechs installed in the office today."

Jacobsen frowned. "It goes against precedent. I should make my report to Congress first. And I've got to get a copy of this memorypak to the Mutant Council. However, I suppose you're right. Horner's set off a wildfire. I've got to put it out first."

"I've reserved the Presidential Room for ten A.M. tomorrow."

"Fine. Get Craddick on my private line, would you, Andie? Then issue a release to all the usual media networks."

The rest of the day passed in a blur as Andie set up interviews after the press conference, fielded other calls, and rode herd on the rest of the office staff. Her nerves felt raw, abraded a bit more each time somebody mentioned the term "supermutant."

At six-thirty, Karim called to remind her of dinner plans. Reluctantly, she canceled. At nine-thirty, she remembered to have a sandwich sent up to the office. Two hours later, she forced herself to go home. Livia greeted her at the door with petulant Abyssinian yowls.

"Sorry, my dear. Tough day at the office. I know you're hungry."

Andie kicked off her shoes, grateful for the luxurious pile of the blue carpet against her aching feet. She fed the cat, adding an extra portion out of guilt, then settled onto the sofa to review her notes for Jacobsen's comments the next day. Livia curled up beside her, purring and licking herself contentedly. Slowly, Andie's head nodded forward. Her eyes closed. But her sleep was uneasy, filled with dreams of golden-eyed Frankenstein monsters stalking her, herding her toward churches whose doorways opened to reveal rows of sharp, grinning teeth.

BETWEEN SHOWS, Melanie leaned against the bar and eyed the crowd at the Star Chamber. Two men in nice suits looked like they'd be generous tippers. Near them was a group of Korean tourists; they always tipped well and they never grabbed very hard. She saw a couple of the regulars and made a note to stay away from the gray-haired chuter. He kept trying to pull off her arrows.

In the two weeks that Melanie had worked at the club, she'd quickly learned whom to avoid and whom to encourage. The chuters were most likely to grab hard. Something about doing chute just made them aggressive. But the joyheads were harmless. They giggled and tickled her, and sometimes they tipped well, if they remembered. She scanned the far side of the club. Oh, no. That weird gork, Arnold Tamlin, sat alone at a table. His eyes looked really unfocused tonight, she thought.

"I see your sweetie pie's here again," Gwen said.

"Get 'waved."

Melanie had kept her distance from the big redhead ever since that first night at the bar when she'd been too green to fend off the other woman's advances. She knew better now. When she awoke at night from tangled, sweaty dreams in which she tried desperately to get away from hands that stroked and mouths that sucked, she told herself she'd had too much to drink. Nightmares. It was nightmares that made her heart pound. Fear, not desire. It had to be.

During the second show, Melanie managed to avoid the chuters' outstretched hands and concentrate on the Koreans. They jammed so many chips into her belt, she was almost afraid to move. She danced carefully, teasing two joyheads, and even eluded that awful Tamlin. What a jerk. She finished her dance with a flourish and decided to have a joystick outside.

The night air was cooling and the sweat she'd worked up evaporated quickly. July in Washington was unthinkably hot, but at least there was some relief in the evening. She leaned against the backdoor of the club and thought of her family. Wouldn't they be surprised if they knew how much money she was making? For a moment, Melanie was happy. She didn't need them. She was fine on her own.

"Ex-excuse me. Miss Venus?"

Oh God, not Tamlin again. He'd followed her out of the club. Now he was blocking the door. Melanie backed away slowly, trying to smile.

"Yes?"

"I wanted to tell you how much I enjoy watching you." He moved toward her, his eyes staring fixedly into hers.

"Thank you."

"I was wondering if you'd dance just for me. . . ." He was coming closer, reaching out toward her.

"Oh, Arnold, I don't know. I'm pretty tired." She kept backing, trying to circle toward the door. Why didn't Dick send somebody out to get her? Her break was over.

"Dance just for me, Venus. Levitate and dance in the clouds just for me." He grabbed her by her shoulders. His grip was hard, fingers digging in.

"Arnold, I can't levitate." She twisted, trying to pull away. "Let go."

"Sure you can. Do it with me now. All you mutants can levitate, right?"

"You're hurting me."

He didn't seem to hear her. Melanie tried kicking at his shins as he pushed her but she stumbled over loose brick and toppled backward to the pavement with Tamlin on top of her. He put his hands around her throat, squeezing.

"Levitate, god damn you! You goddamned mutant! Freak! Levitate or I'll kill you!"

Melanie tried to scream, though she knew the noise in the bar would cloak any sound she made. She struggled desperately, clawing at his hands as the roaring sound in her ears grew louder. Louder. Tamlin's grip was too strong for her. Gasping, she struggled for breath, colors flashing against the inside of her eyelids. Then the colors began to fade. Breathing seemed like too much of an effort. She wanted to let go. But something wouldn't let her.

"Miss? Are you all right?"

Somebody was shaking her. Melanie opened her eyes. A young man with longish brown hair, olive skin, and soulful brown eyes stared at her with concern. She sat up carefully.

"Where is he?"

"Ran off when I slugged him."

"God," she said, feeling her throat. "I think you saved my life."

"Well, I couldn't just watch him strangle you." He helped her stand up, a comforting arm around her shoulder. Melanie leaned back against him gratefully. He was one of the businessmen she'd noticed earlier.

"Are you all right? Do you want to see a doctor?"

She shook her head. "I'm all right."

"Then let me take you home. He might be waiting nearby to follow you."

"Do you think so?"

"Anything is possible with a maniac like that."

"Who are you?"

"My name's Benjamin. Benjamin Cariddi. Ben."

She shook his hand, feeling a bit foolish. "My name's Melanie."

"I didn't think it was Venus." He smiled crookedly.

She smiled back. "Give me five minutes to change. And tell them I'm through for the night."

"I'll meet you by the front door."

He was waiting for her in a sleek, dark skimmer. The upholstery looked like gray leather. Must be a good imitation, she thought.

"Hungry?" he asked.

"Yes."

"Like hamburgers?"

"Real ones? Sure."

"I know a great place to get some." He turned the skimmer down a side street toward a freeway access, punched a code into the dashboard, leaned back in his seat.

Melanie stared at the dashboard. "Is this totally mechguided?"

"Just about."

"Aren't these skimmers outrageously expensive?"

Ben smiled at her. "Yes."

Melanie blushed. Stop asking stupid questions, she told herself. Look out the window.

The landscape was unfamiliar; a quiet residential area to her. At the next exit, the skimmer turned off the freeway and sped along past well-manicured lawns and elegant homes that glowed yellow from recessed lighting. Another turn and they were speeding through a canyon of sleek high-rise buildings. The skimmer pulled up before a green tower whose top floor was obscured by fog and darkness, and rolled into a garage elevator. With a grinding shudder, the lift deposited the skimmer in a parking slot deep underground.

"Everybody out," Ben said, opening Melanie's door.

"Where are we?"

"My place."

"I thought we were going to get a hamburger."

"We are. I make the best ones around." He grinned and led her to another elevator. "Twenty-third level, please."

Before Melanie could count the floors, the lift had stopped and Ben was leading her down a plushly carpeted gray corridor. His palm against the knob-sensor gained them entry into an airy duplex. The atrium living room was filled with green plants and low-slung tawny leather sofas.

"Make yourself comfortable," he said and vanished into the kitchen.

The walls were covered with textured cloth that glinted in subdued golds and greens. There was a hallway connecting the entry hall to three bedrooms, a bathroom and a small study. The master bedroom lay beyond, a somber room paneled in rich, dark wood. The far wall held a private lift which she assumed led to the second floor.

The scent of grilled meat drifted toward Melanie.

"Come and get it," Ben's voice announced from the wall speaker.

The kitchen was long and narrow, lined by gleaming white cabinets. It led to a circular nook, where a table was set with thin black plates and shining utensils. Ben ladled sauce into a bowl near a plate of burgers and gestured toward a chair.

"Sit down. This is my own invention."

Melanie looked at the sparkling plates and glasses, the silverware aligned in neat rows. She'd been eating in soya shops too much lately. Grabbing a burger, she took a huge bite. And another.

"Ooh. Great," she said around mouthfuls. She'd forgotten how good real meat tasted. She added some sauce; it seemed to be part tomato and part onion, with a sweet and sour tang.

"I don't believe in false advertising." He took a swallow of beer, looked at her appraisingly. "What are you doing working in a place like that?"

"It's a job. I needed it."

"Where are your folks?"

"Dead." Melanie concentrated on her food.

"Where are you from?"

"New York." She reached for another burger.

"Don't you have clan members who can help you?"

She stopped chewing and stared at him. "What do you know about clan?"

"I saw some docuvid that said mutants had clan meetings and things like that."

"I don't remember any vid like that."

Ben shrugged. "Maybe it wasn't shown in New York."

"Maybe." She swallowed the last bite and wiped her mouth. "Thanks for the food."

She stood up, grabbed her purse and headed for the door.

"Where are you going?" Ben followed her.

"Home."

"To some fleabag apartment, no doubt."

"No doubt." Melanie tried to open the door. It wouldn't budge. "Let me out."

Ben leaned past her and punched a code on the wall panel. The door slid open.

"You'll never find a taxi at this hour."

"Then I'll take the tube."

"There isn't a station for miles around. And you don't even know where you are." He leaned against the door frame. "Maybe it's not such a good idea to come home with strange men, huh?" He smiled crookedly. Melanie's heart began to pound. What had she gotten herself into now?

Ben shook his head. "Relax. I'm harmless. You're free to leave if you want. Or stay."

"Why should I stay?"

"Because this is a nicer place than where you sleep. Because there'll be a lock on your bedroom door that only you will be able to operate. Because you need help and I can provide it."

"Like what?"

"A better job, for starters."

"And what do I have to provide you with in return?"

Ben flashed his smile again. "I'll think of something. But not tonight. C'mon. It's late."

Melanie allowed him to draw her back into the apartment and close the door. He slid aside a wall panel, revealing shelves heaped with blue towels and sheets.

"Take what you need. Your bedroom is first door on the right. It has its own bathroom."

She stared at him uncertainly.

Ben sighed and walked into her bedroom. He punched a code into the deskscreen in the corner. The screen remained blank, but a minute later, a droning mechvoice spoke.

"You have reached the South DCPD. For emergency, dial seven-three-three, for arrest records, six-two-two; for the drug unit—" Ben cut the connection, then made another adjustment.

"There. I've set it on autoredial. They can trace a call in three seconds, but you'll find my address in the top drawer here if you care to report me for kindness to transients."

"I don't get it," Melanie said.

"What don't you get?"

"I don't know you. Why should you do this for me?"

Ben smiled. "I just happened to be at that bar tonight because a colleague was in from Tennessee and wanted to see exotic dancing. And I certainly enjoyed *your* show." He grinned. "But I didn't enjoy watching some psychopath try to throttle you. And I can't be there every night to protect you." He cupped her cheek in his palm. "You were meant for other things."

First the compliment, Melanie thought. Then comes the seduction. Well, all right. Get on with it. But there was an odd look on his face. Wasn't he going to kiss her?

He traced her lips gently with his forefinger. "You really are lovely, you know. I don't want anything to happen to you." He dropped his hand and moved back.

"If you hear any noise in the middle of the night, don't worry. I frequently work at odd hours. I have several overseas connections; I'm an exporter of specialized goods. Now get some sleep." He walked down the hallway, into his bedroom, shut the door.

Melanie watched him, disbelieving. What was he up to? He'd saved her life, fed her, and now he was sheltering her.

135

He hadn't even tried to make a pass at her, really. Strange. She sniffed the flowered sheets, enjoying their clean scent. Sleep beckoned. But first, she closed the bedroom door behind her, and checked the lock twice.

❦

12

ANDIE AWAKENED with a start. She was lying on the sofa, still fully clothed. The wall clock told her it was seven in the morning. Shit! Jacobsen's press conference was in three hours. She leaped up and ran for the bathroom. Two minutes in the shower, five in front of the mirror, and another five spent pulling on her gray silk suit and pinning her hair back in a severe bun. She grabbed her screencase and ran for the tube, praying that it was on schedule. Luck was with her, and she got to the office ten minutes before Jacobsen came in at eight-fifteen, leaving just enough time for Andie to transfer her notes to the senator's deskscreen.

Caryl looked up from her screen and rolled her eyes. "I've been here for an hour. Ninety calls."

As she spoke, another came in. The answermech caught it: Andie's recorded image assured the caller that Senator Jacobsen would review this call and to leave a message after the tone.

Jacobsen walked in briskly. She looked cool and competent in an ivory suit.

"Everything under control?"

"So far. Your notes are ready."

The senator nodded and disappeared into her office.

The rest of the staff was in house by eight-thirty. Andie began to feel more optimistic. They would carry the day. They had to.

Fifteen minutes before the conference began, Andie went down to the Presidential Room to check the mikes. All five were in place. She watched the reporters file in right on schedule.

She nodded at Rebecca Hegen and smiled at Tim Rogers. In fact, there wasn't a face she didn't recognize, save one. A young man with short black hair, pale skin and old-fashioned tortoise-shell eyeglasses shoved his way past the other reporters, settling squarely into a seat in the middle of the second row. At least one colleague glared at him. Probably saving the seat for somebody else, Andie thought. But the bespectacled man was oblivious to his neighbor's displeasure. He gazed with great concentration at the table where Jacobsen would sit. Then he lowered his head and began to fiddle with a leather screencase.

I'd rather dig ditches than work in cable news, Andie thought. The competition is cutthroat. Any newcomer can shoulder in and take over. If she was to judge, that young man had a promising career ahead. She'd have to find out who he was later.

The noise in the room lessened as Jacobsen entered from a side door. She gave Andie a small nod as she settled in.

"I would like to clarify the statements of my colleague, Senator Horner, concerning the so-called supermutant rumors," Jacobsen said. She looked confident and in control. Andie began to relax.

"We must not allow emotion to get in the way of the facts. And, at the moment, the facts are that no proof has been uncovered revealing any sort of genetic experiments such as the ones to which Senator Horner referred. And absolutely no proof has been discovered of any sort of superman mutant. I fear that my esteemed colleague has been taken in by a hoax and invite him to reveal his sources to me or members of the media."

The video jocks were watching Jacobsen raptly. Andie saw the strange, bespectacled young man in the front row aim what looked like a recorder at the senator.

"It is vital that we see this for what it is; a ghost, an unsubstantiated rumor—"

A shrill whine cut through the room, drowning out the senator's voice. Jacobsen, turning to look for the disruption, froze in midstatement. She was enveloped in swirling white light.

Andie gasped, tried to move. But the room was packed. She was hemmed in. Helpless. In horror, she watched Jacobsen slump forward across the podium.

"That man. Grab the man with the glasses!" she yelled.

But he was jumping over a row of chairs, and dodging between people, running toward the door. Then the crowd erupted.

"Get a doctor!"

"Call security!"

"Get him. He shot Eleanor Jacobsen!"

A burly cameraman in a blue T-shirt tackled the gunman five feet from the door, and both disappeared under a pile of uniformed security guards.

Andie fought her way to the stage. Jacobsen lay sprawled on the floor like a rag doll. Her eyes were open, unblinking, and she was staring into space. A woman in a red dress leaned over her, checking for vital signs.

"How is she? Is she breathing? Does she have a pulse?"

Andie asked the questions mechanically. One look and she knew the truth. Jacobsen was dead. Numbly, she watched as the woman closed the mutant's unseeing eyes.

"Get a doctor! Hurry!" someone yelled.

Andie forced herself to look at Jacobsen's pale face, fighting an urge to smooth the disarrayed blond hair. All that splendid intellect, incisive wit, steady commitment—gone.

The mutant heroine, golden Eleanor, murdered by a nonmutant. Tears stung Andie's eyes. She sank down on the edge of the stage and covered her face. It was the end of everything, she thought. The end of everything.

"HAND ME THE LASER LEVEL," Bill McLeod said, bending over the nose of his antique Cessna.

Joanna rummaged in the tool pack. "What's it look like?"

"It's long and black, with a yellow LED."

"I can't find it," she said. "Did you have to bring this thing with us on vacation?"

"Never mind. Just hand me the whole thing."

Joanna swung it toward him, grinning. She didn't pretend to enjoy working on his plane, but visiting the old airstrip near Lake Louise was part of their vacation tradition. And she did like to see the weekend pilots tinkering with their planes. The glint of bright metallic paint, the clear blue, cloudless skies through which the small crafts soared; she enjoyed being in the midst of it.

Although she'd attended flying school at Bill's urging, and even qualified as a pilot, once the kids were born her interest in flying had faded. She treasured the memories of her solo flight. But she was satisfied to leave them as that: memories.

"Remember when Kelly used to come out here with us?" she asked.

"Yeah. She'd have made a hell of a pilot."

"Sure would. I don't know what she's interested in these days." Joanna let out a sigh.

"Besides knife fights?"

"Bill!"

He held up his hands in surrender, then turned back to he plane. "Just joking. Any news on that little mutant girl?"

"Melanie Ryton? Kelly hasn't said much."

"I noticed. She just moons around since we came up here."

"She misses Michael. That's natural."

"I wish I could say the same for him."

"You know I don't like it when you talk about him that way." She crossed her arms in irritation.

"Hell, Jo, I can't help it. He gives me the creeps. He's a nice kid, but those eyes. That slant on 'em doesn't help much. And I don't know who was more uncomfortable when Kelly made him give that levitation demonstration. He looked like he wanted to crawl under the couch. Can't say that I blamed him, though. Sort of like being a sideshow display."

Joanna chuckled. "Still, it *was* pretty amazing. I don't think I've ever seen a mutant strut his stuff before. I almost envied him. It seemed like fun." Briefly, she imagined floating in the air.

"Maybe. But if you ask me, that mutant didn't look like he was having much fun."

"No, you're right. He's so serious. But I suppose he's worried about his sister."

"Yeah. And now we've got this crazy supermutant thing to think about, if you believe that senator—what's his name? Horner."

McLeod was silent for a moment, which meant he was probably tightening a wire. She leaned against the silvery fuselage.

"Honey, it's almost five-fifteen. Do you want to hear the stock market report?" she asked.

"Sure."

Joanna pressed the stud on her watch. The disc jockey ran through the familiar string of commercials, some small talk about the market, and then proceeded to the closing figures for the day.

"Market prices plunged on the heels of the assassination this afternoon . . . the Dow Jones Industrials closed at fifty-four forty, down seven hundred twenty."

McLeod jerked his head up, nearly banging it on an engine panel. "Assassination?"

Joanna keyed up the news channel.

"And now, this just in from Washington: Arnold Tamlin,

the alleged assassin of Senator Eleanor Jacobsen, was found dead in his jail cell in Washington at one thirty-eight this afternoon. No immediate cause of death has been determined. An autopsy is expected as soon as next-of-kin are located and notified."

"Somebody killed that mutant senator. Bill, I don't believe it." Joanna said. She felt strange, light-headed.

McLeod frowned. "I knew something like this would happen sooner or later—"

"Shhh—listen!"

The newscast continued.

"Tamlin was apprehended moments after Senator Eleanor Jacobsen of Oregon was shot in the midst of a news conference. Senator Jacobsen, a mutant, was refuting comments at the time that had been made by Senator Joseph Horner concerning rumors of a so-called superman mutant. She was struck by a phaton blast at close range and killed instantly. In the scuffle that followed, the suspect Tamlin was subdued and taken into custody.

"Senator Horner had this comment to make: 'It's a tragedy. Just a pure and simple tragedy. But God's will be done, I say. Let's all bow our heads in prayer. . . .' "

Silently, Joanna pressed the red off-stud. A cloud floated across the sun, throwing shadows over the pavement.

"I never could stand that man," McLeod said.

Joanna gasped.

"Is that all you can say?" she snapped. "A great woman is killed, and you make snide comments about some fool reverend!" Angrily, she threw down the tool kit and watched the contents scatter across the black pavement.

"Joanna, what's the matter with you?" he stared at her, shocked.

She turned to face him, hands on hips.

"I'm tired of your attitude toward mutants, Bill. Our daughter is in love with one, and all you can talk about is how creepy you think he is. A brave, brilliant woman has been murdered, and you don't even have a shred of regret. I'm beginning to think Kelly's right. You *are* a bigot."

"Now hold on, Jo. I think that Ryton kid is okay, for all my comments. And I think it's a lousy break for the mutants that their senator was killed. But you can't expect me to get all broken up about it."

"No," she said. "But I do expect you to care."

He swung down from his perch, took her in his arms.

"Jo, I *do* care. Any assassination is disturbing. Frightening. But don't you see that the mutants seem to draw this kind of violence? And they have, ever since they came out in the nineties. I don't want our daughter mixed up in it. Do you?" His gaze was solemn.

Joanna leaned her head against his shoulder. "It frightens me, too, honey. The Ryton kids seem perfectly fine to me. I can't believe the mutants deserve this kind of treatment. And I don't know what to tell Kelly anymore." She blinked rapidly, fighting back tears. "I don't care how many mutants are assassinated, I won't forbid Kelly to see Michael. I can't. And I want you to accept that. Now finish up and let's get out of here." She turned on her heel and strode away toward the skimmer.

JAMES RYTON sat motionless in his office, the deskscreen blurring before his eyes. He'd watched the press conference begin, watched the camera swing crazily as Eleanor Jacobsen fell. Saw blurred faces, yellow curtain, and then a mutant woman in a white suit lying on the floor on her back, eyes open, unseeing.

"I told them we had to be careful," he said to the empty office. His voice was high, almost giddy. "But they didn't believe me. No, they never listen, do they? And look what's happened now. The normals have killed Eleanor Jacobsen. I knew it. I knew it."

And now the assassin was dead too.

He leaned his head into his hands, massaging his temples

143

as the mental flares began their daily clamor. The normals would kill every single one of us if they could, he thought bitterly. And my daughter is somewhere out there, at their mercy.

SKERRY SAT on a wooden stool in the Devonshire Arms in Soho, sipping a Red Jack and watching the satellite broadcast. In replay, he saw the golden-haired woman fall again and again. Then the pale, dead face of the assassin in his cell. The bartender watched with him.

"Too bad about that mutant minister-lady, mate," he said. "She seemed decent enough."

Skerry nodded slowly, his eyes fixed on the screen.

"She was."

He emptied his glass.

"Guess it's time to get going."

He flipped a credit chip toward the bar.

"Keep the change."

STEPHEN JEFFERS rubbed his hand over his mouth and watched the deskscreen in his office.

"Dammit," he said. "This ruins everything."

SUE LI RYTON leaned back in her chair, her eyes on the desk-screen. Trevan, the department assistant, walked into the office and, without a word, handed her an amber glass filled with liquid. She nodded her thanks and took a sip. She could smell the anise, but somehow, the drink didn't register on her tastebuds. She took another mouthful. And another.

"Ouzo," Trevan said apologetically. "It's all I had."

"It's perfect," Sue Li said, handing him the empty glass. "Could you fill it up again?"

BENJAMIN CARIDDI watched the deskscreen in his office until the newscast ended. His face was white. He dialed a private code and cloaked his screen.

"Yes?" The voice sounded strained.

"It's Ben."

"You've heard, of course."

"Yeah. I thought this wasn't supposed to happen."

"Damned fool overdid it."

"I warned you—"

"To hell with your warnings! It's too late now. We'll have to move even more quickly."

"You took care of Tamlin?"

"Of course. You've still got the girl?"

"Lock, stock and golden eyes."

"Then get going."

MICHAEL HURRIED DOWN the dark hall toward his father's office. In each room he passed, a deskscreen flickered yellow, gold, red. The same images repeated again and again.

Michael's eyes burned with dry, angry grief.

They've killed her, he thought. Damn them, they've killed her!

He burst into his father's office.

"What are we going to do?"

His father raised his head from his hands and turned to look at him wearily.

"Do?"

"Aren't we going to demand an investigation?"

"Of course. Halden's probably making a formal request right now."

Surprised, he stared at his father.

"I thought you'd be angrier."

"I am angry, Michael. It's my worst fears come true."

"Are we going to have a clan meeting?"

"Yes. On Tuesday, at Halden's." James Ryton's voice was thin.

"I want to go."

His father nodded. "Fine. Why don't you set up travel arrangements."

* * *

MELANIE PAUSED IN THE SHADE at the vidkiosk, munching a shimiroll. She was on lunch break from the reception job Benjamin had found for her at Betajef. It was fun to meet all the foreign businessmen and she preferred the neat pink company jumpsuit she wore to her Star Chamber costume.

Onscreen, some old fool senator was being interviewed. What was he saying . . . something about supermutants? As she watched, the scene shifted to a conference room where a slim blond woman with golden eyes lay on the floor. Melanie stopped chewing. Wasn't that Eleanor Jacobsen? Her father was always talking about her. But what was the vidjock saying now?

". . . murdered yesterday. Her alleged assassin found dead today in Washington. Mutant leaders across the country are converging on the state house in Oregon to discuss Jacobsen's successor. . . ."

Dead? It couldn't be.

The scene now showed a panel of somber-faced video jocks dressed in gray and black jackets.

The gray-haired reporter said, "Allen, on the heels of this tragedy, I think we can expect to see heightened political activity on the part of the mutants."

"Yes, Sarah," replied a blond man. "There are also fears that this assassination is the first part of a far-reaching plot to eliminate all mutants in public office."

"Damned mutants asked for it, if you know what I mean," an older man with deep wrinkles around his eyes muttered, watching the screen.

Melanie ducked her head quickly, grabbed her filtershades, and moved away from the small group that had gathered in front of the screen. Was everybody looking at her? At her eyes? She told herself they probably hadn't noticed her. She repeated the chant for calmness three times and hurried back to work.

* * *

THE LIGHTS in the hospital corridor blazed with impersonal cheeriness. Andie sat on a yellow chair by the emergency room door, idly toying with stray wisps of hair that had escaped her bun. She felt as though she hadn't slept in days, that she'd been born and would die in that same gray silk business suit. Her watch told her it was 3:30 in the morning. Then 3:31. And 3:32. She rubbed her eyes. The Valedrine the intern had offered her was beginning to work, and the sick numbness was melting into a warm buzz.

Leaning back against the wall, she shut her eyes, resting her head. Once more, she flipped through the day's events like a video schedule.

Andie still didn't believe it. She'd been three feet away. If only she could have saved her. Again, she ran through the events, imagining herself tackling Tamlin before he aimed the gun, then throwing herself into the path of its beam.

A nightmare. So awful. Grotesque and endless.

When Tamlin was found dead in his cell, Andie began to think the world had truly spun off its axis. Despite the video surveillance in the cell, the man had simply clutched his head, keeled over, and died. Preliminary autopsy results showed a massive cerebral hemorrhage. It would take days to locate his medical records, study his history, decide if this was death from natural or unnatural causes.

"Do you always sleep on the job?" a familiar voice asked.

Andie opened her eyes. A young, bearded man, tall and muscular, wearing U.S. Army fatigues and a white Japanese T-shirt, stood next to her.

"Skerry?"

"At your service."

She bristled. "How can you sound so cheerful?"

"Reflex. How are you holding up?"

"Not well."

"Which means better than most." He sat down next to her. "I assume you were there?"

"Oh yes. I had a ringside seat." Andie's voice shook.

"Steady." He put his hand on her shoulder. "Look, I know this has been rough for you, but we've got some unfinished business, and it won't wait."

"What do you mean?"

"That little gift I gave you in Rio. I need it back."

"Tonight? What for?"

"Now that Jacobsen's dead, I'll have to take it to the Mutant Council myself."

"I thought you weren't welcome there."

"I'm not. But there's nobody else who could do the job."

Andie took a deep breath as a wild idea came to her.

"Skerry, let me do it," she said. "I want to. For Eleanor."

"You're crazy."

"No, Skerry. Please. I was in Rio with her. I know as much as she did about it. Perhaps more. And I've still got a few government connections."

"They don't allow nonmutants in the meeting."

"Couldn't we try?"

"You'd never get past the front door."

"Even with you?"

He paused. "Well, maybe with me." A smile began to crease the corners of his mouth. "All right. I don't know what good it would do, but it probably can't hurt. I'm already in it so deep with them, it doesn't matter. They'll only banish or censure me."

"Don't they realize what you're trying to do for them?"

Skerry shook his head. His smile hardened. "Mutant ways are slow, stubborn, and by the book. Our Book. If you don't live according to our Book, you're an outlaw."

"Well, outlaw or not, we'll make them listen to us!" Andie said. She felt hopeful for the first time that day.

"Where is it? The memorypak?"

"In my desk."

"Can we get it?"

"Now?" Andie shrugged. "I guess so. But what's your hurry?"

"I'd just like to get things moving, that's all."

She sighed. She felt dead on her feet, but his gaze was insistent.

"Come on."

The building was half lit and practically deserted. Andie keyed on the lights and opened her desk.

"Damn!" she said. "I could have sworn it was here."

Skerry loomed over her. "What's wrong?"

"I thought I'd left it in the back of my file drawer. I usually keep it hidden."

"Good idea. But it's not there?"

"Well, I showed it to Jacobsen. But then I put it back. I'm sure of it."

"Search all the drawers," he said.

Andie tore apart her desk. Then she searched Caryl's station.

"Nothing."

She turned to Skerry. He looked grim.

"What about Jacobsen's desk?"

"I suppose I could check it."

Reluctantly, Andie entered the senator's office. Skerry picked the lock on the top drawer and the rest opened with ease. A ten-minute search yielded nothing.

"Shit." Skerry leaned back in Jacobsen's chair. Andie sat on the floor, resting her head against the side of the desk.

"What now?" she asked.

"I think we've been screwed." Skerry said. "Any pak would have been safe here."

"I don't understand how it could have disappeared. Somebody would have had to know I had it, and they'd have had to steal it during the assassination. How could they get in here in the first place? And my desk is always locked."

"You saw how quickly I got into Jacobsen's desk. A lock is nothing."

Andie jumped up and keyed on Jacobsen's deskscreen.

"What are you doing?"

"I've got an idea."

She scrolled furiously through the files.

"Damn! Where is it?" she muttered.

After a moment, she typed in several commands, then leaned back with a sigh of relief. "There it is."

"What?"

"I showed Jacobsen the memorypak two days ago. It's still in the screen's memory."

Skerry leaned forward to study the screen.

"Can you make a record of it and kill the memory?" he asked.

"Sure."

He patted her on the back, beaming. "Toots, I take back every unkind thing I ever said about nonmutants. You're terrific. And when we're done with that Mutant Council, they'll probably get *you* appointed as senator."

13

MELANIE SAT on the green watercouch and shivered as she watched the flickering images on the roomscreen. Benjamin leaned over, put his arm around her shoulder, and squeezed gently. The warmth of his hand was pleasant against her arm and she snuggled against him.

"Frightened?" he asked.

"Not really. I just hate watching this over and over. Jacobsen never hurt anybody. And when I think that her murderer was that creep Tamlin, my stomach hurts."

"He must have been psychotic. A crazy mutant hater."

"The way he tried to strangle me at the club. I still have nightmares."

Benjamin cupped her face in his hand. "You don't have anything to worry about now. You're with me."

Melanie smiled, admiring his warm brown eyes and dark hair. If only he'd pull her a little closer. . . .

To her disappointment, he gave her a brotherly hug and stood up.

"Maybe I should go to the police."

"And tell them what?" His tone was brusque. "That Tamlin attacked you? He's dead. The best thing you can do now is forget about him. Otherwise, you'll just get involved in trouble you don't want."

"You're probably right."

Melanie sank back against the tan cushions. She was tired of watching endless replays of Jacobsen's death. Jacobsen was gone. Melanie wanted to forget about her. And Tamlin.

Benjamin yawned and looked at the clock. "I'm wiped, kid. Stay up if you want, but I'm going to bed." He gave her a quick, crooked smile and was gone.

She sighed and dialed up an old movie from the eighties, landing right in the midst of a love scene. Melanie watched it wistfully.

I want Ben to do that to me, she thought. With his mouth, all over. She watched the lovers onscreen couple skillfully, passionately, gasping and writhing. She reached for a joystick, biting off the end for a quicker rush.

Maybe he doesn't like women, she thought. But then what was he doing at the club? And what am I doing here? Why did he rescue me and give me a job? A place to live? She'd been here almost a month. She gave a quick, affectionate look around the sumptuous living room, lingering on the rich wall covering and fine red Navaho rugs.

After the first week, she'd left her bedroom door unlocked, wondering if he'd notice. No reaction. She'd started wearing shimmering, opalescent shifts at home, which revealed more of her body than they concealed. He acted as though she was wearing a dylon box. They lived together like brother and sister. But she already had two brothers, thanks.

The joystick relaxed her and she felt that familiar, persistent warm tickle begin between her legs. Hell, she was tired of masturbating. If she were telepathic, she could implant a few erotic suggestions while Ben slept. But she wasn't telepathic. Melanie sighed. She'd have to take the old-fashioned approach.

She turned off the screen and walked toward Ben's door. There was no light seeping from beneath it. Good. She palmed it carefully and it slid open without a sound. In the dimness, she could just make out his form in bed. He was breathing evenly. Asleep.

Melanie pulled aside the bedclothes. He was naked. As her eyes adjusted to the dark, she admired his compact, muscular build. She touched his face gently.

"Mel?"

He sat up, blinking.

She unhooked her tunic at the shoulder and let it drop in a circle around her feet. Stepping out of it, she leaned over and traced a line from his chest to his groin. He came erect at her touch.

Gently, she kissed him. He pulled back, reaching for the sheet.

"Go to bed."

"I'm not sleepy."

She took his hand and held it against her breast.

"Mel, you shouldn't do this," he said, pleading. But he didn't pull his hand away.

She moved gently, letting him feel her nipple, erect against his palm. When she released her grip, he kept his hand in place, then moved closer, covering the other breast with his free hand. Melanie sighed and closed her eyes. A moment later, she felt his warm mouth licking, sucking, moving from one breast to the other.

She slid down against him on the bed, feeling his pleasing muscularity, the odd, tickling texture of the hair on his chest and arms. She wanted to touch and explore everything. To be touched and explored.

He pulled her closer, kissing her breasts, neck, and lips. She responded, gasping, rubbing against him in an unfamiliar yet compelling rhythm. His hands moved between her legs, slowly teasing at first, then working boldly, quickly. She heard a voice crying out which she realized must be hers, but it didn't matter. He was in her and she was exploding, rippling outward in waves of intense pleasure. And he was hers forever. Forever.

THE CLAN ELDERS assembled around the teak table in Halden's basement were grim and silent. Michael thought he'd never seen a Mutant Council meeting so listless, so depressed. Even the unity pins most of them wore seemed dull, without sparkle. And his father just sat there, his blue shirtsleeves rolled unevenly, toying with his cup of tea.

"We must decide on somebody to nominate to fulfill Jacobsen's term," Halden said. "I meet with Governor Akins on Monday, and we must have consensus on a replacement by then. The faster we move, the better chance of his ratifying our choice."

"Why bother?" Zenora asked. "We'll just be supplying another target for the normals' weapons."

"If we take that attitude, then we really are defeated," Halden said sharply.

"You tell 'em, Unc," a familiar voice said. The group, as one, turned toward its source. Fifty pairs of golden eyes watched a pillar of orange flame rotating slowly next to the silvery-gray floatsofa. Gradually, it coalesced into human form; a tall male mutant wearing black boots, jeans, a purple T-shirt and an army parka, his grin framed by a curling brown beard. Skerry. A red-haired woman in a gray business suit stood next to him looking apprehensive. Michael recognized her as Eleanor Jacobsen's assistant, Andrea Greenberg. What was she doing here, with Skerry?

"Greetings, all," he said cheerily. "Pardon my entrance, but you know I like to make an impression. And I'd like you all to meet a friend of mine. Say hi to the nice mutants, Andie."

She nodded uncertainly. "Hello."

"Skerry, what is the meaning of this?" Zenora demanded. "Bringing a nonmutant to our private meeting, especially now? Are you out of your mind?"

"Not yet, Auntie. I'm only thirty, remember? And this isn't

just any old normal. Andie Greenberg was Eleanor Jacobsen's assistant."

"Relax, Zenora. I'll vouch for her," James Ryton said.

"I still don't see why she should attend."

"You will," Skerry said.

Michael levitated a white folding chair toward Andie from across the room. As she settled into it, he winked reassuringly.

"It's rare that you join us, Skerry. What's on your mind?" Halden asked.

"Take a look at this." Skerry tossed a memorypak onto the table.

Halden frowned. "What is it?"

"You want to stir up our troops here? Get them interested in finding somebody to fill out Jacobsen's term? This should set your mutant hearts thumping, folks. Here's one reason why we should have somebody in Congress as soon as possible. It's proof about mutagen research going on in Brazil."

"Brazil? Those rumors are true?"

Skerry nodded. "They're doing germinal tissue studies. Specific locus tests, on what appear to be human subjects."

"Trying to detect and isolate mutations that can be replicated in a petrie dish . . . this is far more serious than we'd dreamed," Halden said, face pale. He handed the memorypak to Zenora. She clipped it into the roomscreen deck.

The room lights dimmed and the screen scrolled through the pak's contents, flickering with blue light. Michael thought it looked like diagrams from a genetics textbook. But his father was sitting up in alarm, as was Halden, both staring at the screen.

"Double alleles? Splitting zygotes? Are these human embryos?" Ryton demanded.

"So it seems."

"Unbelievable. We can't even get close to this kind of precision," Halden said, his voice thick with emotion. "Not even with psychokinesis."

"Have any of these embryos been successfully implanted or carried to term?" James Ryton asked.

"Don't know," Skerry said. "It's not clear just how far they've come already. Or who is sponsoring these experiments. These records are a couple of years old, and they're incomplete."

"Where did you find them?"

Skerry shrugged. "Let's just say a happy accident enabled me to locate them."

Halden sighed. "I suppose that means you stole them."

Michael hid a smile. Good for Skerry, he thought.

"Spare me the moralizing, Unc," Skerry snapped. "You know damned well that we've always gotten by any way we could. I remember a time when we used to sit around after the yearly meeting and discuss burglary techniques, swindles —and nobody sat there looking horrified. It was business."

"He's right," Michael said. "Besides, we've got the data now. Who cares how we got it?"

With a nod, Halden conceded their points. "However you obtained them, you've done us a tremendous favor," he said. "We've got to take these rumors seriously now."

"What if this is a hoax?" Zenora demanded. "Skerry could have faked these records. He's not exactly the most reliable member of the clan." She glared at him. He returned the look with vehemence.

"Why would I bother, Zenora? I agree that it's hardly worth my time taking any risks to try and save your ass, but since I've done it, the least you can do is believe what I show you."

"If only Jacobsen was still alive," Ryton said. "I'd feel better about supporting action on this if we had her input."

Skerry leaned forward, palms on the table. "I've brought the next best thing, James. Andie went to Brazil with Jacobsen. That's why she's here."

Halden turned to her. "Can you tell us anything about your research?"

"Well, yes," Andie said. Michael thought she looked uncomfortable. "And no. You've just seen the only definitive proof we have of mutagenic experimentation. However, I'm convinced that there is more going on in South America than we could uncover. And I think Senator Jacobsen knew it, too."

"Subjective nonsense," Zenora said.

"Maybe so," Andie retorted. "But where did they get those mutagenic agents? Why did the entire city feel like it was under a mind cloud?"

"Mind cloud?" Halden turned to Skerry. "How much have you told her about us?"

"Plenty. Stop looking so stricken, Halden. She can help us. And we need nonmutant help."

"Why should we believe her?" Zenora asked. "Maybe she's just agreed to help you disrupt the meeting."

"Why would she want to do that?" Michael demanded angrily. He was beginning to think his aunt was getting paranoid.

"I've come to help you in any way I can," Andie said, her voice soft. "Senator Jacobsen's death was a terrible tragedy for nonmutants as well as mutants. And a personal blow to me. I admired her greatly. And I believed completely in her goal of cooperation and integration between mutant and nonmutant. I still believe in it. But do you?"

Silence greeted her words, but Michael could see that she'd reached everybody there. He began to feel more optimistic.

"If you would like further proof that something sinister is taking place in Brazil, you could share my experiences in Rio de Janeiro," she said. "Skerry's explained to me how it's done, and I'm willing to submit to the process if it will help further Jacobsen's work."

"Do you realize what you're offering?" Halden asked.
"Yes."

For a moment, no one spoke. Then, as if by silent consensus, a mild humming filled the room. Michael leaned over and took Andie's hand. He hoped she knew what she was doing.

ANDIE BIT HER LIP. She'd come into this secret meeting prepared for hostility and anger. But she hadn't intended to invite scrutiny of her memories by a group of mutant strangers.

Their suspicion was to be expected, she knew. But if she didn't convince them to trust Skerry's information, the entire Brazilian trip seemed wasted and worthless. And the only way to convince them was to agree to an experience that unnerved her. Skerry gave her a sympathetic glance as he grasped her hand. She took a deep breath and closed her eyes.

Briefly, she felt as though she were floating in a pool of warm, golden light, sliding along a subvocal wave of pulsing harmonies. Why, there was nothing to be frightened of here. Fellowship and warmth sustained her. The raw, sore spot in her memory that was Eleanor Jacobsen's assassination stopped throbbing, the pain subsiding to a mild ache. And gently, ever so gently, the hum faded, the wave lowered and she was sitting in her chair, blinking, holding Skerry's hand.

"That was some visit to Teresópolis," he said, grinning.

Andie blushed and pulled her hand away. "Did everybody see that?"

"Nah. I shielded you. Besides, the groupmind has limitations. It can only look where directed. Or invited. But I couldn't resist taking a teeny stroll around."

Andie glared at him. She should have known better than to trust him entirely. That ridiculous entrance stunt. Skerry was always unpredictable. She tried to ignore the image of him peering at her most intimate memories and concentrated on the group reaction around her.

The large man in the dark-red shirt, the group leader named Halden, smiled at her. "Thank you, Ms. Greenberg. Very convincing indeed." He looked around the table. "Are there any skeptics left among us?"

Fifty heads shook in negation. "Then we concur that there

is unusual, dangerous experimentation taking place in Brazil," Halden said. "I propose that we form our own investigative panel. If we wait for another government committee, it may be too late."

"What's so terrible about supermutants?" Andie asked.

"Nothing," Halden said, "as long as they're not being controlled by undesirable parties."

"Such as?"

He shrugged. "I can name a dozen special interest groups, and so can you, Ms. Greenberg. Terrorists. Fascists. Neo-Nazis, for starters."

"And you believe one of these hostile groups is behind the supermutant experiments?" she said.

"Some hostile group, yes. What other reason for the secrecy? And why haven't they enlisted our help? Mutant geneticists are known for their skill."

"No offense, Unc, but it looks like they don't need our skill," Skerry said.

"Have you ever developed a supermutant naturally?" Andie asked.

Halden shook his head. "So far, the closest we've come have been double mutants such as young Ryton there. But enhanced mutants developed from clandestine, possibly abusive genetic experiments, to be manipulated by who knows what source for unknown, sinister ends, could have dreadful consequences."

"Ms. Greenberg, the armed forces of the world have been courting mutants ever since we revealed ourselves," James Ryton said. "How many secret police services would benefit from the talents of our best clairaudients? How many guerilla wars would be affected by telekinetic intervention? At the moment, our skills are too unreliable to interest the military. But a mutant with enhanced abilities would draw a lot of government attention—you can bet on it. Such a being could be marvelous—or a danger to all humankind. And you've had firsthand experience of how violently some normals react to regular mutants. Imagine the public outcry over enhanced mutants."

"Well," Andie said, "why not approach the federal government about your concerns?"

"We'd hoped that the Brazilian investigation would yield official results which we could use as an opening. But Jacobsen's death has deflected our attention—and the government's."

Andie nodded. "That's true. It'll take years for them to make any further queries. It's a dead issue in Congress."

"And possibly a factor in the assassination," Skerry said. "Which means that we can't afford to draw further attention to this." He took a sip of tea from an old blue mug.

"He's right. We must conduct our own investigation first," Halden said. "Surely there are several among us who are qualified. Dr. Lagnin is on sabbatical from Stanford. And Christopher Ruschas runs his own genetics lab in Berkeley. There are a few others. With your assistance, Ms. Greenberg, we'll follow the trail of the congressional investigation."

"You've got it," Andie said, smiling.

"Skerry, we may need you for this."

"I don't know, Halden. I like to operate on my own."

Andie felt like kicking him. Hadn't he gotten them all involved in this? And now he wanted to pull out?

"Well, try to overcome your natural aversion for our sake," Halden said sarcastically. "If you're not concerned, what are you doing here?"

He shrugged. "Come to visit my old man in the mutant bughouse."

Halden pursed his lips. "It's about time you went to see your father."

"For all the good it does him. They've got him so doped up he doesn't know himself."

"Until we find a means for dealing with the mental flares, when they reach a terminal point, sedatives are the only way we have of controlling the pain."

"How about euthanasia?"

Halden crossed his arms. "We're really getting off the subject here. Skerry, we'd like you to be part of the team. If you want some time to decide, just let me know. But with or without you, we will proceed."

Andie watched the byplay, fascinated. Mental flares? She'd have to ask Skerry about those.

"The next issue is, of course, the assassination investigation," Halden said. "We still don't know who the assassin was working for, or what killed him. It's been over a week since Jacobsen was murdered."

"Halden, working through official lines to get this information seems to get us nowhere," Michael Ryton said. "Maybe it's time to use unofficial means."

"What do you suggest? That we march in and demand information?"

"Why not? Is it better to just sit back and let our leaders be killed?" Several clan members nodded, and a few shouted their agreement.

Andie looked around the room apprehensively. Were they all glaring at her? The mood was turning ugly.

"Michael, you're speaking out of anger," Halden said. "I understand how you feel. But we must proceed cautiously. Of course we'll conduct our own investigation into Jacobsen's death. But I propose we discuss who to support as her successor before I talk to Governor Akins in Oregon."

"And I propose that Ms. Greenberg await us upstairs," Zenora said. "What she's had to share was interesting, but I don't see that the rest of this meeting concerns her."

Andie shrank from the hostility in the woman's voice. This large, dark mutant woman bristled with irritation.

"I don't wish to intrude," Andie said. "Excuse me." She walked up the stairs, shutting the door behind her.

"ZENORA, WHEN WILL YOU LEARN to control your temper?" Halden asked, his voice harsh.

She glared at her husband. "I'm not interested in having Skerry's normal girlfriends intrude upon our private concerns."

Michael felt embarrassed for her. He'd never seen Zenora so irritable before. Was she starting to get mental flares too?

"Let's get on to Jacobsen's successor," James Ryton suggested.

The image of a man in a tan suit with a shock of brown hair, a wry smile, and strong, square jaw appeared in Andie's mind. He looked familiar.

"This is Stephen Jeffers," Halden said. "As you may know, he ran against Jacobsen in the senatorial primary. And once he lost, he became a solid supporter of her campaign. He's been a Washington lawyer for ten years, but maintains a residence in Oregon. He's worked with Jacobsen on several issues. He's solid, dependable. Even the normals like him."

The image faded. Michael remembered that he and his father had seen Jeffers in Jacobsen's office in the spring. He seemed like a good choice.

"We've met him before," James Ryton said. "What's his approach?"

"He's aggressive. Wants to repeal the Fairness Doctrine. Of course, he'd pursue some of the conciliatory programs that Jacobsen espoused, too."

"It's about time," Ren Miller said. "Frankly, I'm tired of this tentative shit. I think we should demand more representation. More voice. What good is the Mutant Union if we don't use it?"

"And what would you have that voice say?" Ryton was on his feet, glaring at Miller. The husky young man returned his stare, rising out of his chair to lean on beefy forearms.

"I'm fed up with kowtowing to these normals—inferiors!" Miller's voice shook the room.

"And put us all at risk? Are you out of your mind?" Ryton was shouting now, too.

"What's our alternative?" Miller demanded. "Let them kill

us with impunity? Then crawl to them asking, 'Oh please, please, could you give us just a little bit of information?' "

Michael jumped up, ready to come to his father's aid if Miller attacked him. Angry voices swelled up around their argument, with Halden's roar louder still.

"James! Ren! That's enough!" The Book Keeper stood, knocking his chair over. Halden was one of their strongest telepaths, and he proved it once more, sending mental echoes bouncing through the minds of all assembled until every golden eye in the room was focused on him.

"We've been over this before," he said in calmer tones. "We're not strong enough to make demands. The only thing we'll do is alienate the mainstream without any gain. We've made a little headway. But we *must* proceed cautiously."

Michael sat down. Halden was right, he thought.

"If we cannot reason calmly among ourselves, we have no right to expect outsiders to deal with us at all," Halden said, looking around the room. "I'm uncomfortable with the growing arrogance I detect toward the normals. I remind you that we are all human, gifted in different ways. I can't stress enough the dangers of overconfidence."

"Well, then don't select Jeffers," Skerry said. "You're asking for trouble."

Halden righted his chair and sat down. "What makes you say that?"

"He's more conservative than you think. And less."

"Stop talking in riddles." James Ryton rubbed his forehead.

Skerry put down his cup. "Don't you have any other candidates? What about you, Halden?"

The big man shook his head. "I don't want that job. What's more, I'm not qualified."

"And what do you really know about Stephen Jeffers?" Skerry said.

"Reports on him are good. He hasn't attended a clan meeting recently, but he's known to be careful, conservative and responsible."

"I think you should choose someone better known, better tested. I don't trust him."

Ryton pushed back his chair. "I'd say that's high praise, coming from you."

Skerry ignored him. "Just take it on faith, okay?"

"You know we could force you to share with us," Zenora said angrily.

"Mindrape? You and what mutant army?" Skerry's voice was loud, scornful. "You know I'm one of the strongest here. Do you really want to try it?"

He looked poised to fight. Michael shuddered. Skerry would be a formidable opponent.

"Of course not. But you're not giving us very much useful information," Halden said, with a sharp look at his wife.

Skerry turned to face him. "I came here to enlighten you about what's going on in Brazil and to vote against Jeffers. I don't have any hard information on him. But I think you're making a mistake about him."

"Perhaps if you attended a few more clan meetings, we'd trust your perceptions more," Zenora said.

"Save it," he snapped. "You know I don't fit in. And if you'd only realize that I'm more useful to you on the outside than in this claustrophobic little circle, you'd know I'm right about Jeffers."

"Skerry, can't you give us any proof?" Michael asked.

"Nothing you'd trust."

"Well, we can't just go on your word," Halden said. "Be reasonable. You're overexcited. Jeffers is a fine candidate."

"It's our funeral." Skerry folded his arms.

Above the table, an image formed of a giant mutant unity pin. Suddenly, every arm that encircled the pin's golden eye rose up, each fist clenched in aggression. The arms stretched, lengthened, reached out toward the assembled clan before turning down at strange angles. The distance between each elbow and wrist elongated. Fists disappeared. Impossibly slender, the limbs pressed against the floor of the air and levered the center disk upward. It was a body now, not an eye. The body of a giant golden spider that scuttled away, mandibles clicking, seeking prey. Skerry smiled. The image faded.

For a moment, no one spoke. Then James Ryton slammed his cup down on the table.

"Enough of these silly parlor tricks," he said. "Regardless of Skerry's opinion, I move that we endorse Stephen Jeffers and support his appointment."

"Seconded," said Sue Li.

Halden asked for a vote, and it was almost unanimous, save for Skerry's abstention.

"Motion passed," Halden said. "The Central-Eastern Mutant Union hereby endorses the candidacy of Stephen Jeffers," Halden said. Beside him, Zenora made notes on a lapscreen jacked into the CST Net.

"Halden, the San Bernadino session and the Berkeley group have selected Jeffers as well," she said. "Alaska, Hawaii and the Midwest also."

"Good," Halden said. "I'll make the recommendation to Governor Akins on Monday."

Skerry stood up. "Well, so much for good intentions." He walked toward the door and vanished. Michael looked around the table. The meeting seemed to be ending. He decided to go find Andrea Greenberg.

"That telepathic linkage wasn't anything like what I expected," Andie said. She sipped coffee from a bright yellow mug, grateful for the warmth.

"What did you think?" Michael asked, smiling. "We'd bolt you to a table and send electricity jolting through you? Turn you into some kind of zombie?"

"Not exactly. But I didn't think it would be so, well, pleasant. I almost envy you for being able to connect in that way."

"It's one of the best things about being a mutant."

"And the mental flares are some of the worst?"

Michael nodded.

"Tell me about them."

"They seem to occur mostly in older male mutants. My father's just starting to get them now."

"Are they fatal?"

"Not on their own, no. But sometimes suicide seems a preferable choice to the noise and pain."

Andie grimaced. "Sounds awful."

"I'm not looking forward to it."

"Any cure?"

Michael shrugged. "Our healers can control it somewhat. After that, we rely on drugs."

"What did you think of our entrance?"

"Typical Skerry. He always does something strange. I like it. And him."

"Doesn't seem like your clan elders share your opinion."

"Well, they're pretty conservative. Traditional. Too traditional." He frowned.

"What do you mean?" Andie thought he seemed exasperated.

"Well, in relationships, for instance. I'm seeing this girl, and since they don't approve, I've got to be careful not to risk their censure."

"Is she mutant?"

"No."

"What would they do to you?"

"Demand that I end the relationship or else be expelled. They want me to marry somebody in the clan."

Andie stared at him in surprise. "Arranged marriages? I thought that went out with the abacus."

"Not in mutant season."

"What?"

"Sorry. Private joke. You see, it doesn't matter what's happening in the outside world. In here, it's always mutant season. Which means that what matters is tradition."

"And I guess it's always an off-season for illicit romance." Andie patted his shoulder sympathetically. "Don't let them discourage you, Michael."

"I won't." He smiled. "To change the subject, what do you think of Stephen Jeffers? That's who we've decided to recommend as Jacobsen's replacement."

"Seems like a good choice to me," Andie said. "Jacobsen certainly liked him. I remember, he was always after her to push harder on pro-mutant legislation. But can your people convince Governor Akins to appoint him?"

Michael leaned back against a kitchen counter, nodding. "Sure. Halden can be *very* persuasive when he has to be. And Akins knows he's got to pacify the mutants somehow or we'll see a replay of the violence in ninety-five, when the Mutant Union was formed."

"God, I hope not."

"If anybody can head it off, Jeffers can. Will you work for him?"

"I doubt it. He'll probably want all new staff. And I could use a vacation. I still have dreams about the assassination. Bad ones. I'm considering a hypnotic implant to screen them."

"If they persist, you might want to ask our healers for assistance."

Andie smiled. "Well, if their treatment is anything like that groupmind thing I experienced, I might take you up on it." She glanced at her watch. "Gods, it's late. I'd better hurry if I'm going to catch the shuttle back to Washington. Good luck, Michael. Keep in touch."

14

ON SEPTEMBER FIRST, Governor Timon Akins of Oregon appointed Stephen Jeffers to serve out the remainder of Eleanor Jacobsen's Senate term. Andie got the news at lunch when the screen in the Senate cafeteria ran an interview with the handsome new senator. She pushed away her plate of curried tofu, her appetite gone.

So Halden had been persuasive, just as Michael had promised, she thought. And now, what happens to me?

"You're not eating," Karim said in mock disapproval. "What's wrong?"

"Nothing," she lied. "I'm thinking about the Brazil report. I guess your boss will give it now."

"Craddick's probably a better choice than Horner. You know I suggested to him that you should present it with him now that Jacobsen's dead."

"Yeah. And he delicately demurred. I don't blame him. After all, who am I? The former aide to a dead senator."

"What are you going to do now?"

"Clean my desk out and go on vacation." She pushed back her chair and stood up. "I think I'll get started. See you tonight."

The elevators whisked her to the fifteenth floor, the air-conditioning raising goosebumps on her skin. Shivering, Andie buzzed open the door to the office.

She'd heard nothing from the mutants since her visit to Denver. Of course, it was only a week ago. But they'd already managed to get their next senator in place. Well, if they needed her, they'd call her.

Jeffers was due to report in tomorrow. How the press would enjoy Jacobsen's successor with his vidstar looks and Italian silk suits.

Andie didn't expect to keep her job, but she was prepared to offer her services as liaison for the transition in staff. Then, maybe, there'd be time for two weeks in Cancun or Mendocino or ClubMoon. After that, well, there was the rest of her life to contemplate.

The buzzer at the door sounded. She heard Caryl talking to somebody. The door to her office slid open and a man with thick brown hair, tan skin, and golden eyes walked in.

"Ms. Greenberg? Good to see you again."

Andie jumped to her feet. "Senator Jeffers. We weren't expecting you until tomorrow. . . ."

Jeffers smiled. He had terrific teeth.

"I apologize for the inconvenience. I'd wanted to meet the staff early and was afraid you'd arrange some kind of stiff, uncomfortable ceremony."

Andie smiled back. He certainly seemed less formal than Jacobsen. She took his outstretched hand and felt the warmth as she shook it.

"I know you were indispensable to Senator Jacobsen, and I'm afraid I'm going to be leaning pretty heavily on you at first. You are staying on, of course?"

"Uh, of course." Andie wondered why she was agreeing. But he was so charming. And after all, taking over for an assassinated senator was a huge task. Of course she'd help him out. She could put off her vacation for a while.

"Great! I'm sure you're busy now, but I'd like to talk with you, get to know you a bit. We're going to be working together very closely." He flashed the smile again. "Do you have plans for dinner?"

Andie thought of Karim. She'd promised him she'd cook tonight. But he'd understand. This was the opportunity to lay the groundwork with her new boss. Jacobsen had never invited her to dinner.

"Nothing I can't reschedule," she said.

"If it's not a problem, I'll send a skimmer around for you at seven." His watch chimed. He looked down at it, frowning. "Hmm, got to run. Meeting a few of my colleagues." He smiled once more, not as much voltage this time. Was it her imagination or did he wink as well? "See you tonight, Andie." He was gone before she'd had a chance to nod back.

Caryl walked in, tucked a stray blond hair behind her ear, and leaned against the door frame. "Not bad, if I may be so bold."

Andie sat down. "Quite a contrast to Jacobsen."

"Well, women in public office have to be more formal. They can't relax."

"I suppose."

"I love his dimples."

"Caryl, you're not supposed to say that about the boss!"

"Maybe not, but why are you primping in that mirror suddenly?"

Andie snapped the mirror shut.

"Don't I hear your screenboard buzzing?"

Caryl turned on her heel. "Have fun at dinner."

TINY LIGHTS set in clerestory niches cast warm tones of amber and rose across the enameled ceiling. Round candles winked in delicate saucers at each linen-covered table. Andie was grateful for the pink silk shirt and leather pumps she kept in her office closet. This was one of the finest restaurants in Washington. A menu sans soya. Remarkable. Her jaw almost dropped at the list of steaks and exotic seafood, some of which she'd thought were impossible to get.

"What do you recommend, Senator Jeffers?"

"Call me Stephen, please. Otherwise, I'll feel uncomfortable." He smiled. His golden eyes were candid, friendly.

Andie smiled back. "All right. Stephen. But you haven't answered my question."

"Well, if you want my opinion, I'd select the peppered oysters, then the abalone-stuffed scallops, but only if you're a seafood fan. Otherwise, the whitened sirloin is superb."

"The scallops, then. And the oysters."

Andie admired his ease with the waiters, his graceful movements. He was unexpectedly charming, with a touch of the exotic. Those golden eyes only accentuated his appeal. She was surprised, and a little embarrassed, to find herself so attracted to her new boss.

"I'm delighted you'll stay on," Jeffers said. "I was afraid you'd had enough of Washington after the tragedy and might want to work in a private law firm someplace else."

Andie nodded, ignoring the voice in her head that asked her when she had agreed to stay on permanently.

"Among my priorities are carrying on my predecessor's work. I'd like what I do to be a kind of memorial to Eleanor, if you know what I mean." His tone was low, confidential.

"I think that's a lovely idea, Sen— Stephen."

"I may not always have agreed with her priorities, but I have great respect for her. Always will. I'm going to start by establishing a memorial scholarship in her name. I've also been thinking about sponsoring an award, the Jacobsen Award, for work by those committed to improving and enhancing cooperation between mutants and nonmutants. This chasm between us is ridiculous."

Andie took a sip of wine, a soft rosé that lingered pleasantly on her tongue. He was making the usual promises. Well, fine, as long as he put them into action.

"That sounds like a good idea," she said cautiously. "It would gain the goodwill of the voters and honor your predecessor as well.

He nodded. "Exactly what I was thinking."

"What about the Brazil report?" she asked, watching him closely.

Jeffers gave her a quizzical look. "The Brazil report? I'm afraid I don't have much information on that."

"The unofficial investigation into genetic experiments in Brazil?"

"You'll have to brief me on it, Andie. But you can bet I'll want to take part in the presentation, representing Eleanor."

Good, Andie thought. Aloud, she said, "Do you plan to monitor the investigation into Jacobsen's murder?"

He frowned. "Of course. I'm going to get heavily involved, you can be sure. We *must* discover the motives behind the killing, who hired the assassin, this Tamlin, and why. I'll make certain everybody realizes that open season on mutants is over." There was a steely tone to his voice, suddenly, that made Andie want to shiver. Jeffers's glance seemed far away. Then he turned toward her, his look less abstracted, and smiled.

"Too grim, huh? Sorry, Andie. Keyed into a bad memory for a minute. Forget it. There's just so much to do and I'm anxious to get started." He reached across the table and took her hand. She saw that his fingernails were neatly buffed, impeccable. "I know that together, we'll be able to accomplish a great deal. We'll make Eleanor proud of us."

Andie nodded. "Of course." Either he was the best politician she'd ever seen, or he was completely sincere. And when he didn't release her hand, she began to think that her new boss was doing more than trying to forge a bond with a valuable employee. What concerned her was not his seductive manner, but the fact that she wasn't sure she minded.

MELANIE STRETCHED LUXURIOUSLY in bed and rolled over, seeking Ben's warmth. When she reached the other side of the bed, she realized he was gone. The wall clock said five a.m. The room was still dark. Where was he?

Yawning, she padded naked into the bathroom and got a drink of water. Flicking on the light, she looked at herself in the mirror. In the warm pink light, she thought she looked transformed; more worldly, more womanly. She'd been living with Ben for over two months now. She felt settled and happy. Each night, he seemed to teach her something new in bed. She loved to please him.

At first, she'd been worried about getting pregnant, but after she'd visited that special gynecologist, Ben had assured her she didn't have to worry. The doctor had given her an ovum block good for two years. Melanie had never heard of the procedure, but if Ben said it was safe, then it must be. So that's what had taken so long, she'd thought. It had felt as though the doctor was planning to poke around in there for a year while she kept her feet frozen in those damned stirrups.

She walked out into the hallway and saw light spilling from under the door of the den. Were those voices she heard? People talking?

"Ben?" She knocked at the door. There was no response. "Ben? I know you're in there. What are you doing?"

The door slid open and Ben grabbed her by the shoulders, his face a red mask of rage.

"You're disrupting a business call," he snapped. "Go back to bed!" He shoved her toward the bedroom.

"Ben! What's wrong?"

"I'm working, dammit. Now stay out of here." He slammed the door.

In tears, she hurried back to the bedroom. What had she done? She lay there sobbing for what seemed like hours until she felt him next to her, touching her gently in the predawn gloom.

"Mel? I'm sorry. You surprised me in the midst of some delicate negotiations."

"At five in the morning?"

"Overseas. Promise me you'll stay out of there."

She rolled over to face him. "Do I ever intrude on your business?"

"No."

"I just missed you and wondered where you were."

"I'm sorry I got so upset." His arms were around her. She felt his fingers beginning to work their magic upon her.

Two days later, she came home early from work and heard voices from the back of the apartment.

"Ben?"

No answer.

Cautiously, she walked toward the den. The door was open. Ben was talking on the screen to a somebody whose voice she didn't recognize.

"Don't get too distracted by this one," the male voice said.

"Don't worry. Besides, you're getting all the benefit."

"Well, I wouldn't say *all* the benefits."

Both men laughed.

"How is she?"

"Inexperienced," Ben said. "But hot. And willing. Once she crawled into my bed, how could I say no?"

Melanie began to shake. Was he talking about her in that snide, offhand tone?

"How did you find her to begin with?"

"Stroke of luck," Ben said. "I just happened to be at that club. Can you believe that Tamlin was trying to strangle her?"

"That crazy gork. Amazing that he hit the right target at all."

"Yeah. And then he blew it anyway."

Tamlin . . . That was the man who killed Eleanor Jacobsen, Melanie thought.

"Well, don't worry about him," the strange voice said. "How much longer before we get the girl?"

"Well, I kind of hate to give her up now that I've got her trained," Ben said.

More laughter.

No, Melanie thought. No. No. No.

"Don't be greedy, Ben. You'll be well rewarded. Maybe we'll even let you have her back when we're finished with her. But there's a doctor in Brazil who's anxious to meet her."

"I thought that supply of ova would keep them busy for a year."

"They want more. You're sure she hasn't been traced?"

"Positive. I checked it out as soon as I got her here."

"Fine. Well, get her ready. We'll want her in a week."

"Okay. I'll tell her we're going on vacation."

Mel staggered backward, stunned. She could hardly believe what she'd heard. Get away. She had to get away. What was he planning to do to her? Brazil? Ovum? She felt like gagging. Somehow she forced herself to palm open the front door, and bolted down the beige-carpeted hallway.

"Mel? Mel, is that you?" She heard Ben's faint shout. Then the elevator door slid closed. Gasping, she rode it to the skimmer port.

She'd drive away. That was it. She'd take his skimmer and drive home. She'd go back to her parents. She had to tell them about what she'd heard.

No.

She'd go to the police. That's what she'd do.

The elevator door slid open and she ran toward the car. As she reached for the door, a hand grabbed her wrist.

"What do you think you're doing?"

"Ben." She gasped. "I, uh, I wanted to go shopping."

"Without telling me? Why are you so pale?" He moved closer, his face hard. "If I hadn't taken the express elevator in the apartment, I'd have missed you. Why don't you come upstairs?"

"I don't feel like it." She pulled back, but he was dragging her slowly toward the elevator.

"I want to tell you about the trip we'll be taking."

The door was open and he was pulling her into the elevator. She saw something silver flash in his hand and realized it was a hypo.

"Let go of me, you bastard!"

Desperately, she kicked out, kneeing him in the groin, hard. He collapsed, groaning.

"I thought you loved me!" She kicked him again. He grabbed her ankle and pulled her to the ground.

"Crazy mutant bitch!" He slapped her across the face. "You think fucking means love?" He reached for the hypo lying on the elevator floor. She struggled for it, frenzy giving her speed, and her hand closed upon the ampule a second before his did. Shaking, she rammed the hypo against his neck and heard the faint hiss of its trigger releasing. Ben's features relaxed. His eyes closed and he slumped to the floor, out cold.

Boldly, she searched his pockets for credit chips and found his wallet. There was enough in there to keep her going for a month. She took the key to the skimmer and got in. She'd have to dump it quickly, but at least it would take her to the nearest tube stop. And from there, she'd get the shuttle.

She backed into the skimmer elevator, waited until she'd been raised to street level, and gunned the motor toward freedom.

15

HUNGRILY, Michael eyed a fat burgundy plum on the tree by the front lawn. Some of the best fruit came in September. He plucked the juicy globe and palmed the door open.

The house was empty. He took a healthy bite of the plum, paused to hang up his gym sack, then checked the e-mail monitor. There was the usual assortment of queries and contracts. He made a mental note to finalize the Haytel negotiation tomorrow. The message light kept blinking. He pressed the play button, and an image of his mother flickered to life.

"We'll be home in two days," she said. "Your father's flares appear to be subsiding, but he needs a bit more rest. See you on Tuesday."

Michael finished chewing and tossed the plum pit into the waste chute by the door. He'd thought his father was too young to start suffering from flares, but apparently he was wrong. What a mixed blessing mutancy was.

He walked into the kitchen and ran a quick survey of the pantry menu, selecting burritos with shoki mushrooms and freeze-dried pork. The refrigerator conveyor engaged. When the bell rang, he levitated the defrosted package into the convection oven, set the timer, and let it cook for three minutes.

As he set the table, he wondered what it was like to have to rely on your hands to do everything. Slow. He chose a Red Jack from the bar and sipped it, waiting for his meal to cool a bit.

Michael set the kitchen screen autodial for ten-second delay. Dutifully the screen scrolled through dancers in black and yellow body paint; antique movies at least twenty years old filled with old-fashioned cars, gun battles, and shrieking women; talk shows in which reporters in somber gray news suits covered world events twenty-four hours a day; the shopping channel flashing kaleidoscopic images at him of skimmers, floathomes; Moonstation condos; mech body extenders; solar-powered orgasm clips; and plastic surgery specials. Michael saw that this week's bargain was chin enhancement.

He took a bite of burrito, savoring the taste of the peppers igniting against his tongue. What he really wanted to do was see Kelly. But she was away on business with her father and wouldn't be home until the end of the week. So he was stuck with the vid. At least Jimmy was visiting cousins overnight.

Propping his feet up on the floatchair opposite him, he settled into the blue, fluid-filled cushions and watched the screen flicker and change, flicker and change. One image caught his interest, and he told the dial to pause at a news show. A handsome young man with a thick shock of brown hair, a sturdy smile, and bright golden eyes appeared onscreen in three-dimensional holoview.

Stephen Jeffers, Michael thought. The new mutant hope. Looks even better in video. Nice chin. Wonder if it's enhanced. Michael asked for another channel and paused, struck by the video jock's familiar appearance.

"I should hope I look familiar," the jock said, frowning at him. "Wake up, kiddo."

Michael blinked. Then he smiled. "Skerry, I should have known. Where are you?"

"Closer than you can imagine. Listen, I need to talk to you, Mike."

"Are you still pissed off because of that meeting?"

"Let's say I'm displeased. That's why I need to see you."

"When?"

"How about now?"

"Okay. Where?"

"Do you know the Hardwired?"

"In Mountain Side? Sure."

"Meet me there in fifteen minutes." The image wavered, and suddenly, the reporter had blond hair and blue eyes. Skerry was gone. Michael finished the last bits of burrito, levitated the dish into the washer, and went to meet his cousin.

The bar was empty, lit by a few red and blue beer signs and a row of blinking white lights. The mechband played a raga by the I-Fours. Michael's eyes began to adjust to the cavelike gloom. It had been years since he'd been in the Hardwired. It wasn't a mutant hangout, particularly, and since the knife incident with Melanie, Kelly had wanted to avoid the place.

He saw an attractive woman at the bar with straight dark hair and a friendly smile. She was wearing a green tunic cut low in front to display her considerable cleavage. Probably a pro, Michael thought. But he felt an unmistakable lustful tingle all the same. Kelly, come home soon, he thought.

A bright yellow arrow distracted him. It pointed toward a booth near the back wall. He walked in that direction as the arrow danced ahead. Skerry was hunkered down in a booth at the back of the room. The arrow disappeared with a chime. Not for the first time, Michael envied his cousin's mastery of telepathy, a sleight of mind that he would never be able to achieve. He sat down on the tan cushion facing Skerry.

"Hi. Have a kimmer." Skerry pressed a button at the table and the server filled a glass for Michael.

"What's up?"

Skerry looked disgusted. "Well, they've really gone and done it this time."

Michael sipped the sour mixture slowly, savoring the tang of the alcohol.

"What do you mean?"

"I mean, dear cousin, that Stephen Jeffers is not what he seems to be."

"No? Then what is he?"

"Ambitious. Dangerous." Skerry sank deeper into his seat.

"Ambitious? That doesn't sound so bad. He seems okay to me. And he sure got appointed easily enough. Besides, I'm tired of mutants going around on tippy-toes, trying not to offend the normals. How do you know this guy's dangerous?"

Skerry drained his glass and ordered another. "Because I reached in and took a look, okay?"

Michael's jaw dropped. "You what?"

"Spare me the reaction, kid. You probably don't believe me anyway. But this guy's got bad vibes."

"Like what kind?"

"He's one of those mutant supremacists. Hates normals."

"So? Half of the members of the clan feel the same way. And most normals reciprocate, don't they?"

"Maybe. But it's better to have somebody in public office who's less prejudiced. Who can deal with nonmutants comfortably. Fanatics make me nervous."

Michael took another sip. "If you're so concerned, why didn't you say something about it at the meeting?"

"I tried. But I can't push our cozy little group too far. Otherwise, they'll fry me. Or die trying. And they didn't want to believe me. Jeffers is too pretty. Besides, everybody's anxious to put the assassination behind them. So now Jeffers is senator." Skerry poured a glassful of the red brew and stared at it morosely.

"Skerry, stop brooding about it. Jeffers might not be so bad. And we need somebody in that Senate seat."

180

"I suppose. Better him than Zenora."

"What is it between you two, anyway?" Michael reached for the pitcher.

"Three years ago, she made a pass at me after the big meeting."

"Zenora?!"

Skerry nodded. "Too much to drink or something. Maybe she and Halden were having problems. Who knows? At first, I tried to ignore her. But she was pretty persistent. Finally I took her up on it. Hey, don't look at me that way, kid. It happens. And it was pretty good between us, too. But I ended it, eventually. I knew it meant trouble. Tried to let her down easy, but she wasn't happy about it. Still isn't. It's one of the reasons I stay away. Scorn a mutant at your own risk, I guess. Don't tell Halden, okay?"

"Sure." Privately, Michael thought the image of his tall, dignified aunt coming on to a younger man, especially Skerry, was hilarious. And painful. He also suspected that Halden knew all about it. There were few secrets in the clan.

"Well, what's your plan now?"

"Canada." Skerry put down his empty glass with a bang. "I'm heading up north in a couple of days. Wanted to know if you were interested. Could use your talent. You know that job at your old man's firm bores the piss out of you."

Michael nodded ruefully. "Isn't that the truth."

"So come along."

Michael paused, glass raised halfway to his mouth. What temptation, he thought. Leave home and clan behind for good. Stop worrying about government contracts and mutant traditions.

Skerry leaned toward him. "There's a group of us who stay in touch about mutant business. A nice underground network. But with Jeffers in Washington and the Mutant Union flexing its muscles again, we'll be burrowing even deeper. He'll have to be watched. And there's still this supermutant threat."

181

"It sounds interesting," Michael said. He put down his glass. Why not? he thought. Why not leave? Work with Skerry. Live outside the narrow confines of the mutant world. He was almost going to say yes when he thought of Kelly. He remembered the satin feel of her skin. Her eyes twinkling as she smiled. The way her laughter warmed him, inside out. Leave her? He couldn't do it.

Skerry frowned, his mouth twisting to one side. "Don't bother to tell me. I know, you're worried about that little normal you're glowing for. Dammit, Mike, stop thinking with your hormones!"

"I'd miss her," Michael said, cheeks reddening.

"You'll forget her in six months," Skerry said. "And you'll meet *real* women. Exotic, exciting, and experienced. . . ."

"Forget it, Skerry. It's not for me. At least, not now."

A number flashed in Michael's head, green numerals winking against his eyelids.

"If you change your mind, you can leave a message for me here. Think about it, Cuz. Adios."

The air around the table wavered. Michael blinked. He was alone in the booth. He sighed, finished his kimmer and paid the mech at the register.

A blue, snub-nosed skimmer was sitting in the driveway when he got home and the front door to the house was unlocked. Feeling uneasy, he entered the house carefully.

The speakers in the living room gave out an unfamiliar, pulsing chant, almost inaudible. Michael frowned. He could smell the acrid scent of joystick. The lights were so dim that he could barely make out the figure of a woman sitting on the couch.

"Mel?"

A silvery giggle was his only reply.

"Kelly?"

"No, silly, it's me, Jena." She stood up and walked toward him. She wore a tight blue plaskin jumpsuit, which showed off her long legs and slim figure. Her blond hair hung loose to her shoulders. Her golden eyes glittered like coins.

"Have a joystick," she said.

"How did you get in here?"

"Your parents called and gave me the door combination. Said I should look in and see how you were." She sat down again, crossing her legs. She was wearing black, high-heeled boots. The air was thick with joysmoke, making him dizzy.

Slowly, Michael sank down onto the couch, confused. The kimmers he'd had with Skerry were buzzing through his head. The chant had a hypnotic, compelling quality. He noticed that Jena's jumpsuit shaded from opaque to translucent just above her nipples. A small voice in his head wondered what it would be like to lick his way beneath that jumpsuit, trailing along all that tawny skin. . . .

"When will your folks be back?"

"Tuesday."

Uncrossing her legs, Jena slid closer to him on the couch, handing him a joystick. He bit down on the end and felt the familiar joyrush sweep him up. After a moment, he leaned back against the cushions, vision blurred. Jena moved even closer, pressing against him.

"So how are you?" she asked. Her voice was husky.

For a moment, Michael hesitated, thinking of Kelly. Then the rhythmic pulse of the chants absorbed him. What the hell, he thought. Kelly was miles away. Jena was next to him, willing and most likely ready. Kelly would never have to find out, he thought, as he put his arm around Jena.

Soft. Gods, she was soft. That jumpsuit felt like silk. Like skin. He ran his hand down her arm, to her waist, then back up, fingers reaching toward even more yielding softness. He pulled at the neckline of her jumpsuit, felt it open, ran an exploratory finger beneath it. Her nipples were hard. Jena sighed and pressed against his hand.

Michael kissed her, feeling her lips part, tongue darting toward his. The kiss seemed to go on forever, the chant

throbbing, Jena moving rhythmically against him. Aware-
ness, like ripples on a pond, flowed outward, swirling in a
circle of sensation and the beating of his blood. When he
opened his eyes, he was lying on top of Jena on the couch.
Their clothes were heaped on the floor.

The insistent lapping of invisible tongues ran along his
skin, seeking out each secret place, each sensitive nerve ending, making him moan with pleasure. Jena was leaning back
on her elbow, watching him lazily from half-closed eyes.

"Do you like that?" she whispered, smiling a cat's smile.

A thousand erotic images danced in his head, a sensual
mandala encircling him in flame. He dug his hands into the
cushions, heart beginning to pound.

"Jena . . . my God . . ."

"Actually, your parents didn't call me," she said gleefully.
"I called them at Halden's and told them I was concerned that
you were alone."

"You did?"

"Sure. Besides, I knew Kelly was out of town."

"You knew?" Michael tried to concentrate on what she was
saying. But it was difficult.

She chuckled. "Of course. I thought you might be lonely."
She put her hand between his legs, lazily stroking. He arched
up to meet each caress.

"I can see I was right." When she withdrew it, the stroking
continued. Michael wanted to tell her she wasn't the one for
whom he longed. And he bit his lip to keep himself from
telling her not to stop.

"Can your normal girlfriend do this? Can she reach inside
and find what you like best, and how, and when, then do it
to you, intensified a thousand times, without even touching
you?"

Michael began to sweat beneath her invisible witch
touches. He became white hot, molten.

"I didn't know you were a double . . ." he gasped.

The cat smile deepened. "Yes. Telepathic and telekinetic.

Your parents were right. We'd make a good pair. Good genetic material." She giggled as she said it. "Maybe we'd even produce that supermutant they're all so hot for."

"But to reach inside is forbidden. . . ."

"Only if they find out . . . and are you going to tell them at the next meeting about how I reached into your mind and gave you more pleasure than you've ever had before?" Jena almost purred. Invisible hands were busy between his legs, teasing, maddening, working him slowly into a frenzy.

The mandala began to rotate, to writhe as multiple coruscating images of Michael and Jena engaged in gasping acts of passion, a living frieze from an Indian temple made of light. Now he was above her, now behind. Here she knelt before him, there she entwined him like a snake.

"I know you're not interested in me. Not now," Jena said softly. She slid down between his legs and slowly began to lick him. Michael hissed with pleasure and closed his eyes. "But you'll remember this. Each time you're with her, you'll know what it can be like with me. And you'll want me, too. You'll see."

Michael pulled Jena up, covered her mouth with his own to stop her from talking. She opened her legs and with a thrust he was inside her, moving, hearing a roar building in his head as he sped toward his climax. He told himself she was wrong. After this night, he would never think of her again. He tried to keep Kelly's image in his mind, but she was blurring, fading, and when he came, crying out, one of a dozen Michaels in an enchanted witch tapestry, gasping, spasming, he didn't know which girl's name he called.

THE SCREEN BUZZED. Andie ignored it. She wanted to finish her notes for Stephen on mutagen research in Brazil for the subcommittee report.

The buzz repeated.

"Caryl?"

No response. Probably on a break.

Andie swore and punched what she thought was the autoresponse key, but missed and hit the answer key instead. The screen lit up to show Karim staring at her.

"Andie?"

"Oh, hi, Karim. I'm really busy right now. . . ."

"I'm sure you are. But this is important."

Andie sighed, trying not to sound as exasperated as she felt. The last thing she was in the mood for was a conversation with Karim. "Okay, what's up?"

"Why don't you tell me?"

"What do you mean?"

Karim frowned. "Look, I'd rather discuss this privately, but ever since your new boss arrived, that has been not only difficult, but nearly impossible. Can we have lunch? A drink? Meet in the corridor for five minutes?"

"Karim, I've got to get these notes finished."

"Please, Andie." He looked so vulnerable, she didn't have the heart to brush him off. She checked her schedule. She could meet him while Stephen went over her notes.

"How about in forty-five minutes?"

"Fine. At Henry's?"

"See you there."

An hour later, Andie hurried into the café. Those notes had taken longer than she'd expected. The main room was half filled despite the fact that it was long past lunchtime. Andie felt sweaty and uncomfortable as she settled into her seat. Karim nodded coolly.

"Thought you'd never get here."

"Sorry I'm late."

He handed her a menu. "Have something to eat?"

"Thanks, I had a sandwich at my desk."

"A drink?"

"Just coffee," she said, dialing the order into the compubar.

Karim looked at her for a moment. As the silence stretched, she began to feel uncomfortable. "Do I have soya in my teeth?"

"No. I'm just wondering what's going on."

"What do you mean?"

Karim leaned forward, eyes hard. "Andie, I haven't seen you in three weeks. I've scarcely talked to you. Don't you think that's strange?"

She started to twist her hair around her finger nervously. "Well, I've been busy—"

"Bullshit. You were never so busy you didn't have time for me when Jacobsen was around. But bring in some handsome mutant and suddenly I'm a stranger."

Andie smiled nervously. "Karim, I think you're jealous."

"Perhaps. But I thought we had something going that was pretty nice. After Rio, I thought—"

"C'mon, Karim. That was just Rio. The stars, the music—it makes you a little crazy. We had some fun. It was very nice. But now we're back in Washington."

"I don't see it that way."

Andie groped for words. "Um, Karim, you know we can't afford to take this kind of thing seriously. We're both much too busy."

He frowned. "I thought we both agreed on the dangers of taking our jobs too seriously. Especially after Jacobsen's death."

"Well, I've found that work helps the healing process. And my boss keeps me busy."

"Yes, I'm sure he does."

Andie's cheeks reddened. "What's that supposed to mean?"

Karim looked disgusted. "I'm not naive, Andie. Anybody can see you've got a thing for your boss. And we know how hard infatuated staffers work." He paused, took a sip of Campari. "Yes, Jeffers is certainly busy. I read about his Mutant Union bill in the Congressional Record. He's not wasting any time, is he? Building support for repeal of the Fairness Doctrine. Angling for an appointment to the Appropriations

Subcommittee. He's been courting Senator Sulzberger, the majority leader, and even the VP."

"What's wrong with that?"

"Nothing, especially if you're a shark interested in diverting funds to special interests."

"Such as?"

"Mutant rights."

Andie felt sweaty again. "I resent that. It sounds like antimutant bigotry. Stephen's not a shark. He's just more capable. More committed. He works so hard because he cares so much."

Karim whistled. "You're beginning to sound like your own press releases."

"Don't be such a cynic, Karim."

"Especially about Stephen, right?" Karim's voice was cold with anger. "You really have changed, Andie. I thought you had more perspective. Sorry I've taken up your valuable time." He stood up.

"Karim. Wait." Andie bit her lip as she watched him walk away. She told herself Karim was just being childish, making more out of a summertime fling than had really existed. She ignored the insistent voice that told her she missed him already. Besides, Jeffers was going to address the Senate about the Jacobsen murder investigation in half an hour. She didn't have time to deal with Karim's pout.

Andie hurried back through the late September sunshine and got to her seat in the chamber with a couple of minutes to spare. Senator Sulzberger was wrapping up what must have been a lengthy filibuster against Bill 173, the bill intended to protect Marsbase against commercial exploitation. His mission accomplished, Sulzberger sat down.

Eagerly, Andie watched as Jeffers, clad in a hand-tailored gray suit, strode to the podium. He put down his notes, and looked around the room.

"Ladies and gentlemen of the Senate, I think you'll agree with me that this investigation has gone on too long," Jeffers said. "I demand that we find some answers to the murder of my predecessor. To allow this case to linger shows a shocking lack of diligence. Is this the message we want to send forth? That a member of this august body can be killed with impunity?"

He stalked the floor of the Senate like a jungle cat, Andie thought. Visions of campaign slogans waltzed before her. Stephen was good, very good. Election would be a cinch next year. And, eventually, maybe even higher office. If only Jacobsen had possessed his charisma. Instead of death threats, Andie was counting the fan mail. Even the nonmutants loved him. The scholarship fund hadn't hurt him, nor had his establishment of the Co-op Foundation. There was already talk of summer games displaying mutant talents.

"Mediagenic," Karim had said with a certain smirk after he met Jeffers. Well, that was undeniable. And what was wrong with being charismatic? It just made Stephen more effective at his job. And he was very good at his job. He'd pounded three bills through having to do with mutant business, and was already being courted by other senators for support.

Applause shook her out of her reverie. She wasn't surprised that Jeffers's colleagues were applauding him. He flashed a grin, made a self-deprecating remark, and hustled back toward his seat, winking at her.

Next on the agenda was the subcommittee report on the Brazil trip. Craddick presented their findings with some additional comments by Jeffers. Horner was absent, which apparently caused little discomfort among his colleagues. Andie had been over the material so many times she couldn't help tuning out most of Craddick's statements. She came awake however, when she heard Jeffers's voice.

"I concur with the findings of the subcommittee. Because there is a lack of substantive evidence, I cannot recommend further investigation at this time."

Huh? Andie rubbed her eyes. She'd expected Jeffers to issue a ringing call for immediate action. She'd shown him all of her notes. Even the memorypak. How could he just sit there nodding, saying there was no evidence to support additional investigation? She'd expected Craddick and Horner to remove any potentially inflammatory material from the report. But Jeffers? Fuming, Andie went back to the office to await her boss.

"That went well." He grinned. "Better than I'd hoped."

"I'm glad you think so," Andie retorted. "Your comments on the subcommittee's report were certainly a surprise to me."

Jeffers looked at her uncertainly. "You sound upset."

"I am."

"Why?"

"I thought you were going to demand further investigation of the genetic experiments in Brazil."

"How could I? The hysteria surrounding Jacobsen's assassination still hasn't died down. To confirm that in fact there may be more mutants, supermutants even, coming soon, would just fan the flames. Even I can't risk doing that, Andie."

"So instead you sweep this under the Senate rug."

"I'm not entirely convinced there's as much there to investigate as you think there is."

Andie was about to say that other mutants felt differently. But a small voice in her head told her to avoid it. This was mutant business, and she was an outsider.

"Well, I wish you'd pursued it a bit more vociferously."

Jeffers reached down, took her face in his hands.

"Andie, I'm sorry. I disappointed you. And this really meant a lot to you, didn't it? Listen, how about if we have a drink at seven, then talk it over at dinner?"

Andie's heart pounded. "All right."

Three hours later, they were sitting in the plush, dimly lit dining room of a two-star French restaurant on Avenue M.

"Stephen, please try to understand," Andie said. "I was in Brazil with Jacobsen, right before she was killed. I feel like

I've let her down somehow, not pushing harder on this issue."

"You did the best you could," Jeffers said smoothly. "It's wonderful to keep her memory alive, and you know how I feel about that. But we can't operate from a daily viewpoint of how Eleanor might handle something."

"But what if there are supermutant experiments taking place in Brazil? It certainly looks that way."

Jeffers threw his napkin down on the table and dialed up the check. "Well, I still don't think that memorypak was conclusive evidence. Besides, I thought you told me that the mutants are conducting their own investigation, privately. So the matter is far from closed."

"Yes, but—"

"Andie, there's only so much we can do officially. Brazil is a foreign country. We can't risk creating a diplomatic incident. I agree that the thought of any experimentation on human subjects is repugnant, but we don't have proof of that. Records of embryo splitting done in test tubes don't mean there are captive women in some clinic in Rio with implanted mutant pregnancies." Jeffers waggled his eyebrows. "Sounds like some horror vid. Dr. Ribeiros and his island of mutant embryos."

Andie laughed in spite of herself and followed him out of the restaurant to his gray skimmer. When he pulled up to the curb near her apartment, she was surprised to see him kill the motor.

"Andie, I can't tell you what your help means to me. You've made this transition very easy."

"I'm glad." She looked down at her lap self-consciously.

"I really enjoy working with you. Being with you."

He reached out and drew her into an embrace. The kiss was warm, deep.

"Would you like to come in?" Was she really asking him up to her apartment? Her boss? A mutant?

"Of course."

Andie led him inside, upstairs; they paused for a quick drink on her sofa. Then they were in her bedroom.

"Come here," he whispered, reaching for her. All of her hesitation disappeared. She moved into his arms easily, as though she'd done it a hundred times.

Once they were in bed, Andie saw with relief that he was a functional, normal human male. Nothing genitally exotic, thank God. Andie felt the muscles ripple under his tanned skin as he moved over her, in her. She'd never been so close to a mutant before. He felt warm, as though his body temperature was higher than normal. The golden eyes, like a jungle cat's, held her with hypnotic power. Was she prey? Did she care? All she wanted right now was Stephen Jeffers in her bed. She sighed gently. Then less gently as she came.

16

MICHAEL CUT THROUGH the clear pool water, arms at his sides, legs motionless. A thin, silvery wake uncoiled behind him. As he passed them, other swimmers watched enviously. He didn't care. One of the nicest things about telekinesis was being able to propel yourself through water without effort. His gift prevented him from competing in swimming competitions, of course. The so-called Fairness Doctrine prohibited mutant participation in sporting events. But that didn't matter to Michael. He loved to feel the water enfold him. The sheer sensual pleasure was reward enough. He wasn't really interested in showing up some poor normal flailing away with arms and legs. If they wanted to keep their silly sports "pure" so that they wouldn't be reminded of their own limitations, let them.

He flipped over onto his back and glided toward Kelly. She was a graceful swimmer, for a normal. He admired the way her dark hair fanned out behind her in the water. Also, he admired the sleek azure suit that clung to her like skin.

"Time for one more lap?" she asked.

Michael looked at the wall clock guiltily. He'd promised Jena that he'd pick her up at the shuttleport at nine. It was seven-thirty now.

"Uh, no. Got to get home early, work on some contracts. But we can come back tomorrow."

"Okay. I've only got a half-day of temp work anyway."

She floated toward him, put her arms around his neck, and kissed him lightly. The quicksilver feel of her as she floated against him was enticing, but he pulled away.

Kelly frowned. "Anything wrong?"

"No. Just getting cold."

"Well, let's go." She swam toward the ladder, then looked toward him mischievously.

"How 'bout a boost?"

Telekinetically, he lifted her gently out of the water and deposited her on a beechwood bench. The lifeguard gave him a dirty look.

What the hell, Michael thought, and levitated himself up and out of the water, landing with a graceful twirl near Kelly. She applauded and threw him a green towel.

Once again the lifeguard scowled. Michael shrugged. He wasn't breaking any rules, aside from a few old-fashioned assumptions about physics. And mutants had proved the physicists wrong, much to the physicists' astonished delight.

"See you in fifteen minutes," Kelly said. She snapped her towel at him and walked toward the women's showers, hips swinging saucily.

Michael watched the steam rise from the heated water and wondered how his life had ever gotten so complicated.

He was not completely surprised to see that a second lock had been fitted through the metal handle of his locker door, securing it against his key. When would they learn? With a sigh, he concentrated his full telekinetic force on the lock. As he increased the molecular movement within the metal it glowed pink and began to melt. The metal pooled on the floor, glinting as it cooled. He slowed the molecules to hasten the process. The practical joker would find a slag heap for all his trouble. Michael had spent years foiling normals who'd pulled such stunts, in high school and at college.

Kelly was waiting for him, wearing a bright-yellow parka that glowed in the November twilight. Michael put his arms around her. She moved suggestively against him as they kissed. Michael felt a pang of guilt mixed with a flicker of desire. Sooner or later, Kelly was going to figure out that he was seeing somebody else. She was already suspicious. He couldn't risk losing her. But how could he break off his affair with Jena and lose the magic of their intoxicating couplings? He promised himself he would end it. Eventually.

The November trees threw skeletal patterns against the deepening purple sky. It was Michael's favorite time of day. He wanted to take Kelly by the hand and just walk off into the cool middle distance. Instead, he got into the skimmer and took her home.

ANDIE ANSWERED THE MESSAGE LIGHT on the third blip. Bailey's hound-dog face stared out at her. Fatigue deepened every line of his jaw.

"Red, I've got something on that mutant girl."

"Melanie Ryton?"

"The same. Don't get excited. It's only a little bitty something."

"Well?"

"Stolen skimmer report lodged two months ago by a Maryland businessman." Bailey squinted at a printout on his desk. "One Benjamin Cariddi claims Melanie Ryton stole his car."

"He specifically named her? How did he know who she was?"

"Says here that she was his girlfriend. They had a fight."

"His girlfriend?"

"Yeah. Says she was employed as an exotic dancer at the Star Chamber." Bailey looked up. "I wouldn't take my worst enemy there."

Andie smiled frostily. "Maybe that's where Mr. Cariddi finds all his girlfriends."

"Anyway, the skimmer was recovered. Abandoned at a Maryland suburban tube station."

"And our girl's long gone?"

"No leads."

"Can you get me a copy of that report?"

"Sure, Red. Anything else?"

"Yeah. Tell me what to say to her parents."

THE SHUTTLE was half an hour late. Michael paced the landing port. A small group of mutants was gathered in the bar but he avoided them. The last thing he wanted to do right now was sit with mutants. Mutancy was responsible for most of his problems these days.

He'd dropped Kelly off quickly, but not so quickly that he hadn't noticed the look of confusion and disappointment on her face. He should be with her right now, he thought.

The shuttle landed with a jolt and taxied toward the port. Within moments, the doors had opened and Jena was striding down the walk toward him, wearing a tight blue opalescent pantsuit. Michael saw that he wasn't the only male in the crowd watching her progress with interest. He had to admit it: she was stunning.

"Michael! God, how I missed you."

She threw her arms around him and kissed him.

Despite his resolve to resist, he pulled her closer, inflamed by the seductive subliminal images with which she teased him.

"Come on," he said at last, pulling away. "Let's go someplace where we can be alone."

ANDIE HAD A FULL AFTERNOON scheduled. But it was going awry already.

The *Washington Post* reporter, Jacqui Renstrow, was ten minutes late. After her, Andie had Jason Edwards of Network Media and Susan Johnson, the late-night vid hostess, stacked up. Both vidjocks wanted to interview Jeffers on his determination to repeal all athletic guidelines and restrictions on mutants. God knew what Renstrow wanted.

"Andie. Good to see you again." Jacqui Renstrow settled into the booth, blond curls bouncing. "Sorry I'm late. Barton was in one of his loquacious moods—"

"And you never know when he'll let slip something that will gain you the Pulitzer, right? What are you drinking?"

"Scotch, neat. Thanks."

Renstrow opened her screencase and pulled out a notescreen.

Andie held up a warning hand.

"Wait a minute, Jacqui. You said you wanted to do some deep background work. I won't have anything for public release on the Fairness Doctrine repeal until Friday."

The reporter smiled brightly. "Relax, Andie. I just want to take some notes. You know we're putting together a retrospective on mutants in public office. Of course, we're concentrating on Jacobsen and Jeffers. I wanted to get a little more background on Jeffers."

Her tone set off Andie's alarm bells.

"Such as?"

"I want to emphasize Jeffers-the-businessman as well as public figure," Renstrow said. "To show his other facets. For instance, I had no idea his private law firm was so large."

"That's on public record," Andie said.

"Of course. And then there's his multinational corporation with all its subsidiaries."

Andie leaned closer. "Don't forget, all of Jeffers's business concerns are being administered by blind trusts for the duration of his tenure in the Senate."

"Can't have any private agendas getting in the way of public business, can we?" Renstrow said, with a laugh that rang more than a little false to Andie.

"That's the idea."

"Honestly, Andie, he must be a superman. I don't know how he did it. All those subsidiaries. Betajef, Corjef, Unijef.

When did the man make time to handle so much import business, his law concern, and run for the Senate?"

"Some people are just particularly capable, I guess."

"Especially if they're mutant?"

"Is that the point of your story?"

"Oh, no. I'm just expressing admiration. He must be an administrative and financial wizard."

"He's a successful businessman. But that's part of public record, too. And not such an odd occurrence among mutants. They tend to be very successful."

"Overcompensation?"

"I'm not qualified to speculate."

"Where did he develop his financial acumen?"

"Well, his father ran a very successful import and export business. And I suppose he concentrated on business studies in his undergraduate work."

Renstrow frowned and looked at her notes. "Well, I don't see how, considering he got a degree in premed."

"Premed?" Andie tried to cover her confusion.

"Yeah. Majored in genetic research. Kind of strange that he went on to law school instead of medical school."

"People change their minds sometimes." What was Renstrow after?

"Don't I know it. I changed my major three times." Renstrow finished her drink. "Well, I'd love to get some more information about how he developed his financial skills."

"Perhaps he's just naturally talented in that area."

Renstrow smiled in a way that made Andie nervous.

"You're probably right," she said. "Look, I realize this is kind of a puff piece. But I need to talk to Jeffers about this. Can you get me in, Andie?"

Andie leaned back and faked a yawn. "Forgive me, I've been talking to reporters all day. I can't promise anything right away, Jacqui. But I'll certainly pass your request along to the senator. What's your deadline?"

"Monday."

"We'll get back to you." She glanced at the bar clock. "Listen, I'm late for an appointment. It's been good to see you." Grabbing her coat, Andie jumped up and, with a wave, was out the door before the startled reporter could say anything.

There were no cabs in sight. Damn. Andie sealed her coat more securely and decided to walk toward the tube. It was just three and there was still a little daylight left.

Renstrow's probing had rattled Andie to her bones. What was she up to, talking about Jeffers's financial skill? Had she uncovered something in the budget? Andie decided to make a quick review of office finances. She'd quiz Jeffers later about his old corporate accounts. Turning down a side street of posh townhouses, doors glowing green with security fields, Andie cut through a brick-lined alley to the tube station.

17

J ENA TURNED OVER in bed and looked at Michael in the moonlight. She sighed. "You're not here with me, are you?"

"What do you mean?"

She sat up.

"I mean, you're someplace else. With somebody else. And I can guess who."

"It's not what you think."

"No? Well, Kelly is a nice hobby. I guess." Her tone was acid.

She's everything you're not, Michael thought. He was beginning to wish he'd taken Skerry up on his offer, and run away to Canada.

Abruptly, Jena switched tactics. She curled playfully around his knees, breasts whispering secret messages to his skin. Michael leaned back as she stroked him, his nerves still tingling from their lovemaking. If only she would just touch him gently now and not say anything. . . .

"Your parents are so pleased that I'm seeing you."

His eyes flew open.

"How did they find out?" he demanded.

"I told them."

"Why?"

"I thought it would make things easier for us."

"For us?!" Michael pulled out of her embrace. "What do you mean?"

Jena looked flustered. "Well, you know. So they wouldn't worry when you stayed over here at night. And so the clan would get used to the idea of us as a couple."

Inside him, something sharp finally crystallized. It was almost a relief. He jumped out of bed.

"Dammit, Jena, what are you trying to do?"

She sat up, eyes big. "What do you mean?"

Michale pulled on his jeans, reached for his shirt. "I mean, you're playing games with me and my family. Why do they need to know about this?"

"Sooner or later, they'd find out."

"You're just trying to encourage their hopes. Build up the illusion that this involvement means something."

"Of course it means something." Her tone wasn't playful any longer.

"To you, maybe." He finished sealing his shirt, slipped on his boots and jacket. "You think that fancy tricks in bed can keep me hypnotized."

"I didn't hypnotize you into bed. You wanted me." Her voice grated.

"That's true. After you literally threw yourself at me."

"And you came back for more."

Michael's cheeks burned. "I know."

"Why are you making such a big deal out of this?" Jena stretched luxuriously, one silken flank exposed. "Come back to bed. We'll do that lotus cluster you like so much."

"No." He ignored the fiery images that flickered before his mind's eye. "We're finished, Jena. This has got to end."

"You don't mean it, Michael."

"I do."

He fled, but her mindspeech pursued him down the hall and into the street. *It's not as easy as that.*

"Go to hell," he muttered under his breath, startling a

businessman waiting for the public screenphone at the end of the block. He didn't care. He knew what he didn't want, and that was a beginning. More than a beginning. Kelly burned in his mind, a beacon of promise. Mutant tradition be damned. After the yearly council meeting, he would ask her to marry him, and that would settle things.

THE TUBE GLEAMED, silver steel, at the mouth of the station tunnel. Andie nodded in satisfaction. Right on time. In minutes, she was at the office.

"Morning." The new receptionist, Aten, smiled politely. Her golden eyes gleamed.

"Is Senator Jeffers in?"

"Yes, and he's expecting you, Andie."

"Good."

Andie flung her screencase down on her desk, grabbed her lapscreen, and strode into Jeffers's office.

"Good morning, counselor," he said cheerfully. "You look ready for action."

She ignored his playful tone.

"Look at this," she said, clipping the memorypak of her meeting with Renstrow into his deskscreen, and watching with grim satisfaction as Jeffers's smile faded. "Good thing I tape every meeting."

Jeffers frowned. "What does Renstrow want?"

"She wouldn't say. Just asked to see you. I think she's digging around trying to make trouble. Maybe you're too popular. Yesterday's *AWC Journal* poll gives you a sixty-three percent approval rating in Oregon. She could just be trying to make trouble and get some byline attention."

"You're probably right," Jeffers said. "When can I see her?"

Andie checked Jeffers's calendar. "Tomorrow. Before the Mutant Union meeting at four."

"Okay. Slot Renstrow in for tomorrow afternoon, early. We try to keep all members of the Fourth Estate happy." He gave her a penetrating look. "Something else bothering you?"

"Stephen, I spent all night going over our budget figures, looking for a possible problem. Do you realize we have spent three times as much as Jacobsen did by this same time last year?"

Jeffers shrugged. "The staff has expanded, Andie. You know that. Jacobsen wasn't on a major Senate subcommittee. She didn't have our needs. So our expenses are greater."

"What if this is what Renstrow's after? Maybe she's looking to expose profligate mutant senators. She was *very* interested in your business background."

Jeffers grinned. "Let her dig."

"Stephen, I'm serious."

"I can see you are. And I'm trying to lighten you up. Believe me, I can handle Renstrow's probe attempts. My affairs are in order. And stop worrying about the budget. That's not your department anyhow."

"Sorry to have troubled you," Andie said. She set her jaw defiantly, closed her lapscreen with a snap, and stood up to leave.

His voice stopped her at the door.

"Andie, wait. Come back and sit down. Please?"

She halted, turned, looked toward him.

"I don't mean to make light of your work," Jeffers said. "Your concern is commendable. I just hate the thought of you losing a night's sleep over this. You work hard enough as it is."

"I'm not looking for gratitude, Stephen. I just don't like being told that this is none of my business."

He leaned over and covered her hands with his. "Andie, you're incredibly important to me. I couldn't function without you. And I know you're disappointed with your current responsibilities, but have patience. That will change."

"Forget it, Stephen."

He didn't release her hand. "I think we need to talk. Can I see you tonight?"

"Not tonight, Stephen. I have plans."

"Break them."

"I'm sorry. I can't."

"Tomorrow, then?" He smiled disarmingly.

"Ask me tomorrow." She stood up and walked out of his office.

THE BUILDING housing Ryton, Greene, and Davis Engineering was low and graceful, built from a blue-gray epoxied granite that Michael's father had requested specifically for its soothing psychic resonances. Windows of blue Plexiglas glinted like jewels, set deeply in the building's walls.

Michael pulled his parka collar up and hurried into the building, his breath leaving clouds of condensation in his wake. A cold morning. He could feel mutant season in the air. Halden had called the council meeting for the third week in December. Early, this year.

"Michael Ryton, call on line two," the mech announced as he walked through the door. He hung up his orange parka, hurried to his desk, keyed on the screen. Andrea Greenberg stared at him somberly.

"Michael, is your father around?"

"He's in a meeting."

"Well, then, I guess I'll have to give you the news." She smiled slightly. "Don't shoot the bearer of ill tidings, please."

"What do you mean?"

"I've got some information on your sister."

"Melanie! What's happened to her? Is she alive?"

"As far as I know."

"What do you mean?" Michael stared at the screen.

"I have no idea where she is now."

"Well, where was she?"

"In Maryland," Andie said. "Living with a man."

"Mel?" Michael sat down with a thud.

Andie nodded. "Apparently, she met him at the club where she worked as an exotic dancer."

"A *what?*"

Michael fought back the urge to laugh. His shy sister dancing almost naked in front of strangers? It was impossible. Ludicrous.

"You know. A stripper." Andie's tone grew impatient. "Anyway, it looks as though they had a fight, and she ran off, taking his skimmer."

"Slow down. She stole his skimmer?"

"Michael, I know this is hard for you to believe—"

"Does she still have it?"

"No. It was recovered the next day."

"And where is she now?"

"I told you. I don't know."

Michael leaned back in his chair.

"I can't believe any of this," he said. "An exotic dancer. Living with some guy and taking off with his skimmer." He shook his head in wonder. "At least she's still alive."

Andie nodded. "I'm afraid I don't know much else."

"What's the name of the man who filed the complaint?"

"Benjamin Cariddi."

"Nonmutant?"

"So it appears." She watched him for a moment. "What are you going to tell your parents?"

"The truth, I guess." He rubbed his eyelids. "Now give me some good news, Andie. Make it up, if you have to."

She smiled gently. "Senator Jeffers is working on the repeal of the Fairness Doctrine."

"About time."

"How's it going with that normal girlfriend of yours?"

Michael brightened. "Great! Kelly's wonderful."

"Sounds serious."

"I hope so. I'd like to get married next year. But she's been talking about going away to school."

"Can't she do both?"

"I suppose," he said. "She might not think so."

"Well, I hope it works out the way you want it, Michael. Mixed marriages can be challenging."

He shrugged. "What kind of marriage isn't?"

"I wouldn't know. Yet." Andie laughed. "Good luck. And send me an invitation to the wedding." She winked and was gone.

Michael sat watching the flickering blue screen for a long time.

18

AT FIVE MINUTES TO THREE, Andie walked into Jeffers's office, notescreen in hand. She nodded with satisfaction at the slim green folder on his desk. He had produced files, figures, and depositions that proved his accounting was completely in order. Andie couldn't wait to see Jacqui Renstrow's face when she realized that her little fishing expedition hadn't worked.

Jeffers looked at his watch.

"She's late."

"That seems to be a hobby of hers," Andie said, settling onto the brown sofa. "Give it five more minutes."

"That's about all I can spare," Jeffers said. There was irritation in his voice. "The Mutant Union will be here soon and that will tie up the rest of the afternoon."

"Well, it's her loss. I'll get your notes together for the meeting while we're waiting."

At 3:25, there was still no sign of Jacqui Renstrow. Andie was furious.

"I knew she was just trying to catch us off guard and cause trouble." She drummed her fingers on the desk.

"Forget it, Andie." Jeffers's brow was smooth, his voice relieved. "She probably found bigger fish to fry. Besides, this works in our favor. I'll have a little more time to prepare for the Mutant Union now."

"At least she could have called."

"Never mind," he said. "Do you have those notes ready? And remember, I want to tape this meeting so we can edit it for distribution later."

"Right. And excerpts for your faxletter, too." Andie clipped her notes into his deskscreen. She'd reserved the Madison Conference Room, a double screen and recorder.

At 4:05, every seat in the room was filled with mutants. Andie lingered in the back, feeling suddenly conspicuous among so many golden eyes.

Jeffers stood before them, boldly outlined by pink and white spotlights.

"Friends, I wanted to share our latest advances with you," he said. "As you may know, I've introduced a bill intended to repeal the so-called Fairness Doctrine."

The audience began clapping loudly, whistling and shouting approval. Jeffers waited for the din to end.

"It's going to be a tough fight. Let's not fool ourselves. The normals are frightened of the mutants. Frightened by our gifts." He paused. "I hardly have to remind you that they killed some of us when we first emerged in the nineties. And this year, they killed one of us again, in this very building. But nothing will stop us from regaining our rights. We are citizens. We must be treated as such. And they will have to kill all of us before we will stop demanding our rights."

Again, applause and cheering washed over Jeffers. The Mutant Union members jumped to their feet, chanting: "Rights now! Rights now!"

At their throats, on their sleeves and lapels, golden unity buttons twinkled. Jeffers nodded in cadence with their incantation. Finally he raised his hands for silence.

"It's time for us to move ahead, into the central arena of public life. Rather than being barred or ignored, we must demand that rules be rewritten, recognition be given. We are not just going to go away."

His audience erupted into applause yet again. Andie wondered uneasily what Eleanor Jacobsen would have thought of her successor's speech. Jeffers wasn't talking about cooperation. A hundred pairs of golden eyes watched him greedily.

"And once we've achieved this goal, we will move on. We'll repeal academic restrictions. And those preventing us from attaining security clearance for sensitive jobs of authority. And we will go on until every door is open to us. Until society cannot shun us, and we have assumed our rightful roles as leaders of society, and as heirs to tomorrow."

His audience was on its feet, a blur of blue and green, red and yellow. Andie prayed that nobody else had heard these comments. Heirs to tomorrow? What was he talking about? She'd have to edit that tape carefully. But listen to them applaud. He must know what he's doing.

After fifteen minutes of questions from the audience, Andie tried to catch Jeffers's eye. It was time to wrap things up. He didn't seem to see her, so she walked toward the front of the room.

"A normal!" an angry voice hissed.

"What's she doing here?" someone else called. "Jeffers, what is this?"

Jeffers stepped forward, smiling, and put his arm around Andie's shoulders in a tight grip.

"My friends, this is Andrea Greenberg, a trusted ally who shares our goals, and you must welcome her as you would welcome me."

He turned to Andie and said, sotto voce, "Smile."

She grinned in a frozen rictus. Her heart pounded. This didn't feel like a senator meeting with members of his constituency. It reminded her of a revival meeting. Or a mutiny. In a controlled voice, Andie thanked everybody for coming, promised them tapes of the meeting, and reminded Jeffers of his next appointment. Then she fled, feeling pursued by two hundred angry golden eyes.

Michael, are you busy?

The mental inquiry was a whisper in his ear, the voice his mother's voice. Even as he looked around, Michael knew he'd find the room empty. Sue Li was downstairs in the living room.

"No." He put the screen on pause and waited for her to continue.

I just don't think it would be a good time to share what we know about your sister with your father.

"Why not?"

He still hasn't recovered well from Jacobsen's murder. And the flares weaken him. Until we get additional information about Melanie, let's keep this just between us.

"Whatever you want, Mother."

Who is this Andrea Greenberg?

"She worked for Senator Jacobsen. Works for Jeffers now."

She's called your father before.

Was there the slightest green tinge of suspicion clinging to that comment?

"Mom, she's done us some favors, that's all."

Why would a normal do mutants favors?

"Why would a normal work for a mutant to begin with? Don't be silly. She's our friend."

If you say so.

Michael felt the mental link fade. It was rare that telepaths could receive as well as send, but his mother's gift was strong. Especially when she was determined to protect her husband. If she chose to bury this clue to Melanie's location, he couldn't stop her.

He told the screen to dial Kelly's number. She answered on the fourth ring.

"Michael?" She smiled, but there were dark circles under her eyes.

210

"Sweet-face, you look sleepy."

"I was up late last night helping Cindy work on a report for school. When am I going to see you?"

"How about tomorrow night?"

"What time?"

"Eight?"

"Great." She paused, looking uncomfortable.

"Anything wrong?"

"Michael, I heard from the Air Force Academy. They want me."

He felt his stomach drop.

"They're not the only ones," he said.

Kelly smiled. "Get serious. I might be able to start as early as June."

"Are you sure you want to do this?"

"I don't know. I want to talk to you about it."

"I'll bet your old man is excited."

"He's already decided what squadron I'll be in."

"Well, listen, don't make any more plans for the future for at least twenty-four hours, okay?"

"Not even if Hollywood calls?" She looked at him archly.

"Put them on hold and wait until I get there. I've got a lot of things I want to talk about with you." Michael blew her a kiss and signed off.

He was almost late for a buzzball game with his cousin Seyn. Michael grabbed his parka, and opened the door to his room, colliding with his younger brother, Jimmy.

"There you are," Jimmy said.

"What's up? I'm in a hurry." Michael headed for the stairs.

"Mike, do you think we'll see Mel again?"

"I don't know."

"Do you think she's alive?"

"Of course."

Jimmy frowned, looking like a smaller version of their father.

"Well, do you think Mom and Dad would let me move into her room anyway?"

"Is that all you're worried about?" Michael's voice grated. He took a deep breath and levitated Jimmy, upside down, toward the ceiling, shaking him. "You little wavehead. You don't give a damn about your sister! Or anybody else!"

"Ow! Michael, stop it!"

An antique jug, one of Sue Li's favorites, flew off its perch by the staircase toward Michael's head. He ducked and it smashed into green and blue shards against the far wall of the hallway. Michael stared at it in horror.

"Knock it off or I'll hang you upside down in the basement," he said.

"I'll tell Mom and Dad—"

"Right after you explain how the pitcher got broken."

"I'll fix it. Just put me down."

With a thump, Michael deposited the squirming boy on the rug. As he watched, the shattered ceramic fragments rose up from the floor in a shining spiral which came to rest atop the hall shelf as the pitcher, its former shape resumed. All signs of breakage had been fused and erased.

"Nice job." Michael had to admit it. Even he couldn't have done as well. Jimmy's telekinetic powers were beginning to outstrip his own. He turned to make peace with his younger brother, but the hallway was empty. He heard the door to Jimmy's room slam.

THE NEXT DAY, Andie met Jeffers coming out of the elevator.

"Morning," he said.

"Morning yourself." She fell into step beside him. "Stephen, what was going on at that Mutant Union meeting yesterday? I've never heard you talk like that before. Do you want to terrify everybody?"

Jeffers chuckled. "You're taking this way too seriously, Andie. I can see I shook you up. Well, aren't you the one constantly telling me to give the people what they want?"

He buzzed open the door and waited for her to enter.

"Yes," she said. "But not to the extent that it sounds like a Nazi pep rally." She strode into his private suite and flung herself into the blue chair by his desk.

Jeffers stood above her. "You're stretching this way out of shape," he said soothingly. "Since the Mutant Union got established, it's demanded strong talk. So when the Mutant Union comes to see me, that's exactly what I give it. I tell the members what they want to hear without making any real commitments."

"What about all those restrictions you promised to repeal?"

He shrugged. "They know I'm not a miracle worker. I didn't give them any timetable. And besides, those restrictions really are unfair."

"What was that bit about 'heirs to tomorrow'?" she said.

"Just razzle-dazzle to get them on their feet."

"And what do you tell your normal constituency?"

"That I'll look out for their best interests and keep their taxes low. That integration of mutants and non will continue in an orderly fashion that benefits the best interests of all involved."

Andie sighed. "You have answers for everybody."

"Two answers in every house, and two votes." Jeffers grinned wolfishly.

His deskscreen buzzer sounded.

"Senator Jeffers. Mr. Canay to see you."

"Send him in."

A dark-haired, dark-eyed man with olive skin, wearing an expensive suit, entered the room. He nodded at Jeffers, then looked at Andie uncertainly.

"Ben. Good to see you." Jeffers shook his hand. "Meet Andie Greenberg, my principal aide and press secretary."

Canay nodded. "A pleasure." His smile was a a bit crooked, but charming.

"Hello." Andie's tone was just the slightest bit cool. Why had Jeffers called her his press secretary?

"Andie, Ben worked with me in Betajef, my import company. I've decided to bring him on staff to help coordinate the election campaign in '18 and to work with me on special projects."

"I see."

"I want Ben to put together that caucus we've been talking about; the one on mutant-nonmutant interests."

Andie's eyes widened in surprise. She had expected to head up that project herself.

"Ben agrees that we need a forum that will bring us all closer together," Jeffers said. He seemed oblivious to her reaction.

"We want to get moving on this quickly," Canay said. "Great publicity potential. Of course, I'll need staff support."

"I'm sure you'll get it," she said icily, then turned away from him. "Stephen, I want to talk to you."

"Can it wait until this afternoon? I wanted to go over some things with Ben."

"The sooner we get to it, the better."

"How's one o'clock?"

"All right."

"Nice to meet you, Andie."

"Ditto." She flashed a furious look at Jeffers, grabbed her notescreen, and strode out of the room.

Fuming, she checked her agenda. Damn! She was already late for the Roosevelt Group meeting.

"Aten, I'll be out until one," she said and hurried downstairs.

The Roosevelt Group, comprising representatives from every senatorial staff in Congress, met on the first Tuesday of every month. Part support group, part gossip session, it kept Andie plugged in to the network of political aides that snaked through the halls of power. In her opinion, more pol-icy-making and favor-trading went on here than took place on the floor of the Senate.

Karim was sitting across the room. He winked at her as she walked in.

"Did you hear he's dating one of Coleman's aides?" Letty Martin whispered.

Andie frowned. "No. Which one?"

"The blonde."

She wondered briefly if she'd let a good man get away, but shook off the thought. Karim had been a passing interest. She'd never felt the passion for him that burned in her for Jeffers. But she did miss bouncing ideas off Karim. And she could use his input now.

She plugged her laptop into the jack on the table and tapped in his code. The answer came back quickly.

WHAT'S UP?

TROUBLE. TALK?

WHEN?

AFTER MEETING.

OKAY.

An hour later, when all the in-jokes and gossip had been swapped, Karim was waiting by the elevator, a quizzical expression on his face.

"So?"

"Let's take a walk."

"Are you 'waved? It's cold outside!"

"Not in the mall."

"All right."

The Capitol Mall bubble was a welcome shield from late-November winds. Busy street traffic and bare lawns and trees awaiting the first snowfall flickered through transparent segments in the blue wall. Andie gazed at them, unseeing, as she walked beside Karim.

"What's the problem?" he asked.

"I think I was just demoted."

"What?"

"Jeffers brought in some guy from one of his companies to work with him on special projects."

"So where's the demotion?"

"He introduced me to him as his press secretary."

"Oh." Karim looked thoughtful. "But I thought you were already his PS."

"Just as part of my other duties."

"So you think this new guy is a replacement?"

"Yeah."

He shrugged. "That'll teach you to get involved with the boss."

"Look, Karim, I didn't ask your opinion to receive a cheap shot." Andie turned and started to walk away.

"I'm sorry, I'm sorry." He grabbed her arm. "Wait. Is this new guy mutant?"

"No." Andie said. "Why do you ask?"

"Scuttlebutt has it that Jeffers is loading his staff with mutants."

Andie stared out at the trees.

"It's true," she said grimly. "Three this month. Five last month. You know Caryl quit. She couldn't take it."

Karim nodded. "Can't say I'm surprised."

"Jacobsen never did this."

"Well, she had a different approach."

"What else does scuttlebutt say?" Andie asked.

"Most of the legislation Jeffers has sponsored has been pro-mutant," Karim said. "But I think that's to be expected. Especially after Jacobsen's assassination."

"Jacobsen had a less myopic approach."

"Well, I think Jacobsen was less influenced by special interest groups, especially the one to which she belonged."

Andie stopped walking. "Are you saying that Stephen is a pawn of the mutants?"

"No. I don't think so. He might be. But maybe he's just much more upfront about mutant rights and .interests. Why shouldn't he want mutants on his staff? Who else has 'em in Congress?"

"Davis."

"That's one."

Karim watched her expectantly.

She bit her lip. "That's it."

"Look, Andie, I think you're making too much out of this. If I were a mutant, alone in Congress, I'd probably want some of my fellows working for me. Are you really worried about your job?"

She shrugged. "I don't know. I didn't like what I heard this morning."

"Then ask for clarification. But I don't have to tell you that. Are you having trouble working with these new staffers?"

"Not yet."

"Then I think you're inventing problems where none exist."

Karim looked at his watch.

"Listen, I've got a lunch date. . . ."

"Thanks, Karim."

He touched her cheek. "Anytime."

Andie watched him hurry off. She walked back to the Capitol alone.

A message from Jeffers was waiting for her on her desk-screen: CAN'T MAKE ONE P.M. MEETING.

Probably at lunch with Canay, she thought. Damn. Andie dialed up the faxletter for December. Might as well get started on it early.

An hour later, Jeffers breezed through the door.

"Andie! Sorry about the delay. Ready for me?"

"That's an understatement." She followed him into his office with her notescreen, closing the door behind her.

"Can Ben sit in on this?"

"I think not."

Jeffers made a mock frown at her. "Sounds serious."

She rounded on him. "Stephen, what did you mean about my being your press secretary?"

"That's what you do."

"It's an element of my job," she said sharply. "In addition to research, administration and accounting."

Jeffers waved his hand dismissively. "Perhaps it was. But you needn't worry about spread sheets and file keeping. Ben will be handling that."

"What?"

"Andie, your people skills are far too valuable to waste on paper shuffling and number crunching. I need you in a more people-oriented position." He leaned forward. "I want you to be full-time media liaison."

"You've got to be kidding." Andie sat down with a thump. "I'm a lawyer, not a public relations flack."

"Your legal background makes you even better suited for this role."

"Stephen, I didn't come to Washington so I could make chit-chat with video jocks."

"I know that," he said sharply. "But what you're doing is acting as my representative. I can't think of anything more important than that."

"I can."

Jeffers frowned. "Frankly, I'm surprised. I thought you'd want a more visible role."

"You know I'm more interested in the legislative process than media presentation," she said.

"Well, there'll be plenty of opportunity for involvement there as well."

"When I'm finished talking to 'Washington Today' and 'Goodnight, Japan'?" Andie folded her arms. "Next, I suppose you'll want me to head up a show on Mutant News and Views."

"It's not a bad idea."

"Stephen." She paused, exasperated. "I'm joking."

"Look, Andie. I've made up my mind. I want you as media liaison. Are you with me?" His tone was sharp.

She stared at him. Unbidden, a memory from their last time in bed together flashed through her mind and, annoyed as she was with him, she felt a prickle of desire. Did she want to quit? Could she leave him? No and no.

"I'm in."

"Good." He smiled. "You'll enjoy it. You'll see. I've left a list of reporters on your screen. Let's try to get some extra coverage of the debate on the Fairness Doctrine repeal.

"Fine." She rose to leave.

Jeffers put his hand on her shoulder. Her heart began to pound as he pulled her back gently against him.

"See you tonight?" he whispered.

She nodded. "Of course."

He slipped his hands under her jacket, cupping her breasts.

"Let's go away somewhere, just the two of us," he said. "I know a lovely hotel on Santorini. We could take a nice, long weekend there around Christmas."

Andie leaned back against him, her resistance ebbing.

"That sounds nice," she said.

"Good."

Jeffers kissed her on the back of the neck and released her. "I'll have Aten make the arrangements."

Andie nodded.

Bemused, she walked out the door as Ben Canay breezed past her. He gave her a crooked grin, walked into Jeffers's office, and closed the door behind him.

19

So MELANIE IS ALIVE and hiding somewhere near Washington?" Kelly asked. She snuggled closer to Michael on the green sofa in the McLeod living room.

"So far as I know."

"Why doesn't she come home?"

"Either she doesn't want to or she's afraid to. Maybe both." Michael selected an apple from the glass bowl on the black rubber table.

"Will you discuss it at the next Mutant Council meeting?"

"I don't think so." He bit into the ripe fruit, then offered it to Kelly. "It'll just upset my parents."

"When is the meeting?"

"December fifteenth."

"That's early. Only two and a half weeks from now."

"And I'm backed up with work until then." he said. "Overtime every night. If I see another schematic on solar-cell factories, I might just develop mental flares myself. This solar reflector job is taking more time than we expected."

"Isn't that the deal my dad negotiated?"

"Yeah. Don't tell him," Michael said. "I think we'll still get it finished in time."

"Okay." Kelly fidgeted, not meeting his gaze.

"Something wrong?"

She shook her head in a quick, nervous motion. Then she looked up at him hesitantly.

"I told you about the academy," she said. "What do you think?"

"Do you want to do it?"

She sighed. "I want to do something."

"Is that a good reason to become a pilot?"

"Mike, I don't want to be a housewife. Or just another computer operator. At least this gives me options."

He traced her jawline lightly with the tip of his finger. "I don't like it that you'll be so far away," he told her.

"Denver is a fifteen-minute shuttle ride. I can see you whenever I get leave. And the way you've been working these days, you won't miss me during the week anyway. Besides, I won't be leaving until June." Her voice had a pleading tone that made Michael uncomfortable.

"Can you get into the accelerated program?" he asked.

"I don't know. Why?"

"I just think you ought to consider it. That'll give *us* more options."

She smiled uncertainly.

"All right. I like it when you talk about 'us.' "

"Me too." He hugged her gently. "I'll try to see you before I have to leave for the council meeting."

"Are you going to discuss Jacobsen's death again?"

"Probably."

Kelly squeezed his hand. "It seems so far away now."

"Not to me. Or to the other mutants. But at least now we have Jeffers."

"Yeah, I saw a video of him. Cute." She giggled.

"You just have a weakness for mutant men." He kissed her gently and felt her heart beating against him. Deftly, he unsealed her tunic and ran a friendly hand over her breasts. Kelly sighed happily. Michael nuzzled her neck, then moved lower, covering each taut nipple with his mouth. When Kelly's moans began to fill the room, he paused.

"What time did you say your folks will be back?"

"Not for two more hours." Her eyes were luminous.

"Let's go upstairs."

They made love eagerly, teasing and laughing. Kelly reached a gasping climax, thrashing beneath him. Michael closed his eyes, feeling the burning approach of his own orgasm. Suddenly, the image of Jena, naked and provocative, flashed in his mind. He repressed it savagely.

This is my life now, he thought. This. I want this.

His climax, when it came, was a weak one, remote, unfulfilling. But Kelly didn't seem to notice his momentary hesitation. She curled happily against him and he held her, spoon fashion, for a long time, until her even breathing convinced him she was asleep. Slipping out of bed, Michael dressed quietly and left her to her dreams.

He drove home slowly. The unexpected mental intrusion into his lovemaking troubled him. Had Jena planted a trigger image to plague him? Or did he just miss her?

As he entered the house, he felt fatigue settle into his bones. One more week of overtime, he told himself. Then came mutant season.

He stopped in the kitchen and dialed up a Red Jack from the bar inventory. The lid popped with a hiss and he drank the tangy brew in quick, grateful gulps. Once the Mutant Council meeting was over, he could get on with his life. The thought cheered him and he hoisted the silver can in a toast: "To Kelly and me. And the future."

He finished the can and levitated it into the disposal unit.

On his way upstairs, Michael passed his father's study. Blue light seeped out into the darkened hallway through a crack between door and frame. He peered in. James Ryton was talking with someone on his deskscreen: Andrea Greenberg. Michael looked at his watch. It was late. Why was she calling at this hour? And why was she talking to his father?

James Ryton made an inaudible comment, Andie nodded, and the screen went dark. Michael knocked gently at the door. His father turned to face him.

"Come in. Just getting home?"

Michael nodded.

"It's late," Ryton said. "Don't put in too much overtime, son. Bad for the brain." He rubbed his chin. "I've just had a most peculiar conversation with Andrea Greenberg."

"I don't want to intrude."

"She wouldn't mind. I think she might have wanted to talk to you anyway. But she got me instead."

"What did she want?"

"It's damned peculiar. She wanted some advice about mutant-nonmutant marriage."

"Why from you?"

"I suppose she thought there was no one else to go to." He shook his head. "She thinks she's in love. With one of us."

"Really? Who is it?"

"Jeffers."

"What?" Michael stared at him, nonplussed.

"I was as shocked as you."

Michael sat down on the plush beige chair by the door.

"Maybe it would be a good thing."

"For whom?" His father demanded. "I'd expect you to say that, given your romantic inclinations. Frankly, I think it would be disastrous. For him and her. And I tried to discourage her."

"Why? Intermarriage can work," Michael said.

His father sighed. "I know you think so. But I've never seen a really successful match between mutant and non. There's always trouble. Besides, Jeffers hasn't asked her."

"Now I'm really confused."

"Well, you're not alone. I hope that girl isn't setting herself up for heartbreak."

"I thought you didn't like normals."

"Mostly, I don't. But she's a decent sort. I'd regret it if she got hurt. And Jeffers can't possibly risk alienating his mutant constituency by marrying outside the clan."

"Maybe it would be a good thing," Michael said stubbornly. "It could bring everybody closer together. That's what I think we need to do."

His father smiled sadly. "The young should always be optimistic," he said. His voice was gentle. "Of course it could be a fine thing, if it worked the right way. But it won't."

Sue Li appeared, yawning, and leaned against the doorway, red kimono wrapped around her. "James, who were you talking to?" she asked.

"Andie Greenberg."

Michael watched his mother's eyes narrow in suspicion.

"That woman who works for Senator Jeffers? Why is she calling you again? And so late?"

"She wanted some advice."

"About legislative matters? Why consult you?"

"It was a personal matter," Ryton said. "Regarding a mutant."

"Personal?" Sue Li lingered over the word.

"She's in love with a mutant," Michael said.

His mother's eyebrows arched in surprise.

"Is it Skerry?" she asked.

"No," Ryton replied. "That's what I suspected. In a way, that would have made sense. But it's not Skerry. It's Jeffers."

"Jeffers?" Sue Li closed her eyes. "Poor girl."

Faintly, Michael could hear her telepathic chant for composure.

Sue Li blinked rapidly, then gave Michael a mournful look.

"I wish we were ready for intermarriage," she said sadly. "Perhaps someday we will be. Come to bed, James."

She turned and was gone.

"Good night, son."

Michael's father patted him on the shoulder and followed his wife down the hall. Michael thought again of Andie and Senator Jeffers. Strange match. But perhaps no stranger than his own. The more mixed couples, the better. He palmed off the light switch and walked in the darkness to his room.

SIDE BY SIDE, the blond woman and red-haired man stared intently at one another, nodding occasionally. Clad in matching brown suits, they swayed gently in their seats, shoulders touching. When they stood up to exit the tube, Andie saw without surprise that their eyes were golden. Just two mutant telepaths communing in public, she thought, and followed them out onto the station platform.

Ever since the Mutant Union meeting, she'd seen, daily, more and more public displays of mutant abilities. In the tube, in the street, at the bank, at work. Andie hardly blinked now when a golden-eyed businessman hurried past her, a stack of discpacks trailing in midair behind him. But other nonmutants reacted with less tolerance, glaring and muttering to their companions.

She planted her feet firmly on the walkway flowing into the Capitol annex and pondered her feelings for Jeffers. Did she love him? Memories of their lovemaking left her dreamy, indecisive, and longing for more. But what could she look forward to? Her conversation with James Ryton had not given her much hope.

Andie jumped off the walkway and just made it into the crowded elevator before the doors closed with a whoosh. She saw Karim in the back and waved. He sidled over to her.

"Hear about Jacqui Renstrow?"

"No. What's there to hear?"

"They found her body in the Potomac."

"What???" Andie's stomach contracted.

Karim shrugged. "Yeah. I think she was investigating the Pai Gow poker syndicate on ClubMoon. As they say to nosy reporters in the Sea of Tranquillity, sayonara." He grabbed Andie's shoulder in alarm. "Hey, are you okay? You look like you're going to faint."

She pulled away.

"You're sure she's dead?" she asked.

He nodded.

"Karim, I just saw her last week. I can't believe this."

The elevator stopped at their floor and Karim propelled Andie through the door.

"I didn't think you'd get so upset," he said. "Were you two good friends?"

"No. But I'd worked with her before on stories. She was bright. Going places."

"Not anymore." Karim's mouth was a grim line. "Are you sure you're all right?"

Andie brushed her hair out of her face. "Yes. I'm fine. Just a little shook up." She squeezed his hand. "I've got to go."

"Okay. See you." He watched her walk down the hall.

She was early, the first in the office. Andie sank into her chair. Her last meeting with Jacqui Renstrow was still vivid in her mind. Lord, but she'd been a pain in the ass. And a good reporter. Despite her irritating persistence, Andie had liked her.

A thin-faced young woman in a dark-blue suit peered in the door. "Miss Greenberg? Is Senator Jeffers in?"

"Not yet. Can I help you?"

The dark-haired woman moved forward timidly, clutching a lapscreen. "I'm Nora Rodgers. General Accounting Office, Section R. We've been handling the audit on your office since Senator Jacobsen's death."

"And?"

"Well, I have some questions for Senator Jeffers. His budget overruns for this quarter are high. Very high."

"May I see your spread sheet?"

"I really shouldn't."

"I'm sure Senator Jeffers wouldn't mind." Andie reached for the notescreen, smiling. Her smile vanished as she scrolled through the audit records.

The figures were astronomical. They almost quadrupled

what Jacobsen had spent over the same time period the year before.

"Impossible," Andie muttered. "I haven't seen the spread sheets in a while, but he told me that everything was in balance. We'd been running a bit over, I know, but this is impossible. You must have made an error in computation."

"I've checked it three times."

"Well, check them again, before you waste Senator Jeffers's time," she said heatedly and flipped the screen back toward the auditor.

"I'll try to contact the senator later," Nora Rodgers said, and retreated, vanishing through the door.

With relief, Andie watched her go. Those figures had to be wrong. They just had to be.

The morning was getting off to a bad start, she thought. First Renstrow. Now this.

Jeffers bustled in the door.

"Stephen, we've got to talk."

He bowed with a mock flourish. "Your place or mine?"

She marched into his office with Jeffers a step behind her. "What's up?"

"Jacqui Renstrow's dead."

"That reporter for the *Post?*" Jeffers dropped his screencase on the desk. "My God, when?"

"I don't know. They found her body in the Potomac."

Jeffers looked toward the floor. His mouth was a grim line. Finally, he gazed toward Andie.

"Let's get a note of condolence over to her family."

"Right."

"Was that all?"

Now it was Andie's turn to look at the floor.

"No. An auditor from the GAO was here."

"The GAO?"

She faced him squarely, hands on hips. "Stephen, the first-quarter figures are horrifying. We can't possibly be spending all those credits. According to their figures, we've already blown two-thirds of our budget for the fiscal year."

Jeffers expression turned explosive.

"That's ridiculous," he snapped. "They're wrong."

"I thought you told me you'd checked out all our budget figures."

"I did. We're fine."

"Maybe you'd better call the auditors," she said.

"Just stop worrying about this, Andie." Jeffers's voice was harsh. "I told you, this is no longer your department."

"But—"

"No buts."

He stood up and gestured toward the door.

"I suggest you concern yourself with your own area for a change." His tone was dismissive.

Angrily, Andie stood up. "Fine. Excuse me for caring." She turned to go.

"Andie?"

His tone was lighter, almost caressing. She looked back at him.

"What is it?"

"I'm sorry," he said, smiling warmly. "You do a great job. Don't overburden yourself with this. I'll deal with the GAO."

Andie's temper cooled. All right, she thought. Let him handle the budget if he feels so strongly about it.

"Apology accepted."

Jeffers leaned forward.

"I think we both really need that vacation."

Andie smiled. "That's an understatement."

"Would you send Ben in on your way out?"

"Sure. If he's here."

"Andie?"

She paused in the doorway. "Yes?"

"Two weeks to Santorini and counting." He winked at her.

20

THE DECEMBER WIND dusted the blue beach shack with snow, rattling the windows. Inside, the space heaters glowed, red conductive crystals filling the room with false summer.

The chant for linkage boomed from the wall speakers. The soothing basso tones reverberated throughout the room. Michael leaned back in his seat at the wide table, enjoying the peaceful afterglow of the sharing. He saw Jena watching him from across the room, face somber. Even she couldn't dislodge his calm. He smiled at her and looked away.

Halden was back in the head chair as Book Keeper; he'd been reelected easily. In his deep, sonorous voice, he called for attention.

"To recap," he said, "you all know the severe loss we've suffered this year. Devastating. Our beloved sister, Eleanor, can't be replaced. But thanks to Stephen Jeffers, we can live with hope."

All heads around the table nodded.

"The repeal of the Fairness Doctrine is a major step towards equality," Halden said. "Senator Jeffers isn't wasting any time."

"I told you he was the right choice," Ren Miller said happily.

"That was the good news," Halden said. "But there's bad as well. The FBI investigation of Jacobsen's murder has gone off track. The official inquest was closed on December first. They think Tamlin worked alone. But everything we've turned up in our search leads us to suspect that he had help."

"Working alone? That's a joke," Zenora said, sourly.

"What about our own investigation?" James Ryton asked. "Did we turn up anything there?"

Halden nodded. "There's no question that Tamlin was disturbed, with a distinct pathological hatred for mutants. But he couldn't possibly have faked those press credentials. Somebody gave him access to Jacobsen."

"How can you tell?"

"We've attempted to replicate his ID ourselves. And failed completely, even with the efforts of our best holo artists. There's only one holoshop in all of Washington that makes the press passes, and it's under direct contract to the government. His credentials were made in that shop."

"And the FBI can't figure this out?" Ren Miller asked.

"Perhaps it doesn't want to," Halden replied.

"Are you saying there's a conspiracy to cover this up?"

"Possibly."

"I say Horner did it," Tela said, her voice harsh.

"Ridiculous," Ryton retorted. "We have no proof of that."

"Well, isn't he a likely suspect, with all his born-again Fold blather?" Tela said hotly. "And his weak attempts to recruit some of us? He's the one that publicized the supermutant rumor. Maybe he's working with a bunch of other senators who feared Jacobsen and decided to bring her down."

Paranoid, Michael thought.

"We've already investigated Horner," Halden said in a weary tone. "He's clean. Of course, we'll continue to pursue this."

"What about the supermutant investigation?" Michael asked.

"Doctor Ribeiros has disappeared, along with his clinic's records." The Book Keeper paused. "No sign of him in Brazil. We've got other groups alerted, especially in Southeast Asia. We assume he'll surface sooner or later. We'll be watching."

All around the room, the clan stirred restlessly.

Halden held up his hands. "If there's no other business—"

"Uncle Halden, I request the right to speak," Jena said, her voice husky.

Michael glanced at her, wondering what was on her mind.

"Right is granted," said Halden after a moment.

Jena stood. She wore a clinging green velvet synthsuit. Her face was set in a curiously grim way. Everyone was looking at her now.

"I claim the right of betrothal," she said firmly.

Halden's eyebrows shot upward.

"Betrothal? To whom?"

"To Michael Ryton," Jena said, pointing across the space between them.

Astonished gasps, both audible and mental, filled the room. Michael's heart began to pound. What the hell was this? He looked toward his parents, but they were staring at him, mouths open in astonishment. Michael shoved his chair back from the table and stood up.

"I refuse," he said angrily, barely recognizing his own voice.

Jena stared at him. Her eyes were fierce.

"Nevertheless, I claim the right."

"This is a difficult claim to make when the designate is unwilling," Halden said.

"Unwilling?" Jena flung her shoulders back and stood with hands on hips. "He wasn't so unwilling when he came to my bed! When he placed his seed within me! From which I have conceived his child."

The words slammed into Michael like physical blows. Jena pregnant by him? It couldn't be. No. No. No.

"Prove it," Sue Li said in a voice that sounded raw and ready to crack.

"I invite you or your designate to share with me," the girl replied. "You'll see I speak the truth."

"The truth, yes," Sue Li cried. She rose quickly and set out toward Jena. Michael thought his mother meant to strike the girl. But Zenora intercepted her.

"Keep back, Sue Li," she said, her voice calm. "Let me share with her. You're too angry." Firmly, she pushed Sue Li back into her seat. Michael gripped the table. This was a bad dream. It had to be.

Zenora took Jena's hands. Michael knew that her mind was traveling the paths, the nerveways of the other's body. Would she sense a quickening at the center? New life forming in the uterine nest?

Zenora dropped her hands and moved away from the smaller woman, rubbing her forehead.

"It's true. There is life within." She paused. "But is that life, in part, Michael's? That still must be proven."

Michael sank back into his chair.

"I have proof," said Jena, reaching into a screencase by her chair. She held up a green memorypak. "These are the results of the blood and chromosome tests done a week ago. They show who the father is, all right."

"Let me see that," James Ryton said. He took the memorypak and inserted it into Zenora's lapscreen. Halden joined him, watching intently as the screen flickered blue light, scrolling through the file.

"Hmmm. The fetus appears to be female," Halden said. "And there's the aberrant chromosome." He tapped the screen. "The centromere position is acrocentric. Undeniably pinched."

"All this proves is that the father is mutant," James Ryton said irritably.

"It proves more, James. You know the location of the centromere can indicate paternity as clearly as a blood test." Halden turned to Zenora. "Can we access Michael's chromosomal records through the Net?"

"Yes."

"Use the spare roomscreen."

Michael sat frozen like a condemned prisoner, watching as the scaffold from which he would hang was constructed.

Time ticked endlessly by. Then Zenora nodded grimly and looked up from the screen. "It's a match, Halden. We have parity of the dominant alleles, centromere location and configuration, and blood type." She turned toward Michael. Zenora's generous features flickered as she gave him a sad half-smile. "I'm sorry."

All noise in the room ceased as the clan waited for Halden's pronouncement. The Book Keeper looked at Michael strangely. It was as though he'd never seen him before. Nearby, James Ryton stared into space, his face drained of all emotion. A muscle jumped in Sue Li's cheek. Silence enveloped the room. Finally, Halden stood.

"Betrothal is granted," he said, lips puckered oddly. The words themselves might almost have been bitter in taste. "New life must be protected by the clan."

Michael came to his feet.

Marry Jena? No. This wasn't in his plan at all. He had his entire life waiting for him back home. With Kelly. He couldn't marry Jena. But to defy the clan meant expulsion. Shame for his parents. What would happen to them? To him?

And if he didn't defy the clan, what would happen to Kelly and him?

"I won't marry her," Michael yelled, half surprised to hear himself say it. In sudden rage, he kicked over his chair and bolted out the door into the snow, shoving aside the telepathic cries of the clan.

He would go to Canada. Find Skerry. They'd never catch

him. Never. Running for his life, Michael pounded down the street, away from the meeting, into the gathering dark.

Stunned, Sue Li watched her son disappear out the door. She couldn't think. Couldn't feel. She looked across the table at Jena. The girl also watched the doorway as though expecting Michael to return at any moment. Then, a bit sadly, she looked down toward the floor.

"Well, I suppose it's all for the best," Zenora said.

"Best? How do you know what's best? I certainly don't," Sue Li snapped.

"He'll come back. Don't worry," Tela said.

"Perhaps it would be better for him if he didn't," Sue Li said, her voice rising.

Face pale, Jena stared at her.

Sue Li rounded on the girl.

"You tricked my son," she said. "You have won right of betrothal and you may be able to enforce it if he returns. But I will never forget what you did nor forgive you."

Tears filled Jena's eyes.

In fury, Sue Li looked around the room for her husband.

James Ryton was staring at the roomscreen, scrolling through the memorypak's contents again. He looked pleased, Sue Li thought. Wasn't he concerned about Michael?

"I declare a recess until we know Michael's real intentions," Halden said.

"But that could take days," Tela said. "We have to get back to our homes. Our jobs."

Halden wiped his forehead. "Michael must have time to adjust. I will give him three days to make his decision. After that, if he does not return, we will declare him outlaw and resume the council."

Released from the formality of the meeting, most of the clan lingered in the main room.

"Sue Li, don't worry. He'll be back," Tela said. "Come over to my place and we'll chant."

"Maybe later, Tela."

A small group gathered around Jena.

"How wonderful," one cousin said.

"When is it due?" asked another.

When they saw Sue Li watching them, the group moved toward her.

"Congratulations, Sue Li," said Cousin Perel.

"Spare me your congratulations," Sue Li said angrily.

She looked around the room. Ren Miller stood nearby.

"Ren, would you go after Michael?" she asked.

The dark-haired young man almost choked on the soya roll he was eating.

"Uh, Sue Li, no offense intended. But I don't want to get involved in family problems." Miller turned away.

Frustrated, Sue Li moved toward Halden. The Book Keeper was sitting, eyes closed, in a faded blue floatchair.

"Halden?"

His eyes flew open.

"How can you just sit there?" Sue Li demanded. "Aren't you going to try and find Michael?"

Halden raised his hands helplessly. "What good would that do? Would you like me to bring him in, trussed up like a turkey? No, Sue Li. What you're asking is completely inappropriate. As Book Keeper, I have to remain neutral. Michael must return because he wants to. I'm sorry." He returned to his meditations.

Sue Li looked around the room. No one would meet her eye.

"Well," she said. "If nobody else will do it, then I'll go."

Grabbing a thick red and gold thermal wrap from the rack by the door, she hurried out into the snow.

IT WAS TWO WEEKS since Jacqui Renstrow's body had been fished out of the Potomac. The controversy over the Fairness Doctrine was heating up. Bill Edwards, Katharine Crewall, and all the other major video jocks were practically camped out on Jeffers's office doorstep. Andie counted down the days to vacation, eager to get away from the endless phone calls and repetitive questions. Five days alone in Greece with Jeffers—she almost hugged herself with delight.

A sleek gray skimmer pulled up to the curb with Ben Canay at the wheel.

"Taxi, miss?"

Andie got in and closed the door carefuly.

"I really appreciate your giving me a lift to the shuttleport, Ben."

He gave her a quick grin as the skimmer cut quickly across into the speed lane.

"Glad to do it, Andie. Wouldn't want you to drag your bags on the tube, and since Stephen is going to meet you in Santorini for your Christmas r-'n'-r, I thought the least I could do was to offer myself as cabbie."

Canay was working so hard at being ingratiating that she tried to warm up to him.

"Nice car."

"Thanks," he said. "I just had the interior redone."

"All this leather? My god, that's an indulgence."

Canay smiled crookedly. "Well, it was more like a necessity. You see, my girlfriend trashed it."

"This skimmer? Does she do that often?"

"That was her parting shot. After she stole it. Good thing I have insurance." Canay gave a harsh laugh.

Andie frowned. Canay's personal life sounded messy.

At the traffic light near the shuttleport, a shapely mutant woman with long blond hair crossed in front of them. Canay watched her progress, sighing.

"Gorgeous," he said.

"You admire mutant women?" Andie asked. "Most nonmutant men don't."

"I know. Although, just between you and me, I think most nonmutant men wonder what mutants are like in bed." He turned toward Andie and winked.

She looked away. "No doubt."

"Well, I consider myself a connoisseur," Canay said, oblivious to her coolness. "My girlfriend was mutant."

"Really?" Andie swung around to stare at him. "I didn't think mutants behaved so hysterically."

Canay shrugged. "She was upset. We'd had a fight."

Must have been a lulu, Andie thought. Aloud, she said, "Mixed couples aren't all that common."

"Present company excluded?" Canay said. "Well, I just got lucky."

"Sounds like you miss her."

He smiled.

"Yeah. I guess you could say that."

To Andie's relief, the shuttleport loomed into sight, orange terminals dotted with blinking lights. Canay pulled the skimmer up to the Olympic Air entrance near a mechporter.

"Need help with your bags?" he asked.

"No thanks," Andie said. She jumped out of the skimmer.

"Have big fun with the big man," Canay said. "We'll take care of business until you get back." He waved and drove off.

The mechporter took the bags, processed Andie's ticket, and told her that the shuttle was loading. She strode toward the gate, eager for a few days in the sun. Canay's comments haunted her oddly. So what if he liked mutant women? If he was foolish enough to get mixed up with people who stole and ruined his possessions, that was his business. Why should she care about his stupid girlfriend and car? Shrugging off her uneasiness, she ran for the shuttle.

21

MAKE ME INVISIBLE, Michael thought. Sweep me out to sea and let me float. I want to become seaweed and seafoam. Shivering with cold, he stared at the gray breakers as they crashed upon the shore. He'd been hiding out for two days now, ever since that nightmarish moment in the clan meeting when Jena had tried to claim him.

Any minute now, he prayed, Skerry would send a sudden telepathic summons to come away. Skerry always knew when he was in trouble. And Michael would go. He'd become outlaw to the clan. He'd get a message to Kelly, and she'd fly to Vancouver for a clandestine wedding, to become his outlaw bride.

If only he'd been able to reach Skerry. But the number he'd been given months ago was out of service. He'd tried it for two hours yesterday, dialing and redialing.

Michael?

It was the faintest whisper in his mind. He turned, gasping. "Skerry?"

Michael, can you hear me?

"Yes, Skerry." He almost wept with relief. "Where are you?"

Not Skerry, dear. Mother.

"Oh." Despair enveloped him.

Sue Li walked up the beach toward him, her cloak billowing in the wind like bright red and gold wings. Michael's dreams of escape crumbled with each step she took.

"Come back," she said.

"No."

"Surely you don't want to become outlaw? Do you understand what that means?"

She sat down beside him on the damp sand.

"Yeah," he said. "I won't have to attend these damned meetings any more."

Sue Li's face crinkled in a smile. "That may be one of the few benefits. But do you really want to leave all of us? To shed family, friends, even your job?"

"I could do it if I had to."

"But do you want to?"

"I don't know." He stared off into the waves.

Sue Li kept her voice calm. "Then come back."

"Why?"

"It's our way."

"I don't give a damn about our way. She tricked me."

"I know."

"Don't you care?" He turned to face her. "Do you really want Jena as a daughter-in-law?"

Sue Li sighed.

"This goes beyond what I want or don't want. In some ways, I wish you and Kelly had just run away together. I could stand to be the mother of an outlaw."

"Really?" Michael stared at her in amazement.

She brushed a lock of hair out of his eyes.

"Yes. But I can't endure being the grandmother of a half-outlaw child," she said gently.

"I don't love her."

"I know that, too. But you have a responsibility now to more than what you want."

"You mean the child?"

"Yes."

Angrily, Michael pulled away from her touch.

"Dammit, why can't Jena just get an abortion?" he cried.

"You know why. It's forbidden in the clan."

"What about *my* happiness?" His voice was ragged.

Sue Li smiled sadly. "You may find that happiness comes with time. And when you least expect it."

"I could run away."

"You could. There's a tube station around the corner. I'll even give you money for a ticket. But where will you go, Michael? What will you do? And what shall I do if I lose yet another of my children?" Her voice was soft.

Michael drew his knees up to his forehead. He rocked back and forth in the damp sand. Tears trickled out from beneath closed eyelids.

Kelly, he thought. Kelly, I'm sorry. I'm so sorry.

He felt his mother's hand on the back of his neck. Choking back a sob, he raised his head, dashing away tears with his fists. He stared at the green-gray waves as they pursued their eternal, rhythmic dance with gravity. Finally, he nodded.

All right.

"I'll come back. For the child. And you."

"You mean that?"

Again, Michael nodded.

He stood up, helped his mother to her feet.

"I love you, Michael," she said, standing on tiptoe to kiss his cheek. "I grieve with you."

"I'm always going to love her."

"I know."

She took his hand. Together, they walked back to the clan meeting, Sue Li's cloak flapping around them.

As they entered the meeting room, Halden greeted them with a sigh of relief.

"Found him? Good. I didn't want to delay another day." He sent forth a mental summons for order. Then he spoke to Michael.

"Have you returned of your own free will?"

Michael was silent. He gazed around the room at his clan. A hundred golden eyes glittered back at him.

"Yes," he said. "I ask forgiveness for the disruption."

"I should think so," Tela said sharply.

"I think we should be understanding of our younger brother's confusion," Halden said benignly.

All around the table, heads nodded.

Michael sat down next to Jena. She smiled tremulously at him, face aglow.

She really does love me, he thought. Enough to have bound me to her in this way. Even to risk my anger. My hatred and rejection.

He looked at his betrothed. She was beautiful. Tall and cool and blond. Michael thought of another woman, shorter, with dark hair and a lively smile. His mouth tightened with pain.

Kelly, he thought. I waited too long.

Jena squeezed his hand. Michael looked at her again. I don't love her, he thought. But maybe I don't hate her. And perhaps I can be kind to her. Someday.

Michael clasped her hand and closed his eyes as Halden began the closing chant that sealed his fate.

> Within the clan, we are family.
> Within the inner circle, we are one.
> From past ages to final future,
> We go forth as we have gone before,
> Together, hand in hand, heart in heart,
> mind in mind. The right of new life
> joins us as one.

THE BEACH was dark volcanic sand, sparkling with glints of mica. On this unusually warm winter day it soaked up the heat of the pale sun and felt too hot to walk on. Andie raced

241

toward the blanket, yelping. Stephen looked up from his notescreen, smiling from beneath a Panama hat.

"Ah, paradise," Andie said ruefully, rubbing her toes. "When you suggested Santorini, I never thought I'd get blisters on my feet."

"Here, have a sip," Jeffers said, passing her a silvery squeeze-jug of retsina. "It'll ease your pain."

He went back to his notescreen.

Andie took a swig of the light-green, pine-scented wine. The cool, sour taste was refreshing. She stretched out on the beach chair and admired the turquoise waters of the Aegean. What a good idea it had been to come here. They'd spent the past three days exploring the ash-shrouded ruins of Akrotíri, wandering along the upper ridge of the island, and making love in their private suite in the whitewashed grand hotel perched on the hillside of the ancient volcano. Washington was thousands of miles away. Andie closed her eyes and let the sun caress her into drowsiness.

A shout brought her out of her reverie. Two heavyset women in black bathing suits were standing at water's edge, shrieking and pointing. Far out from shore, where the water turned a deeper blue, a small, dark head bobbed in the surf. Too far out. The small head went under. Came back up sputtering. Went under again.

"Stephen! That child's drowning!" Andie cried.

She jumped up and made for the surf. She was a fair swimmer, good in a pool. But this was the ocean, cold and powerful. The waves were relentless. As soon as she was in the water, the tidal pull began working on her. That little head was so far away. Andie gasped for air. Then another swimmer passed her, feet motionless, a clear wake streaming out behind him.

Andie fought her way back to shore and stood, gasping, as she saw the little head go under again. She waited for it to bob up again, holding her breath. Then another, larger head, lighter-haired, was there.

Jeffers.

How did he get out there so fast? Andie wondered.

He dove, his back flashing in the sun. Vanished. The spectators watched anxiously. Time dragged by. Suddenly, a spout of green water flumed, and up popped the child, like a cork, with Jeffers right behind him. In moments, they were on the beach, a noisy crowd encircling them.

Jeffers gasped for breath. But the boy was motionless, lips blue. Andie began CPR. Should she call for a medmech? Was there time? The child remained still, unresponsive.

"Please," Andie whispered. "Don't die. Please."

Cool hands on her shoulders drew her away.

"Let me."

Jeffers bent down, placed one hand on the child's chest, the other on his head, and closed his eyes. His forehead furrowed with concentration. He muttered something guttural, indistinct. His lips drew back in a grimace. The child jerked convulsively. Jeffers's neck muscles stood out in cords. The child coughed and began crying. His young mother sank to her knees and clutched the boy to her chest. She wept joyfully as the crowd cheered.

Pale and dazed, Jeffers fell back, breathing heavily. Andie grabbed the retsina squeeze-jug and handed it to him. He drank eagerly. In a moment, his color deepened and his breathing slowed.

"Had to go pretty far down to find him," Jeffers said.

"Was it deep water out there?" Andie asked.

"Not the water. His mind. Almost gone." Jeffers took another gulp of retsina. "Tried to get his heart started first, but he'd been under a long time. Had to call and call. I'm not very good at it. But my mother was a healer. She taught me some of what to do."

Andie felt a chill running down her back.

"How'd you get to him so fast?" she asked.

"Telekinesis. Almost too late."

"I'd say your timing was perfect." She put her arms around

him and led him back to the blanket, oblivious to the hot sand beneath her feet. Jeffers lay down in the sun, utterly drained.

"Think I'll sleep for a while," he said. His eyes closed and he was gone.

Andie glanced at the notescreen he'd tossed aside. It lay on the dark sand, half-covered with black grains. She brushed it off. A list of medical clinics in the Cyclades glowed in amber letters on the screen.

She let him sleep for half an hour, then prodded him awake with a toe.

"C'mon. Let's go inside. It's almost five."

Inside their room, Andie peeled off her synthskin and set the timer and water temperature for the shower. The twin shower heads shot liquid silver threads at the red tile.

"Care to join me?" she asked archly.

He gave her a roguish grin.

"I was hoping you'd ask."

He slipped into the tub behind her and pressed her against the wall.

"Stephen!"

Jeffers kissed her hard as he slipped a hand between her legs. Warm arousal fanned upward from his touch. Andie gasped as Jeffers lifted and entered her. She shuddered with pleasure, wrapped her legs around him, letting the hot water caress her neck, her breasts. She came quickly, crying out in her frenzy. With several deep thrusts, Jeffers followed her. They sank to the tile floor, arms and legs tangled. In a minute, the water clicked off. Andie reached for a towel.

Wrapped in its soft, pink, cottonsynth folds, she sank down onto the bed. Jeffers lay down, naked, beside her. Dreamily, she ran her hand down his chest.

"Tell me about your mother," Andie said.

The peach-colored sheets were deliciously smooth and cool under them. She felt the welcome lassitude that usually followed their lovemaking.

Jeffers shrugged. "I told you. She was a healer."

"Just for the mutants?"

"No. She worked as a psychologist. So I suppose she healed nonmutants as well."

"Where is she now?"

"Killed in the riots in '95."

"My God! Were you there?"

He turned away from her, facing the wall. "Yes. The crowd just flowed up and over us. She made me get under a skimmer and told me not to come out until it was safe. I watched her body lying there. Finally, the police moved her."

His voice was soft, but Andie could feel the horror of the moment almost as though she had been there. Chilled, she pulled the bedcovers up.

"How did you get away?"

"My father found me, after it was dark."

Jeffers turned over and looked at her. In the half-light of the room, his eyes gleamed eerily.

"You don't remember the riots, do you?"

Andie shook her head. "I was only eight years old. I remember my parents talking about the trouble. And I had to stay home from school one day when I was supposed to give a report, so I was angry. But no, I don't remember the riots."

She looked at him, thinking of the child he'd rescued. Of that day, twenty-two years ago, when he waited, longing for rescue, watching his mother's body. Andie felt a pang of strange emotion. It felt like love. Or pity, perhaps.

Sprawled on the bed, he was was a golden idol. A pagan sculpture from a sun-worshiping cult. Light glowed from him, from his tanned skin, golden eyes, tawny hair.

He was splendid today, Andie thought. I could marry a man like that.

Marry this golden man? She watched him from beneath half-closed eyelids. For the first time, she believed in the possibility. They could be together. Yes. And good together. They could bring mutants and nonmutants closer. Work for the same goal. Love each other. Yes, somehow she would marry him. Yes. Yes. Yes.

She leaned back, drowsy. "That felt good. Maybe I'll take a nap."

"Fine." He squeezed her shoulder and got out of bed.

Andie slipped into strange dreams. Stephen was saving the little boy, over and over. Then his face changed. It was Ben Canay's face, and he was trying to save a little boy. No, it was a little girl now. A little mutant girl. Or was he trying to drown her? And the little girl looked strangely familiar.

"No!" Andie cried in the dream. "Save her. Save her."

She sat up in bed. Her heart was pounding and her hair clung stickily to her back and shoulders. The place beside her was empty. She could hear Jeffers's voice coming from the far end of the suite, but his words were indistinct. Probably on the screen to somebody in Washington, she thought groggily.

She lay back, trembling, until her pulse slowed.

It was a dream, she thought. Just a dream.

Slowly, she drifted back to fitful sleep, haunted by the image of a young mutant girl, drowning.

THE TRIP HOME from the Mutant Council was quick. Too quick. Michael dreaded every moment, from lift-off to touchdown. But once in his own room, he could delay no longer.

With numb fingers, he keyed up his deskscreen and dialed Kelly's code.

Please don't be home, he thought.

She answered on the third ring.

"Michael! You're back early," she said. Her face glowed with pleasure. "I thought you'd be away through New Year's. How'd it go?"

"I want to see you, Kelly."

Her smile dimmed. "Is anything wrong?"

"I have to talk to you. Can you meet me at the aqueduct in fifteen minutes?"

"Tonight?" She looked startled. "Of course. Michael, are you all right?"

"I'll explain everything when I see you." Hands shaking, he closed the connection.

A five-minute ride and he was at the aqueduct. The pavement was crazed with lines, like the glaze on one of Michael's mother's favorite old ceramic pots. An abandoned Christmas tree lay forlornly on its side in a snowbank, the glitter leaching slowly from its ribbons of tinsel.

Sunk in gloom, Michael kicked at loose pieces of ancient gray asphalt rimmed with tar and burrowed into his gray parka. The sun was going down and another winter storm was brewing.

I wish I were in Canada, he thought. In South America. Anywhere else, doing anything else.

The old aqueduct was a favorite gathering place for high-school kids who wanted to hypo or do joysticks. Luckily, the place was deserted now.

Hurry up, Kelly, he pleaded silently.

A deep-blue skimmer pulled up. Kelly grinned brightly at him from behind the wheel, cut the batteries and jumped out. She wore a red parka, black leggings, silver boots. She looked wonderful.

"Gods, I've missed you! I thought you'd never get back from that meeting."

She threw her arms around his neck. He kissed her gently. The back of his throat felt like sandpaper. Then he pulled out of her embrace.

"Let's walk." His voice grated.

A furrow formed between Kelly's brows.

"What's wrong?" she said.

He sighed. All his half-formulated lies fell away. "Everything."

"What do you mean?"

He turned to face her.

"I can't see you anymore."

247

Her eyes were huge.

"Can't or don't want to?"

"Can't. Don't look at me that way, Kelly. It's so hard to explain." He clenched his fists. She covered them with her hands.

"Try."

"It has to do with mutant business. I have to get married." Kelly stopped walking.

"Have to get married? What do you mean?"

"There's a mutant girl. She's pregnant. . . ."

"By you?" Kelly's voice cracked.

"Yes."

He watched as she struggled to maintain control.

"Can't she get an abortion?" Kelly asked.

"No."

"Why?"

"It's not allowed in the clan."

"What do you mean, not allowed? What kind of clan is this? A police clan?"

"It's not like that at all. Dammit, I knew you wouldn't understand."

She sat down on a jutting piece of concrete.

"Do you love her?"

"No."

He kneeled beside her. She took his face in her hands.

"Do you love me?" she whispered, after a very long time.

"Yes." Michael looked away, fighting tears. "But it doesn't matter. I can't marry you, Kelly. Not now. Even if I wanted to."

He stood up.

"Why not?" she demanded. "What would they do?"

"I'd be outcast. It's never happened before. My family would be shamed. If I didn't honor my responsibilities to the clan, my folks would be shunned. I can't do that to them."

"So instead, you're going to commit yourself to a woman you don't love and destroy your own life? For them?" Kelly's voice rose. "For those mutants? What are you doing to your-self?"

"You don't understand."

"You're damned right I don't. Michael, how can you throw yourself away like this? How can you throw *us* away?"

She started to walk toward the skimmer. Michael reached for her and caught her by the shoulders.

"I knew I should have lied to you," he said bitterly.

Kelly shook her head, dark hair flying wildly.

"I'd never have believed you. Listen to me, Michael." She grabbed his hands. "We can run away. Tonight. We can get married in Delaware. Then they won't be able to do any-thing."

He took a deep breath. Tears stung his eyes, and the back of his throat. "I wish I could. Oh, Kelly, if only you knew how much I wish I could do it. But it's not as easy as you make it sound."

Her eyes flashed. "It's only difficult if you want to make it difficult."

He thought of Mel, gone now for half a year. Of Skerry, who'd asked him to come to Canada. He was glad Skerry wasn't around to see the mess he was in now. He could imag-ine the sour grin on his cousin's face as he said, "They've caught you, kiddo. Should've run when you had the chance."

"I don't want it to be difficult!"

He turned from her, angry now. Why couldn't she under-stand and let him go? She was just making it harder.

"There's nothing I can do. It's the mutant way, Kelly. I'm sorry. I love you and I'd hoped to marry you, but now every-thing's changed. It's out of my hands."

She stepped back. Her expression was cold.

"I can see you believe it. And I guess that's all that matters, then. Good luck, Michael." She hurried away. Michael heard the door slam, then the roar of the accelerator. Bleakly, he stared after the skimmer, watching his future disappear in the dust of its wake.

22

ANDIE SAT in Jeffers's office, facing him across the desk. She scrolled quickly through her daily agenda. It was three weeks since their return from Santorini, three weeks into the new year. Already, the trip was no more than a pleasant, fading memory swallowed up by the usual controlled frenzy of interviews, position statements, speeches, and press releases.

"Don't forget your speech to The Fold on the morning of the twentieth," Andie told Jeffers. "We'll get good coverage of that. And it's not too early to start thinking about getting Akins's endorsement for the Senate race this fall."

"Halden assured me we'd have it." Jeffers leaned back in his chair, arms behind his head. "Which reminds me, Andie. What's this about attending a wedding after the fund-raiser in New York?"

She looked up from the deskscreen. "Michael Ryton's wedding. God, it's the Saturday after next. I almost forgot. You remember the Rytons, don't you? The mutant father and son who lobbied Jacobsen about government restrictions on space engineering?"

"Those two? And the son is getting married?"

"Yes. He told me he was pretty serious about some girl. I'm surprised the clan is making such a fuss."

"Why? Most mutant weddings are fancy affairs."

"Well, the bride's not mutant."

Jeffers raised his eyebrows skeptically.

"What?"

"The girl Michael wants to marry is a normal. I think it's terrific that the clan has rallied behind him. To tell you the truth, I'm flattered to be invited," Andie said.

"I doubt the clan is supporting intermarriage," Jeffers said. There was an odd tone to his voice.

Andie shrugged. "Maybe times are changing. The clan may be more progressive than you think."

"Maybe." He sounded unconvinced.

"What's a traditional gift for a mutant wedding?"

"Credit chips."

She burst out laughing.

"What's so funny?" he said.

"It's nice to know that, in some ways, we're not so different after all."

THE DOOR CHIMED its familiar minor key triad. Michael moved toward it, but his mother was quicker. Sue Li, dressed in the traditional gold of the groom's family, hurried to open the door and greet their wedding guests.

"Halden, Zenora. A joy to see you."

Michael's aunt and uncle entered, elegant in their glittering finery. Zenora's graying hair was aglow with purple cryolights, which matched her floor-length tunic. Halden wore a flowing gray suit that almost disguised his portliness.

Zenora hugged Michael briefly. Halden slapped him on the back with such heartiness that Michael nearly fell over.

"Ready for the big show?" Halden asked, his deep voice booming.

Michael stared at the floor. "I guess."

"Nothing to it. You'll see."

"Come downstairs," Sue Li said, taking them each by the arm. "We're still waiting for a few guests before we begin."

Halden winked before he disappeared around the corner. Michael sighed with relief and eased the collar of his formal golden suit. He felt as though the neckpiece was slowly strangling him.

The three-note chord sounded again. Michael opened the door and stared in amazement. Senator Jeffers and Andrea Greenberg stood outside, both dressed in subdued business suits. Snowflakes danced around them.

"And here's the groom," Jeffers said with a grin. "Congratulations, Michael. Good to see you again."

Dazed, Michael shook his outstretched hand.

"Senator Jeffers! Andie. Uh, come in."

"Michael, you look wonderful," Andie said. "Where's the bride?"

"Upstairs getting dressed."

"This is what you've been hoping for, isn't it? I'm so happy for you."

"Thanks." Michael's voice was hoarse.

Andie looked at him strangely. Jeffers put his arm around her.

"Come on," he said. "Let's leave him to his last moments of freedom and see the clan."

They moved off. Michael was alone in the hallway. He started toward the bar to get a joystick.

A deep croon wafted up the stairway toward him.

Damn, he thought. The chant's starting already?

Michael turned, took a deep breath, and walked downstairs. His father, clad in gold robes, met him at the doorway. Together they walked toward the improvised altar against the fireplace where Halden stood waiting. Great masses of yellow flowers festooned the walls.

The room was filled. Michael saw Zenora looming in her seat near the center, on the left. To her right sat Chavez and Tela. The entire clan was here. Even a contingent of mutants from the West Coast, the ones with oddly greenish skin, was seated in the back. In the front row, his mother nodded to the chants as she watched Michael approach. A wreath of red carnations crowned her dark head. Senator Jeffers sat with Andie in the front row as well. Andie winked at Michael as he took his place by Halden.

With a nod, Michael's father sat down. The chants shifted in tonality, soprano tones gaining ascendance over baritone and bass.

Jena walked into the room, holding her mother's arm. She strode down the aisle wearing a gown of silken ivory petals shimmering with delicate metallic threads. Her hair had been gathered into an intricate spiral in back, interwoven with lavender orchids and silver ribbon. Her face was alight, golden eyes glittering. All her attention was on Michael. He could feel her joy.

How lovely she looks, Michael thought. How happy.

As if in a dream, he took her arm and turned toward Halden.

"This is an occasion for rejoicing. For thanksgiving," the big man intoned. "As we increase in number, so we increase in strength."

Halden placed a hand on Michael's head, another on Jena's. The folds from his robe enclosed them like dark wings.

"Share with me, and share with one another as you will do each day, for the rest of your lives."

Michael's head throbbed. A strange sensation rippled through him with an electric, almost erotic force. Beside him, Jena gasped.

Halden smiled a quiet smile. His eyes sought out each of them, in turn. Then he lowered his hands.

"It's done. Michael James Ryton, take the hand of your spouse, Jena Thornton Ryton."

The linkage vibrated down Michael's spine as he turned toward the golden woman at his side.

Michael? Do you feel it? Can you hear me?

253

Yes.

Isn't it wonderful? Will it last? Oh, I love you so much. . . .

Hush. Halden isn't finished yet.

The mental speech came easily. Michael felt too giddy to do more than wonder at it.

"The rings?" Halden asked, raising one eyebrow.

Michael searched his pockets. Empty. But he'd put the ring box in there just an hour ago!

He turned around and looked at his mother. She closed her eyes. With a desperate wrench, his brother Jimmy jumped out of his seat beside her, face red. He pulled the missing gray velvet box from his jacket pocket.

"Here. Ow, Ma! I'm sorry. I'm sorry!"

Michael smothered a smile and took the box from his brother. Jimmy hurried back to his seat as the clan chuckled.

Halden nodded. Michael opened the box and slipped the smaller golden circlet upon Jena's ring finger. She took its mate and placed it on his finger. Cool opalescent fires danced upon the surface of the rings.

Jena smiled up at him, mind open to him.

Michael, I love you. I'll make you happy. You'll see.

He kissed her lightly as Halden led the ritual chanting. Then the ceremony was over, and Michael turned toward the sea of faces with his wife.

ANDIE WATCHED THE CEREMONY with fascination and confusion. Michael looked dreamy, almost hypnotized. His bride was certainly beautiful. She gazed at Michael with obvious adoration. But when the couple turned to face the crowd, Andie saw that Jena had golden eyes. A mutant! What had happened to Michael's plans to marry his nonmutant sweetheart? No wonder he'd looked at her strangely when she'd congratulated him.

Andie took Jeffers's arm and followed the wedding party into the light-filled dining room. Chairs lined the walls, and the large table in the center was covered with plates of delicacies and exotic flowers. Halden's wife, Zenora, the large woman in purple, had prepared the feast. Andie remembered how Zenora had protested her presence at that other mutant meeting, after Jacobsen's death. Wait until she discovered that Andie had been at the wedding.

Self-consciously, she straightened the jacket of her dark business suit. The mutants were arrayed in glittering, colorful tunics. The women's flower-bedecked headdresses winked with cryolights. Andie felt like a wren in the midst of an exotic flock of jungle birds.

Jeffers had explained to her that a mutant wedding was a time of high celebration. The continuation of the clan, and the expected additions as the marriage bore fruit, were traditionally considered reasons to celebrate. And Andie was a stranger at the feast. She stayed close to Jeffers as he congratulated the newlyweds, greeted old friends, and worked the room. Halden came lumbering up in shirtsleeves and pants. He'd shed his official robes after the ceremony.

"So, Senator. I suppose you're already planning for the election in November?"

"Of course. And with your help, Halden, I believe we'll make it."

The Book keeper squeezed Jeffers's shoulder. "You've given us new hope, Stephen. Provided balm in a season of pain."

"I'm glad."

Zenora walked up. "Senator Jeffers, we're proud of you. What's this I hear about you sponsoring the repeal of the Fairness Doctrine?"

Jeffers smiled at her. "We're definitely going after it. Once the election is over." He turned and put his arm around Andie. "This is Andrea Greenberg. You may remember her from Eleanor Jacobsen's tenure."

"Oh, yes. I remember her." Zenora said. She nodded coldly. "Welcome."

Halden gave Andie a warmer greeting, patting her hand genially. "Good to see you again, Ms. Greenberg."

"Please call me Andie."

"Of course."

"I'm surprised that you're not with Skerry," Zenora remarked, her tone acid.

"Skerry?" Jeffers looked confused.

"Excuse us, please," Halden said. "Delighted to see you, Andie. I hope we'll get a chance to talk later." He took his wife firmly by the arm and led her away, out of earshot.

"What was that all about?" Jeffers asked.

Andie shrugged. "Who knows?" She held up her empty glass. "Think I'll get a refill."

"Fine. I want to have a few words with the young bridegroom." Jeffers moved off.

Andie was halfway to the bar when a shimmering glass flute of champagne floated toward her.

Don't just stand there, toots. Go ahead. Take it.

Startled, Andie nearly dropped the glass she was carrying. She grasped the narrow stem of the levitating goblet carefully.

Let me get rid of your empty.

The other glass was whisked out of her hand and deposited on the bar.

Andie surveyed the room, trying to locate the source of the mindspeaker.

"What's new?" a light tenor voice asked from behind her.

"Skerry!" Andie whirled around, sloshing champagne.

"At your service." He bowed deeply. His blue suit was shot through with silver lightning bolts.

Andie smiled. But the bearded face that greeted her was grim.

"I didn't think you were here," she said.

"Let's talk."

Andie followed him through the main room to a small library. Skerry closed the door and settled heavily into a floatchair. Andie found a bench and sat down, grateful to ease her aching feet.

"So you're working for the magnificent senator?" Skerry asked.

"Yes. What's wrong with that?"

"If I thought you'd listen, I might actually try to tell you." He sniffed the green carnation in the ribbon lapel of his jacket.

Andie slammed her glass down on the table.

"I have really had enough of your mysterious hints and oblique references," she said. "You dumped that memorypak on me in Brazil. Then you left me holding the bag at the Mutant Council meeting. Why should I listen to you now?"

"Because I know some things you don't. And I'll tell you straight out. You're making a big mistake."

"And I think you're jealous of Stephen," she retorted. "You objected to his appointment—God knows why. But you're right about one thing. I won't listen to you. He's a fine man. A hero. He's brought hope to all of us who thought it had died with Jacobsen."

Skerry nodded sarcastically. "Oh yeah, he's the prettiest thing the mutants have been able to hang their hopes on in a long time."

"I love him. I want to work with him and help him."

"Don't mistake worship for love, babe."

Andie stood up, hands on hips.

"What do you know of love?" she asked hotly.

"Enough to want to help somebody who deserves it."

In two steps, he was next to her, staring intently into her eyes.

"You know, I really like you." He took her face in his hands.

Andie's heart began to pound. She tried to pull away from his embrace. "Skerry. Don't."

"Don't struggle so much. I'm not going to hurt you. I want to help you. Now, close your eyes. Close them."

Against her will, Andie's lids shut tight.

"Good. Lean back. Don't worry, I'll support you."

She felt his arm around her back.

"Attagirl."

His hand was on her forehead, palm cool.

"Count backwards from one hundred, Andie."

"What? Don't be ridiculous—"

"Just do it!"

"Ninety-nine, ninety-eight—"

"Mentally."

She complied. The pressure of his palm increased.

Suddenly she felt light-headed. Blue stars danced behind her eyelids. A roaring sound filled her ears.

NINETY-SEVEN, NINETY-SIX, NINETY-FIVE . . .

A hundred people, an army of voices, chanted with her. It was hypnotic. Deafening. Thought was almost impossible. And then the chorus receded, sound waves slowly moving backward, out of range, into silence.

Andie opened her eyes, blinked twice. Her throat was dry. "What happened?"

Skerry released her. "I implanted an autochant, with a spontaneous trigger should anybody start prying."

"Prying?" Andie sat down, reached for her drink. "You mean telepathic snooping? I thought it was considered bad manners in mutant circles. Don't they respect mental privacy?"

"Some do. But not all."

Andie shuddered at the implication.

"Don't be scared, toots. I just wanted to give you a little added protection." Skerry smiled gently. "You probably won't need it."

"What about this spontaneous trigger?"

"The chanting will begin as soon as a telepath tries to gain access to any level of your conscious infrastructure. That chant will drive them away, and it'll cut off as soon as they withdraw. Or you can trigger it yourself by thinking the word 'defchoir.' Make sure you close your eyes when you do. It'll cycle for fifteen counts of one hundred, but you can interrupt it just by opening your eyes again." He held up his hands. "Presto. Guaranteed privacy."

"You really think I need this?"

"Let's hope not."

Andie stared at him skeptically. He seemed sincere. Maybe she could trust him.

"Skerry," she said, "why did Michael marry a mutant girl?"

He laughed bitterly.

"He got screwed. Or, rather, she did. Literally."

"She's pregnant." It wasn't a question.

"Yep. And he's the proud poppa. So they got hitched, since the clan's motto is flourish and multiply. And vice versa."

"Oh." The closer she came to mutants, the less Andie understood them.

"You look like you could use another drink." Skerry hauled her to her feet. "Come on."

MICHAEL HAD EXPECTED a large crowd. But he'd never expected Senator Jeffers to come to his wedding.

The office suited him, Michael thought. He was so confident. Twice as dynamic as poor Jacobsen had been.

A crowd of mutants clustered around Jeffers. When the senator turned away from them to address him, Michael was flattered.

"Feeling a little dazed?" Jeffers asked kindly.

"Yes. More than a little."

"It'll pass." Jeffers patted him on the shoulder. "Your wife is very pretty."

"Thank you."

"Your parents tell me you're a double mutant. The same as your bride. Those are great odds."

Michael felt confused. "Odds?" he asked.

Jeffers winked. "To pass the trait along. The more double mutants, the better."

"Oh. Right." Michael smiled. "We'll find out soon."

The senator rewarded him with a chuckle. "That's the spirit," Jeffers said. "We need more young men like you in the Mutant Union. Are you a member?"

"I've been thinking about joining," Michael said, although up to that moment, he'd never given the idea much thought.

"Good. If you come to Washington, make sure you contact my office." Jeffers handed him a memorychip. "Here's some information that might interest you." His smile warmed Michael.

Halden appeared on their left. "Senator, there you are," he said. "About the campaign . . ."

"Michael, will you excuse us?" Jeffers asked. Without waiting for an answer, he turned away.

Michael looked around the room. Jena stood in a far corner, balancing two plates of food in midair, chatting animatedly with a turquoise-clad, greenish-skinned cousin from Petaluma whose golden eyes bulged distractingly.

Jena? he queried mentally.

No answer.

Perhaps the mental link Halden had forged between them was only effective when they were in direct proximity.

Michael chewed a piece of spice bread without tasting it. For just a moment he imagined Kelly's face framed by purple orchids. Then he banished the image.

No more Kelly, he thought. *This* is my life now. Maybe I will join the Mutant Union. Why not?

"Meditating on matrimony?" a familiar voice asked. Skerry's bearded face appeared, floating disembodied by the banquet table.

Michael fumbled the plate of food he'd been levitating, nearly dropping it before his control stabilized.

Skerry's full image coalesced in a welter of miniature thunderbolts. Grinning, he stood next to the banquet table.

"I thought you were in Canada," Michael said. "For good. Why didn't you tell me you were coming?"

"I like to make surprise entrances. But I'd say you're the king of surprises today, kid. Marriage? To her? I thought you were brain-bonded to some normal."

Michael tried not to wince. "Yeah. Well, something came up I didn't expect."

Skerry shook his head. "Caught you, did she? I thought so." He moved his head closer, voice conspiratorial. "You can still split with me after the feast. The hell with all this. Get away. Start a new life."

Michael smiled sadly. "You're a little late."

"I'll be in the neighborhood for a while if you change your mind," Skerry said, shrugging. He looked over his shoulder toward Jeffers. "So what's his grandness, the senator, doing here?"

"Impressive, huh?" Michael said. "He was making a speech in New York, and Halden got hold of him, I guess. Besides, I wanted Andie to come."

"She likes working for Jeffers?"

"Yeah. What's wrong?"

For the first time since he'd known Skerry, Michael thought his cousin seemed speechless. Finally, Skerry shook his head.

"Nothing."

"Don't tell me you've got the hots for her," Michael said.

Skerry gave him a sharp look. "I'm not the one with the taste for normal nooky."

Michael glared back. "Goddammit, Skerry, leave it alone!"

"Sorry, Michael. Forget it. I'm sorry I said anything." Skerry took a sample of salad from Michael's plate. "Hmm, not bad. Zenora hasn't lost her touch. Well, I wanted to pass along my commiserations. Talk to you later."

He sauntered away.

James Ryton gave his son a quizzical look.

"Talking to yourself?" he asked.

"Maybe." Michael smiled. Perhaps he'd been the only one to see Skerry at all.

"Damned flares." His father rubbed his head. "I'm going to see the healer next week. Michael, you know we've gotten that house all ready for you and Jena. Are you certain you don't want to take a week off? A honeymoon is an acceptable absence, you know."

"And you know we're behind schedule on that microwave transmitter," Michael said. "Half the second shipment of those damned calibrators was cracked. I want to visit a new supplier starting up in Virginia. You're not up to the trip."

"But we've been using Kortronics for years."

"Well, they're slipping," Michael said. "You need me at work. I'll take a honeymoon later."

His father patted his arm. "You do what you want, Michael. You're a grown man now. I suppose the honeymoon will keep until you're ready for it."

He started to walk away.

"Dad?"

"Yes?"

"Do you think Senator Jeffers can really get elected?"

James Ryton spoke with vigor. "I certainly do. The man has real vision. And we've put a mutant in the Senate before."

He nodded and moved off.

Michael allowed his plate to float gently down to rest upon the white, linen-covered table. Was it his imagination, or was his father already walking with an old man's careful steps?

VAINLY, ANDIE SEARCHED THE ROOM for Jeffers.

I've had enough of this party, she thought. Skerry's gotten me good and rattled.

She walked into a quiet room, empty save for a lone figure silhouetted against the window. The bridegroom. He had his back to her and was resting his head against the plasglas.

Andie hesitated for a moment. Was this some other mutant

ritual? The isolation of the bridegroom? Oh, the hell with it, she thought.

"Michael? Why aren't you downstairs celebrating?" she asked, voice gentle.

He turned and gave her a quiet smile.

"Andie. Having a good time?"

"Sure. You didn't answer my question."

"Maybe I need some time to myself." He glanced back at the window. "I love watching the snow. These February storms can be fierce."

"I'm glad you like them," Andie said. "Give me a warm beach somewhere and an attentive cabana boy."

"Sounds nice," Michael said. He seemed very far away.

"Are you happy?" Andie asked.

Michael smiled a half-smile. "That would be telling."

"What happened?"

"What do you mean?"

"To the nonmutant girl you were in love with?"

Michael stared off into the distance, jaw clenched. "It's over," he said.

Andie felt a pang of pity at his tone.

"Because you wanted it to end?" she asked.

"No." He closed his eyes.

"Michael, I'm sorry."

"Me too."

"How did she take it?"

"Kelly? Not well. I heard she's gone away. To the Air Force Academy. Going to be a shuttle pilot someday, no doubt." His voice rang with bravado.

Andie touched his arm. "Do you want to talk about it?"

"Not really."

"Sorry, again."

"Forget it."

He looked at her with sudden intensity. "You're in love with Jeffers, aren't you?"

Andie blushed. "Michael, I—"

"No, that's okay. I don't want to pry. But Andie, promise me that you'll follow your heart. Don't let anything stop you from doing that. Promise me."

"I promise, I promise."

He looked out the window at the falling snow and the gathering darkness.

"That's the most important, and hardest thing anybody can do," he said. "Know what's in your heart and follow it."

THE WEDDING GUESTS lingered long into the evening. Michael couldn't blame them. Mutants rarely had a cause for such celebration.

He'd rejoined the party to find Halden dominating a corner of the room. The Book Keeper was strumming his ancient banjo and roaring out the lyrics to a ribald song. A dozen mutants sat around him, clapping and singing along.

With Tela's help, Zenora floated the main table against the far wall to clear space for dancing. Joyfully, the mutants flung themselves into the air, touched the ceiling, hovered, floated down again, to repeat the process with elaborate spins and flourishes until they were red-faced and breathless. Those without powers of levitation received a boost from the more talented in the group.

Without thinking, Michael bounded into their midst, leaping and spinning.

"Here's the groom!" somebody shouted. "Where's the bride?"

"She's upstairs," another voice cried. "Let's bring her back to the party!"

Guided by Chavez, the group levitated Jena down the stairs. She giggled with pleasure as they deposited her on her feet by Michael.

He bowed with a deep flourish. "My dear, will you dance with me?"

"Honored," she said, and took his hand.

Together, they floated up and up, turning in a slow arc as

they spun about the room. Jena's tunic billowed gently. She gave Michael a saucy smile, then waved flirtatiously at Halden as they passed over his head.

"None of that," Michael said with mock possessiveness.

He pulled her closer, stared into her eyes for moment, then kissed her tenderly. Below, the onlookers cheered.

Maybe this won't be so difficult after all, he told himself. In fact, it might be fun.

Wrapping his arms around his wife, he kissed her again. And again.

23

AFTER THE WEDDING, Jeffers spent three days fund-raising and speech-making along the Eastern Seaboard, stopping by every mutant community between Baltimore and Bangor. By the time he drove Andie back to her apartment from the shuttleport, they were both exhausted.

Andie leaned back against the skimmer's rich, dark-blue upholstery, savoring its softness.

Jeffers rounded a corner with precision.

He does everything neatly, she thought. Lulled by the rhythm of the motor, she slipped into a drowsy reverie of their time together on Santorini.

Jeffers's voice cut through her dreams. "I wonder how Ben's been doing at the office."

Andie's eyes snapped open. "Fine, I'm sure."

Jeffers gave her a sidelong glance. "I wish you liked him better."

Nettled, Andie sat up. "So do I," she said tartly.

"He's been a terrific help to me."

"How long have you known him?"

"Oh, years."

Jeffers slowed the car at an intersection, then scooted through before the light changed.

"So you knew his mutant girlfriend?" Andie asked.

Jeffers looked at her oddly.

"No," he said, voice controlled. "No, I never met her."

"Well, he told me all about her and what she did to his car. Sounds wild."

Jeffers's smile seemed cramped. "Well, that's Ben." He stopped the skimmer by her front entrance. "Curb-to-curb service, my dear."

"Not bad. Want to come in?"

"Not tonight, Andie. I've got some business to take care of."

"All right." She kept the hurt out of her voice.

Jeffers blew her a kiss and drove away.

Inside the apartment, Andie greeted Livia, kicked off her shoes, and punched up her e-mail. She dispensed with the usual junk notes and saved the message from her mother to play back later. A priority message from the office blinked impatiently at her and reluctantly she keyed it up.

Ben Canay's green-tinged image flickered and formed on the screen.

"Andie? Jacqui Renstrow's replacement, Rayma Esteron, wants to see you ASAP. Said she'd be waiting for you tomorrow morning. Just wanted to prepare you." Ben winked and was gone.

Oh, hell, Andie thought. Another snooper.

She dialed up a bourbon from the mechbar and began to unpack. Livia wound in and around the clothing on the bed.

"Blue is simply not your color," Andie told the Abyssinian. "Maybe red. Those of you with golden eyes should stick to red. The mutants certainly do."

That was some wedding, she thought. Must have cost them a year's income. Well, why shouldn't the Rytons celebrate something? Losing their daughter and all. . . .

She froze. An image had entered her mind: a mutant girl with mixed Caucasian and Oriental features, who held a knife in one hand and was using it to slash the fine leather upholstery of an expensive skimmer.

Melanie.

Ben Canay.

No, she thought. It can't be.

She drained her glass in three gulps and dialed up another. It could be, she thought. And I have to know.

She checked the wallchron. Six o'clock. Early enough on a Tuesday evening for Bailey still to be in. She keyed up the Washington police and punched in Bailey's private code. It took five rings for him to answer. The dark circles under his eyes seemed even deeper than usual.

"Red?" He nodded a greeting. "It's been a long day."

"I'm sorry, Bailey. I've got something that won't wait." She gave him a pleading look. He sighed.

"Okay. Gimme."

"Benjamin Canay."

"A-Y?" Bailey turned to a keyboard at his side, entered the name, waited. In a moment, he looked up.

"Nothing."

"Nothing?"

"No record. Does not exist."

"I want to see his face when I tell him that," Andie said. "You mean he doesn't come up at all?"

"That's what I thought I said," Bailey answered testily. "Have you got any other ID?"

Andie frowned. "No . . . wait a minute! Can you use a voice print to make a search?"

"Maybe. Takes a little longer."

"Try this." She hit the e-mail replay.

"Okay, I've got voice and image dupe," Bailey told her. "Hold on." He faded from view. In his place, an image of a smiling policewoman on a horse appeared. Andie sat on the couch, sipped her drink nervously, and waited. Five minutes later, the policewoman vanished. Bailey stared at her.

"You sure know how to pick 'em," he said.

Andie put down her drink with a splash.

"You found him?"

Bailey nodded. "Three kilobytes worth. Benjamin Carrera, a.k.a. Cariddi, a.k.a. Canay. He's got a rap sheet that'll straighten your hair. What do you want to hear first?"

"Start at the beginning."

"Age thirty-four. Nationality unknown. Possibly Canadian, or maybe Brazilian. Incarcerated in juvenile hall, 1997, judged incorrigible. Tore up three foster homes before they could get him into juvey. Released 2003, on his eighteenth birthday. Two years later, indicted for illegal transportation of minors over state lines. Not convicted. Suspicion of trafficking in controlled substances. 2010, arrested after skimmer search yielded half a kilo of breen. Mistrial declared due to illegal search procedures. 2013, indicted on two counts of kidnapping. No convictions.

"Suspected agent for foreign interests. Most recently thought to be involved in labor trafficking from U.S. to Africa, Far East, Brazil. Five indictments on terms of child labor law violation, transporting minors across state lines for illicit purposes. No convictions."

Bailey looked up from his lapscreen. "This is not a nice person, Red. How do you know him?"

"He's working in my office."

"For Senator what's-his-name?"

"Jeffers. Yes."

Bailey stared at her.

"I don't like it," he said. "Does the senator know about this character?"

"I don't know. I don't think so." Andie gnawed at her lower lip. "Bailey, what was the name of the guy who reported his car was trashed by Melanie Ryton?"

"Who?"

"That mutant girl I had you check out last year."

Bailey punched a code into a keyboard, cursed, looked up. "Cariddi. How'd you know?"

"Just a hunch." She smiled wryly. "Well, it's been fun doing your work for you, Bailey. Let me know if you'd like to come do public relations for the senator sometime."

He looked chagrined. "Cute. You have any problems with this Canay?"

"Not yet."

"Try and keep it that way, Red. He's slippery."

"So it seems. So I thought."

"Anything else I can do?"

"Go home and get some rest. Thanks, Bailey." She blew him a kiss.

"Be careful, Andie," he said, all teasing gone from his voice. "And stay in touch."

"I will."

The screen went dark.

Andie finished unpacking and had another drink.

Wait until I tell Stephen, she thought, grimly satisfied. Won't he be surprised.

She put the drink down and started to walk across the room. Stopped. Covered her mouth with her hand.

What if he's not surprised?

What if he's known about Ben all this time?

What do I do now?"

ANDIE SPENT MOST of the night sitting on the couch, running through the same questions over and over again.

How well does Stephen know Ben? How well?

Long before dawn, she gave up any pretense of trying to sleep and got dressed.

The tube station was eerie and deserted, lit by blue cryolights. Andie felt as if she were the only person alive in Washington. She was at the office before six.

A dark-skinned woman wearing a mauve suit was standing outside the office door as though it were two in the afternoon.

"Ms. Greenberg?" she asked. Her voice was a pleasing alto.

"Yes?"

"I'm Rayma Esteron, *Washington Post.*" She flashed her press credentials. "Could we talk someplace privately?"

Andie stared at her. "Isn't it a little early, Ms. Esteron? How did you get in here? And did you camp out all night?"

The dark woman smiled conspiratorially. "Not quite. I know a few people. . . ."

"Well, I really can't see you without an appointment," Andie said crisply.

"This is very important, Ms. Greenberg," Esteron said. "Are you sure you couldn't spare a few minutes?"

"I'm afraid not."

"It concerns Senator Jeffers. And Mr. Canay."

"Oh?"

Esteron's face was impassive.

"All right," Andie said carefully. "Would you like to talk *inside* the office?"

Esteron shook her head. "Someplace else would be better. My skimmer. It's parked outside."

Andie stared at her in astonishment.

"That's highly irregular."

"Please indulge me," she said pleasantly.

Andie shrugged. "Lead on."

Esteron's purple skimmer was parked in the service entrance of the North Hall. Shivering, Andie followed the other woman into the frigid February air.

She must know a lot of people, she thought. By now, my skimmer would have had five tickets.

The reporter touched a button at her wrist and the doors sprang open. Andie slid into the passenger's seat.

"Well? We're locked up safe and sound," she said. "What's up?"

"Let's go for a drive," Esteron said. She programmed the mechpilot and leaned back to face Andie. The skimmer sped down the street and toward an approach to the Beltway.

"Ms. Greenberg, at the time of her death, Jacqui Renstrow

had developed quite a file on the senator's financial dealings. Have you ever noticed any irregularities in the senator's accounting practices?"

Andie's pulse pounded. "Why ask me? I'm the media liaison."

Esteron gave her a knowing look. "You're also very close to the senator."

"I think you'd better talk to somebody in bookkeeping," Andie said quickly. "I have nothing to say."

The other woman sighed. "I'd hoped you would cooperate." She reached into her purse, pulled out a slim wallet, flipped it open. A gold badge covered with bluegreen holocircuitry winked at Andie.

"Ms. Greenberg, I'm with the FBI," Esteron said. "We're conducting a probe of Senator Jeffers's finances. It appears that great sums of money are being siphoned out of the office."

"What? Where is it going?"

"That's what we'd like to find out."

"Why are you telling me? Aren't you afraid I'll tell him?"

Esteron nodded. "Frankly, yes. We know about your relationship with the senator. However, you're one of only two nonmutants working in his office. And we can't approach Canay, as you know."

"What do you mean?"

"Joe Bailey is a friend of mine," the agent said quietly. "And yours. He's worried about you. After your conversation with him last night, he called me. We put a camera on your apartment. That's why I was waiting for you this morning."

"Bailey told you about Canay?" Andie shook her head. "I'll kill him." She clenched her fists. Then her eyes met Esteron's, and she almost smiled.

"Don't tell me about it if you do." Esteron's voice held the hint of a warm chuckle. But her face stayed sober. "Ms. Greenberg, we suspect that Canay is implicated heavily. The senator may be blameless. If you doubt my statements, I can show you the financial records. But I think you believe me."

"You're right."

"Good. Then I'd like to ask you to work with us."

"What?" Andie stared at her in disbelief.

"Just report what you see, once a day."

"I don't think I can do that."

Esteron smiled gently. "You realize that if we do indict the senator on fraud, or Mr. Canay, you could also be indicted as an accessory?"

"Don't threaten me with phantoms," Andie snapped. "As your records undoubtedly show, I'm also a lawyer. I know how to defend myself in a courtroom. I think I'd start with deliberate discrimination against and hounding of the only mutant senator in Congress. Besides, if you've been snooping around as much as I think you have, then you'd know I'd never turn against Stephen for you. Ever."

"I was afraid you'd say that." The agent stared beyond her, out the window. "Will you tell him about this?"

"I don't know." Andie threw up her hands. "Why do you have to involve me in this? Why can't you just do your job?"

"We need your help."

"Well, find somebody else to help you."

"You're the only one who can."

"Then I guess you're out of luck." Andie's voice was harsh. "Was Jacqui Renstrow working with you?"

"She was an informant, yes. We're afraid that her death may be linked to this."

Their eyes locked for a moment.

"I can't believe that," Andie said. "I won't. Stephen couldn't have been involved in any of this."

"We hope not."

Andie fought to maintain her self-control. "I don't want to discuss this further. I'd like to get back to work now." She crossed her arms and gazed out the window at the first wavering rays of sunlight.

"If you wish." Esteron's voice was soft, regretful. She pushed a button and the skimmer turned the corner, winding its way back toward the Capitol. Neither woman spoke for the remainder of the ride.

The skimmer pulled up by the North Hall service entrance. As Andie got out, Esteron handed her a holocard.

"In case you change your mind." The agent gave her a quick salute and drove off.

Andie hurried upstairs. It was well past seven. Had she been talking with Esteron that long? Head throbbing, she fixed a cup of coffee. What should she tell Jeffers? It had to be Canay's doing. Stephen would never do anything illegal. Never.

Ben Canay strode into the office. He smiled brightly when he saw her.

"Good morning! You're here early."

She forced a smile in return. "Just couldn't stay away, I guess."

Her deskscreen buzzed loudly. It was a call from Jeffers. He was sitting in his skimmer.

"Andie, thank God I found you. I tried you at home first."

"What's wrong, Stephen?"

"I've left one of my screencases at home and I've got to make an eight o'clock breakfast meeting. Can you send a messenger for it?"

Inspiration struck her with the swiftness of a data shunt.

"I don't trust those messengers," she said. "Why don't I run by and pick it up? I've got a light morning."

Jeffers gave her a relieved smile. "You don't mind?"

"My pleasure."

"It's on the hall table by the door. I'll tell the lock to admit you."

"Fine."

"Andie, I owe you one." He winked and was gone.

. . .

274

THE CAB RIDE to Jeffers's exclusive neighborhood took fifteen minutes. Quickly, the landscape changed from the marble nobility of the government buildings to neat suburban homes set off by dense trees and careful landscaping. It was picturesque even in winter, Andie thought.

As she alighted at Jeffers's townhouse, the sun broke through the morning's clouds. She fitted her palm over the diamond-shaped scanner at the front door. The lock clicked and she was in.

The front hallway was well lit by opaque ivory panels. Jeffers's screencase was exactly where he'd said it would be, lying on a burnished-oak side table near the door.

Andie had never seen Jeffers's house. Grasping the screencase, she walked carefully up the dark-green-carpeted stairs and emerged into a large, sun-filled room paneled in teak. A long hallway branched off to the left. The first room she came to held a deskscreen, file drawers, and a gray floatsofa.

She set down the screencase and stared at the screen.

I've got to know, she thought.

She tapped out an experimental code on the keyboard.

The screen stayed blank.

Jeffers's office screen code brought no response either.

She stared at the screen. Jeffers had programmed the lock to admit her. How could she convince the deskscreen to do the same? Her eye strayed to the palmpad at the side of the keyboard.

What if his house electronics were all on the same circuit? Could he have inadvertently programmed his own screen to admit her? She pressed her hand against the pad. The screen burst into light.

Andie scrolled through the menu. So many files. Where to begin?

An entry tabbed "Jacobsen" scrolled past. She brought it up. What appeared was a spread sheet indicating funds reserved for A.T.

"Clarify A.T.," Andie requested.

"Arnold Tamlin," the screen replied. "See March file."

Tamlin?

Andie's hands began to shake.

She requested the file. It was a series of instructions to Tamlin from Ben Canay, corrected by Jeffers.

My God, Andie thought. Jeffers masterminded Jacobsen's murder!

Her legs went out from under her and she sat down with a thud in the desk chair.

No. I can't believe this.

Andie covered her face with her hands.

What should I do now?

I could just leave, she thought. Pretend not to know anything.

No.

Andie turned and stared at the screen.

I can't leave, she thought. And I've got to know how far this goes. With a deep breath, she began scrolling through the menu again.

An hour later, she'd located the spread sheets that showed where the money was being diverted.

Brazil. Medical clinics in and around Rio de Janeiro.

The supermutant research, Andie thought. He's behind that too. She felt a hysterical urge to laugh. But the only sound she uttered was a sob, high and thin.

I need a copy of this, she told herself. But where should I stash it? My office screen is too accessible. Even my home-screen could be broken into.

For a moment, she thought of Brazil. The gentle palm trees. The lovely natives. Karim.

Karim!

She could transmit this to his homescreen. She still had his private code. And even if he found it before she could contact him, he wouldn't erase it without talking to her first.

With a sigh of relief, she duped the evidence and made the

screen-to-screen relay, erasing the transmission code behind her. Then she sank back in her chair.

"Looking for something?" a familiar voice asked.

Andie gasped.

Jeffers was leaning casually against the door. He wasn't smiling.

Her heart pounded in terror but she kept her voice calm.

"Stephen, I thought you were in a meeting." Feigning nonchalance, she reached over and cut off the screen's power.

"My meeting was canceled," Jeffers said. "Ben got worried when you didn't come right back. How did you get into my screen?"

Andie shrugged. "It was on when I got here. Maybe you forgot it."

"Maybe I did," Jeffers said, frowning. "But why were you using it?

"I needed to reprogram my mechmaid and I thought you wouldn't mind if I did it with your screen."

"Didn't you bring your own notescreen with you?"

"I left it at the office," Andie said, knowing that her screencase was tucked out of sight on the far side of the sofa.

"Well, no harm done," Jeffers said.

He drew her up into an embrace and pressed against her suggestively.

"As long as we're here, I ought to offer you the grand tour. Have you seen the bedroom?"

He nuzzled her neck. Andie's stomach contracted in a peculiar combination of terror, revulsion, and desire. She pulled back.

"I'd like to see your bathroom first," she said. Smiling nervously, she fled down the hall into the john. Once she'd locked the door behind her, she studied her reflection in the blue-tinted mirror and counted out thirty seconds, and then thirty more.

You can't stay in here forever, she thought. Maybe you can plead a headache and get out the door.

Stay calm and keep moving, she told herself.

When she reentered the study, Jeffers was sitting on the sofa, holding her screencase in his lap. He watched her the way a cat watches a bird alight.

"I thought you left this at the office," he said. His voice was soft.

Andie felt the color draining out of her face. "Oh, uh, yes. I guess I didn't."

"Don't bother lying, Andie. I just checked the screen memory. You forgot to erase the record of files most recently used."

He put the screencase aside and stood up.

"I suppose you're shocked," he said.

She tried to bluff. "What do you mean?"

"About Tamlin."

"What about Tamlin?"

"Don't play games with me, Andie." His voice was steely. "It was all Ben's idea anyway."

Andie relaxed slightly.

"You mean Ben arranged Tamlin's access to Jacobsen?" she said.

"Yes."

"You didn't know what he was up to?"

"He handled everything." Jeffers's gaze never wavered.

"Thank God," she said. "I knew it. You couldn't have set up Jacobsen's murder."

Jeffers smiled triumphantly. Andie's relief faltered.

"No, I never intended her death," he said. "Tamlin was just supposed to wound her. But he was too unstable and overdid it."

She stared at him. "You wanted her wounded? You did plan the attack on her?"

"Yes," Jeffers said. "I had to get her out of the way. I should have won that election to begin with. I had a clearer grasp of the issues. The needs."

"What needs are you talking about?"

Jeffers took her hand. "Andie, surely you see that the schism between mutants and nonmutants must be closed, and quickly."

"Of course."

"Jacobsen was too slow. She didn't realize the forces of history were bearing down upon us."

"That's hardly a reason to kill her."

Jeffers shook his head impatiently. "I told you. I never wanted her killed. Stunned. Temporarily incapacitated. There would have been room later for her to play a part."

"A part in what?"

"My government. She would have been a fine Secretary of State. Or she could have selected any cabinet post and I would have been pleased to grant it."

Andie pulled her hand free from his grasp.

"Cabinet post? What are you trying to say?"

"Andie, what better way to unite all of us than under a mutant President?"

"A—mutant—President!" Her laughter was shrill, almost hysterical. "We've only just gotten around to electing a woman, finally. What do you intend to do? Push President Kelsey off a parapet at the White House?"

Jeffers continued as though he hadn't heard a word she'd said. "A mutant President," he repeated. "With a nonmutant wife." He turned toward her eagerly. "Marry me, Andie. It's not too late. You could work with me. Help me achieve my goals. Bring us all together."

She backed away into a corner of the floatsofa. It was all too much. "Marry you?" she said, astounded. "Help you? Stephen, what about the murder? What about the money you've stolen for human experimentation?"

Jeffers squinted at her. "You know about the supermutant program?"

She nodded.

"I had to do it," he said, speaking rapidly. "My own resources were overextended. It was the only way. If I'd had a little more time, I could have buried the evidence and the GAO never would have found it." He paused, then hurried on. "Don't you see that an enhanced mutant is the next logical step in human evolution? It would be criminal to prevent the flow of human progress."

"What *you've* done is criminal," Andie said. "Stephen, you've financed kidnapping, illegal experimentation and murder. Doesn't any of this bother you?"

"The ends justify the means."

Andie studied him as if he were something from another world. "What ends? You've killed a courageous mutant leader. What could possibly justify that? And where's your supermutant?"

"We're very close. It will happen."

"It hasn't happened yet," she retorted.

"Are you sure you won't work with me?"

She realized she was being offered her life. But the price was too great.

"I can't."

Jeffers shook his head regretfully.

"What a shame. For a normal, you're really quite talented." With a sigh, he sat down next to her. "What am I going to do with you?"

Panic gripped her. "Let me go, Stephen," she pleaded frantically. "I swear I'll never say anything—"

"Andie, I'm not naive. Even if you really meant it, sooner or later, you'd feel compelled to report what you've learned. So I suppose the logical thing to do is make sure you won't be in any condition to do anything."

"No."

She sprang up and raced toward the door. But he was after her with catlike agility. Halfway down the stairs, he caught her in a powerful grip.

"You murderer! You used me!" she cried.

"Did you really think I was interested in you as anything

more than a sexual experiment?" Jeffers's tone was disdainful.

Desperately, she clawed at his face.

He reeled backward as she struck a telling blow, giving her enough time to scramble out of his grasp. With strength born of fear, Andie leaped up the stairs, her momentum propelling her down the hallway and into his bedroom. She slammed the door, locked it, and cast around the room for a piece of furniture to further block his way.

But even as she shoved the heavy oaken chest of drawers toward the door, Andie heard the lock give, and the door slid open; she'd forgotten his telekinetic powers. Unseen hands laid hold of her now, propelling her toward the door, where Jeffers stood waiting.

With a harsh laugh, he grabbed her, shoving her against the wall, knocking the wind out of her.

Andie gasped, fighting for breath. His golden eyes drilled into her, draining her of the will to struggle.

"You're a telepath?" she said, her voice faint. "But what about the telekinesis?"

"I have both gifts," he replied. "Didn't you wonder how I healed the boy on the beach?"

"I just thought all mutants were latent healers."

Jeffers snorted. "Normals! You never really understand us, do you?"

Weakly, she sagged in his arms. Jeffers placed a hand on either side of her head.

"Such a shame," he said. "Senator Jeffers's press secretary had a complete mental breakdown just before the election. Must be kept medicated. A vegetable, really."

Abruptly, his expression changed.

"Maybe hypnosis would be better," he said. "That way, you'd still be useful."

He pulled her down next to him on the bed, drawing her close.

She was caught, helpless in his shimmering gaze.

"You know I'm innocent," Jeffers said softly. "You know that Canay has been working with my enemies to discredit me. He's falsified all this information. And you've helped him."

His tone was silky, insinuating. He put his hand on the side of her cheek in a caress. Left it there.

"Yes, you and your network of saboteurs. You've been working against me all this time, probably in league with Horner. You hate mutants. And you've subverted young men like Canay who are filled with self-hatred."

"Self-hatred?" she asked groggily. "Who?"

He cut her off. "You'll call Cable News tonight and make a full disclosure, admitting your guilt."

"My guilt." His words were beginning to echo in her head. She wanted to argue, but her tongue felt thick, unwieldy. Her thoughts were confused. Her guilt. Yes, her guilt. She closed her eyes.

"NINETY-NINE, NINETY-EIGHT, NINETY-SEVEN, NINETY-SIX . . ."

A cacophany filled Andie's head: voices, hundreds of them, chanting numbers. Jeffers's voice, yelling at her, trying to overcome the strident chorus. Failing.

"EIGHTY-SIX, EIGHTY-FIVE . . ."

Jeffers released his hold on her. Still, she kept her eyes closed.

"SIXTY-TWO, SIXTY-ONE . . ."

The chorus faded to a whisper and was gone.

Andie opened her eyes.

Jeffers lay sprawled on the floor, unconscious.

I'll be damned, she thought. It worked. Skerry's crazy mental defense worked!

She stood up carefully. The room whirled around her. She staggered past Jeffers and out into the corridor, stopping only to grab her screencase. With each step, her balance improved. By the time she reached the stairs, she was running.

Andie bolted out the front door, jumped a hedge, splashed

through a half-frozen backyard wading pool and jumped another row of bushes into a narrow street.

There was no sign of pursuit.

She ran for another five minutes, gasping with each step. Finally, lungs burning from the cold air, she slowed her pace.

It took a moment to locate the card in her purse, and another moment to open her lapscreen. Andie's hands shook as she punched in the code.

A cheerful, pink-cheeked young woman appeared onscreen.

"FBI, Special Crimes Division."

Andie took a deep breath.

"Rayma Esteron," she said. "And hurry. It's urgent."

24

BEN CANAY WAS ARRESTED that afternoon. But Stephen Jeffers proved to be more elusive. He did not return to the office nor accept calls at home. When the FBI burst into his townhouse, they found it empty, the deskscreen and files missing. The mutant senator had vanished without a trace.

It was a week before the FBI lifted its seal on the office and Andie could get back to work. When she opened the door, she was appalled. The place was a shambles. Chairs lay on their sides. Drawers hung out of desks at crazy angles. Paper, memorypaks and discs were scattered everywhere. Ben Canay had left a wake of destruction behind him before the FBI intervened. Apparently, they hadn't bothered to clean anything up.

Andie stood alone in the chaos. Somewhere in the mess, a deskscreen buzzed. She ignored it.

Her own screen lay blackened, shattered.

I'm glad I wasn't here when they arrested Canay, she thought. He had a little too much time to try and destroy evidence. Thank God for Karim's homescreen.

Footsteps. She whirled to confront the intruder. Skerry stood in the doorway, surveying the damage.

"Nice mess," he said. "I think Hurricane Andie came through here."

She put her hands on her hips.

"I should have known you'd show up after the excitement was over!"

Grinning, he enfolded her in a bear hug that left her breathless.

"Whoa. Take it easy," she gasped. "I'm still recovering from my footrace through exotic Maryland."

"You did it, toots! You flushed out Jeffers!" His tone was exultant. Despite herself, she hugged him back.

"Thanks to 'defchoir.' Skerry, your implant really worked! If not for that, I'd have been a hypnotized zombie by now, in federal custody, claiming I arranged Jacobsen's murder. Jeffers was going to frame me."

The bearded mutant nodded with grim satisfaction.

"I *knew* he was bad news," he said. "Any word from the authorities on his location?"

"Cable News reported sightings in Panama, Seoul, Fiji, Moonstation and Place Pigalle. Personally, I think they should look in São Paulo. Or the Potomac."

Skerry leaned against an overturned desk. "So what will you do now?"

She shrugged. "I'll testify for the prosecution when Canay comes to trial. And I've been asked to assist the FBI in their investigation of Jeffers's conspiracies. They impounded his townhouse, you know. Of course, he was long gone. Taking his credits and records with him."

"They'll find him," Skerry said grimly. "Or we will."

"I hope so." She shivered. "I don't know if I'll ever feel really safe until Jeffers is apprehended."

"You've still got defchoir to protect you," Skerry said. "And if you need me, get on the screen to Halden."

"After what I've done, would any other mutant even want to talk to me?"

His eyes flashed. "The smart ones realize you saved us all.

The stupid ones will lick their wounds and mutter about losing their crown prince. And a few probably even agree with what Jeffers was trying to do. But don't worry about them." He touched her face gently. "Just take good care of yourself, toots. I'll be in touch."

Andie reached out to take his hand, but her fingers closed on thin air. Skerry was gone.

So long, will-o'-the-wisp, she thought. Now to contact support services and get some mechmaids in here to clean up this mess.

Her shoes crunched over debris as she stepped gingerly past her own desk to retrieve her screencase. A few typed commands, and she had arranged for the entire office to be cleaned and repaired. It took the rest of the afternoon to set everything to rights.

KELLY McLEOD strode out of the Akuda boutique in the Cherryhurst district of Denver, looking smart in her navy fatigue jumpsuit. She checked her watch. Twenty minutes until she was due back on the tarmac for preflight instruction. Where was the tube entrance? She looked behind her for a moment. No sign of it.

Distracted, she bumped into a young woman hurrying past.

"Forgive me," she said. Then she paused. The young Oriental-Caucasian girl looked vaguely familiar.

"Melanie?"

The girl removed her sunglasses to peer at Kelly with bright-blue eyes.

"Excuse me?" she asked uncertainly.

"I'm sorry," Kelly said. "I thought you were somebody I used to know. Can you tell me where the tube station is?"

"Down the block on your left."

"Thanks." Kelly waved and hurried away.

The young Oriental woman watched the dark-haired girl in the blue jumpsuit move past her, out of sight.

I didn't know Kelly was in the Air Force, she thought. Maybe I should have said hello. She always *was* nice to me.

For a moment, she was tempted to go after her. She took two steps toward the tube station, then stopped.

What good would that do, Melanie thought. Reopening my old life just when I'm starting over? That's all finished now. A closed chapter. Everything about the past is a closed chapter now.

She pulled out a mirror and checked her reflection.

Perfect, she thought. Those lenses really work. Maybe I will get them affixed permanently, after all.

Smiling in satisfaction, Melanie Ryton tucked the mirror back into her purse and faded into the crowd.

When Andie got home, she was exhausted.

Wearily, she palmed the roomscreen on, setting it to autodial, and sank down on the floatsofa. Images raced across the screen in flashes of red, blue, purple. For a moment, Andie lingered on the central channel, her attention caught by a blond reporter.

"Senator Stephen Jeffers's disappearance has raised rumors of conspiracy, fraud and murder in the nation's capital," he said. "Unofficial reports have the FBI engaged in a massive manhunt for the mutant senator. For mutant leaders' responses, see 'Evening Report' with Don Cliffman."

The front door buzzed. Andie cut off the news.

Odd, she thought. I'm not expecting anybody. Who could it be?

Her heart began to pound as she thought of Stephen Jeffers. Was it Jeffers? Was he standing outside her door, eyes glittering, waiting to abduct her? Hands shaking, Andie switched to the door circuit.

The face onscreen was a mutant face. But it did not belong to Stephen Jeffers. Andie let out a deep breath and relaxed. Michael Ryton stood on her doorstep. As she watched, he buzzed again.

"Hello? Andie? Anybody home?"

Andie keyed on audio.

"What are you doing here?" she asked.

"I'm in town on business. Wanted to see how you were."

She unlocked the door. "Why aren't you at home with your new wife?"

Michael shrugged. "Jena came down here with me. She's shopping at the Georgetown Mall."

Andie studied his face for a moment. His eyes looked shadowed from weariness. The youthful mutant she'd seen only weeks ago was vastly changed. Dressed in a dark-gray suit, he seemed more solid. More thoughtful. Older.

"Sit down," she said. "What can I get you?"

"Vodka."

Andie dialed up his drink and a bourbon for herself.

They sipped quietly.

"How are you, really?" she asked.

His golden eyes met hers candidly. "I'm all right. A little surprised at how things have turned out, but all right. Being married is nice, actually."

"You sound as if you've settled in quickly."

Michael shrugged. "I guess I've accepted the way things are. Not much choice, was there?"

"And your father?"

"The mental flares have increased." He glanced away. "He's only working half-days now. Under sedation most of the time. So I'm busier than ever."

For a moment, neither of them spoke. Then Michael turned back to her. "What about you? From what I've heard, Jeffers's people really trashed your office. Sounds like you've been through a bad time."

"To put it mildly." Andie shuddered. "Michael, I feel like such a damn fool. A naive damn fool."

"Why?"

"I was in love with a madman. With a dream. Saint Andie,

the bridge between mutants and non." She struck a noble pose and chuckled bitterly.

"Your dream was the right dream," Michael said. His voice was gentle. "You just picked the wrong mutant."

"I feel so embarrassed. Ashamed."

He patted her shoulder awkwardly. "Don't. I'd like to think that love is the only answer to our questions. And maybe I still believe that mutants and nonmutants will be able to live and love together. It'll take a lot of work, and we might not make it. But your instincts were good. Just a little premature, perhaps."

"When do you think we'll be ready?"

"Soon, I hope. Let's take it up with my daughter in a few years, when I bring her to visit Aunt Andie."

"I'll drink to that." She hoisted her glass and clinked it against his. Her smile only wavered for a moment.

"Do you really think that your daughter will accept a non-mutant as her aunt?" Andie asked.

"If I have anything to say about it." Michael squeezed her hand affectionately. "And we've got to start somewhere. I can't think of any place better than here. Can you?"

ABOUT THE AUTHORS

Robert Silverberg is a native New Yorker now living near San Francisco. Considered one of the best editors in science fiction, he produced the *New Dimensions* series of original anthologies and is coeditor of *Universe*.

Among Silverberg's novels are the bestselling *Lord Valentine* trilogy, *Star of Gypsies* (his most recent), and *A Time of Changes*, for which he won one of his five Nebula Awards, more than any other writer. He has also won two Hugo Awards, a Jupiter Award, and the Prix Apollo.

Karen Haber was born in Bronxville, New York, and grew up in the suburbs of New York City. She has lived in such exotic locales as Paraguay, Brazil, Pennsylvania, Missouri, and Texas. She now lives in the San Francisco Bay area with her husband, Robert Silverberg.

Haber worked as a nonfiction writer specializing in art-related topics before moving to fiction. Her short fiction has appeared in *The Magazine of Fantasy and Science Fiction*, *Full Spectrum II*, and *Women of Darkness*. She is also coeditor of the original anthology, *Universe*.

BOOKMARK

The text and display types for this book were set in Compano by Berryville Graphics Digital Composition of Berryville, Virginia. The typography and binding design are by Paul Randall Mize.